Elizabeth Hoyt is a *New York Times* bestselling author of historical romance. She lives in central Illinois with her husband, two children and three dogs. Elizabeth is always more than happy to receive missives from her readers. You can write to her at: P.O. Box 17134, Urbana, IL 61873.

Visit Elizabeth Hoyt online:

www.elizabethhoyt.com
www.twitter.com/elizabethhoyt
www.facebook.com/ElizabethHoytBooks

Praise for Elizabeth Hoyt:

'Hoyt's writing is almost too good to be true'
Lisa Kleypas, *New York Times* bestselling author

'Hoyt brings steamy sensuality to the slums of early 18th-century London in this engaging series . . . enhanced by earthy, richly detailed characterisations and deft historical touches' *Publishers Weekly*

'Hoyt has made Maiden Lane a place where danger and desire merge and legend, love, fairy tale and classic romance all seamlessly blend together'
Romantic Times

'Hoyt's exquisitely nuanced characters, vividly detailed setting, and seemingly effortless and elegant writing provide the splendid material from which she fashions yet another ravishingly romantic love story.'
Booklist (starred review)

By Elizabeth Hoyt

Maiden Lane series:

Wicked Intentions
Notorious Pleasures
Scandalous Desires
Thief of Shadows
Lord of Darkness
Duke of Midnight
Darling Beast
Dearest Rogue
Sweetest Scoundrel
Duke of Sin

Elizabeth Hoyt

Duke of Sin

A Maiden Lane novel

piatkus

Elizabeth Hoyt

Duke of Sin

A Maiden Lane novel

piatkus

PIATKUS

First published in the US in 2016 by Grand Central Publishing,
A division of Hachette Book Group, Inc.
First published in Great Britain in 2016 by Piatkus

1 3 5 7 9 10 8 6 4 2

All characters and events in this publication, other than those clearly in the public domain, are fictitious and any resemblance to real persons, living or dead, is purely coincidental.

A CIP catalogue record for this book
is available from the British Library.

ISBN 978-0-349-41234-4

Printed and bound in Great Britain by
Clays Ltd, St Ives plc

Papers used by Piatkus are from well-managed forests
and other responsible sources.

FSC
www.fsc.org
MIX
Paper from
responsible sources
FSC® C104740

Piatkus
An imprint of
Little, Brown Book Group
Carmelite House
50 Victoria Embankment
London EC4Y 0DZ

An Hachette UK Company
www.hachette.co.uk

www.piatkus.co.uk

*This is for everyone who ever fell hopelessly in love with…
the Villain.*

Acknowledgments

Thank you as always to the people who help me write my books: my wonderful beta reader, Susannah Taylor, and my inexhaustible editor, Amy Pierpont.

Special thanks to Facebook friends, Lara Mansfield, who named Pip the dog; and Desiree Cleary-Lacasse, who named Hecate the cat.

Thank you all!

Duke of Sin

Chapter One

Once upon a time there was a king who had no heart. . . .

—From *King Heartless*

OCTOBER 1741
LONDON, ENGLAND

There are few worse places for a housekeeper of impeccable credentials to be caught than kneeling on her employer's bed. But two factors conspired to make *this* situation particularly fraught, Bridget Crumb reflected. One, that the employer in question was His Grace the Duke of Montgomery, widely regarded as the most wicked man in London. And two, that she happened to be clutching a just-purloined miniature portrait in her right hand.

Really, she was going to need a very strong cup of tea after this was all over—always assuming, of course, that she actually *survived* the duke's ire.

"Tell me, Mrs. Crumb," His Grace drawled in a voice filled with honeyed menace, "what are you looking for?"

The duke was neither a particularly large man, nor

what one would normally think of as intimidating—quite the opposite, in fact. His face might've been carved by a Greek sculptor, so perfect were his cheekbones, lips, and nose. His eyes were of the clearest azure. His curling hair was the color of polished guineas and quite gorgeous—which the duke obviously knew, since he wore it long, unpowdered, and tied at the nape of his neck with an enormous black bow. He wore an elegant purple velvet coat over a cloth-of-gold waistcoat embroidered in black and crimson. Fountains of lace fell from wrists and throat as he lounged in a winged armchair, one long leg thrust forward. Diamonds on the buckles of his shoes glinted in the candlelight. His Grace was urbane male sophistication personified—but anyone who therefore dismissed him as harmless was a rank fool.

The Duke of Montgomery was as deadly as a coiled adder discovered suddenly at one's feet.

Which was why Bridget made no sudden moves as she stood up from the bed. "Welcome home, Your Grace. Had I known you'd be returning from the Continent, I would've had your rooms aired and prepared."

"I was never on the Continent, as I'm sure you're *quite* aware." The duke gestured with an indolent hand to a shadowed corner of the room.

Bridget was too good a servant to let her eyes widen at the sight of a small half-open door cleverly set into the paneling. She'd never noticed the door before. She'd had her suspicions, but until this night she'd had no real evidence. Now she knew: he'd been here all along—*hiding* in the walls of his own town house. How long had he been watching her—days? Weeks? The entire three months that he was supposed to have been gone? More to the point, how long had he been watching her *tonight*? Had he seen her find the miniature portrait in a hidden hole in the bed's headboard?

Did he know she clutched it in her hand right now?

The duke smiled, flashing white teeth and deep dimples on both cheeks. "I'm afraid I never left."

"Indeed, Your Grace," Bridget murmured. "How very brave of you, considering the Duke of Wakefield banished you from England."

"Oh, *Wakefield*." The duke flicked his fingers as if shooing a fly instead of one of the most powerful men in London. "He's always taken himself *far* too seriously." He paused and eyed her as if she were an agate discovered in gravel. "But what a very sharp tongue you have for a housekeeper."

Bridget's heart sank—she knew better than to speak so frankly. It was never good for a servant to be noticed by a master—particularly *this* master.

"Come." He beckoned her closer with his forefinger and she saw the flash of a jeweled gold ring on his left thumb.

She swallowed and opened her right hand, silently dropping the miniature to the lush carpet. As she walked toward him she nudged the little painting under the enormous bed with the side of her foot.

She stopped a pace away from him.

His lips curved, sly and sensual. "*Closer.*"

She stepped nearer until her plain, practical black linsey-woolsey skirts were crushed against his purple velvet knees. Her heart beat hard and swift, but she was confident her expression didn't show her fear.

Still smiling, he held out his hands, palms upward. His hands were long-fingered and elegant. The hands of a musician—or a swordsman.

She stared down at them a moment, confused.

He quirked an eyebrow and nodded.

Bridget placed her hands on top of his. Palm to palm. She expected searing heat or deathly cold and was a little surprised to instead feel human warmth.

She'd been hired little more than a fortnight before the duke had supposedly been banished. In that time he had never struck her as human—or humane.

"Ah," His Grace murmured, cocking his head with interest. "What feminine hands you have, despite your station in life."

His blue eyes flashed at her from under dark eyelashes, a secretive smile playing about his mouth.

She met his gaze stonily.

His lips quirked and he looked down again. "Small, plump, with neat, round nails." He turned her hands over so that they now rested palms-up in his. "I once knew a Greek girl who swore she could read a man's life story from the lines on his hands." He dropped her left hand to trace the lines on her right palm with a forefinger.

His touch sent a frisson along her nerves and Bridget couldn't hold back a shudder.

The duke's dimple deepened beside his mouth as he examined her palm. "What have we here? Calluses, earned, no doubt, in my service." He tapped the thickened skin at the top of her palm. "A life of good, honest labor for a Scottish lass."

She held herself very still. How did he know where she

was from? Or at least very *nearly* where she was from? She'd worked very hard to hide her Border accent since coming to London, and she was sure she'd never mentioned her place of birth to either him or the man of business who had hired her.

"And this"—the duke stroked the mound beneath her thumb—"do you know what this is called?"

Bridget cleared her throat, but her voice emerged a bit rusty nonetheless. "I could not say, Your Grace."

"The Mount of Venus." He arched his eyebrows at her. Devastatingly beautiful. Lethally charming. "My Greek girl told me that this foretells how passionate a woman may be. You, Mrs. Crumb, must have untold depths of sensual need within you."

She narrowed her eyes at him.

He bent and bit the base of her thumb.

She gasped and snatched her hand away.

The duke laughed and sat back, smoothing his bottom lip with his beringed thumb slowly. "But then I was much more interested in the Greek girl's titties than her twitterings about palm reading."

Bridget stared at him, cradling the palm he'd *bitten* in her other hand. Though he hadn't actually hurt her, her palm tingled as if she still felt his teeth—his tongue—against her flesh.

She took a steadying breath. "May I go, Your Grace?"

"Naturally, Mrs. Crumb," he said, no longer looking at her. He appeared to be examining his ring. "Have a bath prepared for me. In the library, I think. I've a fancy to read as I soak."

"At this time of night?" Bridget glanced at the darkened

windows as she picked up her candlestick. It was past midnight and most of the servants would be in bed.

But of course rousing the servants from bed wasn't any concern to a duke—or to most aristocrats, come to that. "Yes, now, if you please, Mrs. Crumb."

"At once, Your Grace."

Bridget paused, her hand on the doorknob. She couldn't resist a curious glance back, for the duke had been in hiding for months now—was he out for good?

His azure gaze met hers, amused and wicked, and apparently reading her thoughts. "Oh, no, I'm quite done with the walls. Well"—he pursed his lips, shrugging—"for now at least. They're crowded and dusty, but oh, what a lovely site for spying. I do so like to spy upon people. It gives a delicious sense of power, don't you think?"

"I couldn't say, Your Grace."

"Couldn't you?" He tutted, his sensuous lips curving as he murmured, "Oh, Mrs. Crumb. You imperil your immortal soul with lies, you know."

Bridget fled.

Sadly there was no other word for it. She strode swiftly through the upper floor of the town house, past alabaster statues and gold-framed mirrors, her heart pounding in her chest, and descended the grand staircase. He couldn't know for certain, otherwise he'd have had her immediately dismissed, surely? That would be very bad for her future work prospects, if he dismissed her without reference. Or worse—declared that he'd let her go for theft. She shuddered at the very thought. That would completely destroy her good name. She'd have to leave London, start anew in some other, smaller city, and perhaps change her name.

More importantly, if the duke dismissed her, she'd be unable to help the lady who had given birth to her. That was the real reason she'd taken this job: Bridget was the bastard daughter of an aristocratic lady being blackmailed by the duke. She had vowed to find the letters the duke was using as his hold over her mother. Blackmail was a nasty, vile crime and the duke was a nasty, vile man.

She wasn't leaving until she fulfilled her self-imposed mission.

Bridget halted before the door to the kitchens, taking a deep breath and making sure her skirts and mobcap were in order—a housekeeper always looked completely neat, even when the master had just bitten her. Another deep breath. There was no point in borrowing trouble. Right now she had a house to run. One with its master newly returned—or at least newly emerged from hiding.

She entered the vast kitchens of Hermes House, the duke's London town house. At this time of night the fire was banked in the huge hearth. Shadows lurked at the edges of the ceiling and in the corners of the kitchen, but she found the sight soothing. Everything was as it should be back here.

Bridget woke the poor bootblack boy, sleeping on a pallet by the hearth, and sent the yawning lad up to wake the scullery maids and the footmen. She stirred the fire, building it until it roared, and then lit several candles, the mundane task further calming her nerves.

By the time the footmen and scullery maids arrived a few minutes later, the kitchen was bright and hot and Bridget was in full control. She immediately set her troops to drawing and heating the huge amount of water needed for a despot's bath.

Then she retraced her steps to the front of the house.

Hermes House was newly built by the duke himself and the town house was as extravagant as the man. The wide, curving staircase was white marble, the landings gray-veined pink marble checkerboarded with black marble, and the entire thing highlighted with gilding. The stairs opened onto a wide hallway on the first floor, the walls a pale pink, detailed in white and gold foil.

Bridget paused before the duke's bedroom and listened. No sound came from within. Either he'd already gone to the library, or he was lurking inside, ready to pounce on her.

She narrowed her eyes and pushed the door open.

The room was dark. She raised her candle high—the duke had already caught her by surprise once tonight. Her candle lit shell-pink walls, a ceiling painted with gods and goddesses reveling in debauchery, and the ridiculously huge bed hung with sky-blue draperies and gold tassels. Next to the bed was a delicate secretary inlaid with ivory and gilt. Over the secretary hung an enormous, life-size painting of the duke.

In the nude.

Bridget scowled at the portrait, quickly slipped into the bedroom, and closed the door behind her. She hurried to the bed and knelt down, sweeping aside the bed-curtains to reveal the floor beneath.

Bare floor met her gaze. The miniature was gone.

VAL STUDIED THE miniature in his hand. It depicted a family: an English aristocrat, his wife—an Indian noblewoman—and their infant child. There were much more valuable pieces in his house if one wished to steal. Ergo, Mrs. Crumb was working either for the owner of the miniature or their agent. He remembered the look of bland aplomb she'd given him as she'd slid off his bed. The corner of his mouth curved up as he slipped the gilt-framed miniature into the pocket of his banyan. Had his little housekeeper truly thought she could fool *him* of all people?

Well, not so little, he conceded as he remembered Mrs. Crumb standing rigidly at attention before him. She was a bit over the average height for a woman, with what he suspected was a bounteous pair of tits. Sadly, she hid her glory beneath tightly laced stays, black wool, a white-pinned apron, and a neatly tucked white fichu. Add to that hair entirely covered by an enormous white mob-cap that tied under her chin, pronounced black eyebrows, an unremarkable nose and mouth, a chin that *might* give one a bit of a pause due to the determination of its set… but on the whole an ordinary piece, really—if one didn't notice those intense dark eyes.

Hers were the eyes of a religious fanatic—a saint or a heretic.

Or perhaps an inquisitor.

A woman with complete confidence that she knew right from wrong—in herself and in others. A woman not afraid to suffer—perhaps die—for her beliefs.

Did she then recognize in him her opposite: the very Devil? A man who neither knew nor cared about that delicate difference between good and evil? While others carefully balanced their scales, debating the various weights of sins and good deeds, he chose to dash the entire apparatus to the ground. Why entangle himself with a game whose rules he neither understood nor particularly approved of? Better to make his *own* rules in life. Much more fun, at any rate.

Val's upper lip curled as he wondered if Mrs. Crumb knew the meaning of the word *fun*. Most likely she dismissed it as something vaguely shameful and leading to *sin*—which, at the best of times, it *was*.

Still, Mrs. Crumb was somewhat entertaining in her very novelty—a *housekeeper* attempting to match wits with him—and even with all his plans and plots he was sadly lacking in amusements.

Thus he'd let her stay and play for the nonce.

Meanwhile he had power and position in society to regain—and in order to do *that*, he was about to blackmail the King. He would demand the King's acknowledgement—only that—but more than enough to guarantee an end to exile.

He'd agreed to banishment from England in the first place only because the wretched Duke of Wakefield—a pompous parliamentarian with an overblown sense of his own importance—had threatened to have Val charged with kidnapping if he did not. All because Val had taken the man's sister once. Or twice. Or perhaps three times. Did it really matter? She'd not been harmed in the end—despite Val's intentions—and in fact had married some lowly retired dragoon captain. *Really*. Val had had *much* better plans for her.

But now, *now* he had finally obtained letters with which he could threaten the King. He would go straight over bloody Wakefield's head and to the King himself and there wasn't a damned thing Wakefield could do about it.

Val swung swiftly to a writing desk that he kept in a corner of the library. It was elaborately carved in yellow-and-brown spotted marble, swirling and twirling in quite a ridiculously extravagant way. He'd won it off a Prussian aristocrat in a game of cards—in which he'd bluffed—and paid a king's ransom to have it shipped to London, where it clashed terribly with the walls of his library.

He patted the desk fondly as he seated himself and rummaged in the drawers for paper.

He dabbed a quill in an ink bottle and wrote in his large, flourishing hand, saluting a Mr. Copernicus Shrugg, who happened to be the personal secretary of His Majesty, George II of England. The letter was short but florid—and rather graphic in its threat. Val smiled thinly as he swept his initial on the bottom third of the page.

The door to the library opened and a ragamuffin boy entered.

Well, Alf *presented* herself as a boy in any case and, as far as Val knew, most people seemed to be bamboozled by her trifling ruse. He, naturally, had taken only a minute—if that—to realize her true sex. One had but to look at the slenderness of her neck, the lack of an Adam's apple, the angle where her jaw met her neck, et cetera, et cetera. Amazing how few people truly examined the world about them.

Val gave respect where respect was due and a disguise carefully maintained over years was certainly deserving of some small kudos, so he never made mention of Alf's true nature. That, and he couldn't bestir himself to be particularly interested in street urchins—male or female. He did, however, have much interest in—and use for—an intelligence-gatherer and runner. Alf had fulfilled this position in the months that Val had been perforce hidden in his own walls, often delivering letters, food, and books.

"Yer Grace," the boyish girl muttered when she neared. "You wanted t' see me t'night, if'n I remembers aright."

Val ignored her as he lit his sealing wax and dripped hot wax over the folded edge of his letter. He blew out the sealing wax, set it down, and chose his seal: a crowing rooster. It was a personal jest: the rooster was a symbol of the god Hermes, whom Val had taken as his own patron god. Hermes was the god of travel and of commerce.

He was also the god of thieves and trickery.

Val bit his lip. Too, the base pun on *rooster* was so obvious that even the most unintelligent should be able to parse it.

He turned to Alf.

She was standing hip cocked, weight on one leg, wearing, as far as Val could tell, the same clothes that she'd been wearing for years: a too-large coat and waistcoat, both an indeterminate dark color, much patched and frayed, baggy breeches, mud-stained stockings, enormous buckle shoes the exact color of dried horse dung, and a wide-brimmed floppy hat. Beneath the hat her dark hair was untidily clubbed back and one cheekbone was darkened by either dirt or a bruise.

Val briefly wondered what Alf did with the money he paid her—for he paid her rather well, considering—and then he dismissed the thought from his mind.

He thrust the letter at her. "Take this to Mr. Copernicus Shrugg"—he recited the address—"and make sure you hand it to him personally—no one else, mind."

Alf took the letter, but wrinkled her nose. "It's th' middle o' th' night, you do know that, don't you?"

"And what of it? A man roused from bed is even more prone to fear and excitement, I find. Oh, and tell Attwell and the boy they can quit the inn they've been staying at and attend me here." He glanced over as the door to the library was once more opened and a troop of footmen carried in his bath. "Now off with you, imp. I've the dust of weeks in those damnable walls to wash away."

The girl hesitated, eyeing him speculatively. "Then yer out o' yer 'idey-'oles, are you?" She tilted her head with significance at the servants, now pouring the bathwater before the fireplace.

"Out and soon to be restored to my rightful place in society," Val said. "Run along."

He turned to his bath without waiting to see if she obeyed his command. Few people had the nerve to refuse his orders. Ah, but he was forgetting the winsome Mrs. Crumb. What *was* her Christian name anyway? He must demand it of her at the first opportunity. Not only had his housekeeper attempted to steal from him, but she'd refused to answer his questions, and—he surveyed the servants sent to wait upon him—if he wasn't mistaken she'd made sure to hide away the comeliest of his maids and footmen. Did she think him a satyr?

Well, perhaps she wasn't *entirely* mistaken in her judgment...

Val smirked as he shed his banyan—the only article

of clothing he wore—and sauntered nude to the bath. He crooked a finger at the eldest and most worldly-looking of the footmen. If Mrs. Crumb thought to curtail his bedsport, she was going to be sadly disappointed.

HUGH FITZROY, THE Duke of Kyle, yawned widely as he followed a linkboy's wavering lantern through a darkened courtyard at the back of St James's Palace. It was near four of the clock—too early yet for a servant to be awake and too late for all but the most determined revelers to be still abroad. That left him, newly roused from his warm slumbers by an urgent royal summons, and the poor linkboy, who would guide night travelers with his lantern until dawn.

Both bound by the needs of their masters.

Hugh smiled wryly to himself. *Master* in his case wasn't quite correct, but it was close enough.

He and the linkboy neared an obscure rear entrance and a guard came to attention. Hugh paid the linkboy off and then turned to the guard to give his name.

The guard shot him a curious glance as he let him in. This was an odd entrance for a duke.

But then Hugh was rather an odd duke.

Inside he was met with a footman who had apparently been waiting for his arrival. "This way, if you please, Your Grace."

Hugh followed the man down a service passage. Unlike the front of the palace, the hallway was uncarpeted, the walls simply painted.

The footman opened a door at the end of the hall and bowed him into an office, murmuring, "The Duke of Kyle."

A bandy-legged man wearing scarlet breeches, a dark-blue banyan, and a soft cap swung around from where he'd been pacing before a fire. "Damn me, Kyle, it took you long enough!"

Hugh arched an eyebrow. "I came as soon as I got your note, Shrugg." He glanced back at the footman. "Bring coffee and tea, will you? And something to eat."

The footman hurried away.

"Forgive me, Your Grace." Copernicus Shrugg shook his head. He was a man of middling years, but he'd always looked like an old man. His ears protruded from his skull on either side like the handles of a jug, and his head was round, wrinkled, and bald, and sat almost squarely on his shoulders without benefit of a neck. He stared at Hugh with bloodshot eyes the color of cornflowers. "It's this damnable matter. I had to wake *him* up over it and you know he never likes that."

They both glanced reflexively at the ceiling, where the royal apartments resided somewhere above them.

Hugh dropped his gaze to Shrugg again. "How is the King?" Technically the man in question was also Hugh's father, though no one ever made mention of that fact.

"Talking in French," Shrugg replied. "He's quite beside himself. Thank God you're back in London—I don't know who else I would have summoned."

Hugh raised an eyebrow.

Shrugg's face darkened. "Though, of course, the circumstance of your return from the Continent is naturally a sad one. I was sorry to hear of the death of your duchess."

Hugh tightened his jaw and nodded once. "Is it the prince?" The Prince of Wales—whom Hugh had met only once—and the King loathed each other.

"Not this time," Shrugg said grimly. He held out a letter.

Hugh took it and walked over to the desk, where several candles burned. He tilted the piece of paper to the candle and read:

Dear Mr. Shrugg,

I trust that you have had a restful night up until this point because I doubt it will be so hereafter. Let me at once get to the point: certain letters have come into my possession concerning W which, if they were made public, would bring great embarrassment to—and possibly the Downfall of—the Gentleman you serve. I, of course, am most anxious that this occurrence not come about. To prevent this Terrible Event I have merely one request: that I be Acknowledged in Hyde Park at a time mutually agreed upon.

So simple, really.

I am, your servant, & et cetera, et cetera,
M

Hugh read the letter once quickly and then again more slowly.

When he looked up again, a steaming cup of coffee had been placed on the desk in front of him.

"Thank you." He took a sip. "'M'?"

"The Duke of Montgomery," Shrugg said.

"He made sure not to sign his name." Hugh's mouth

twisted wryly. "A blackmailer who knows to be circumspect in letters. 'W' is Prince William." Prince William, the Duke of Cumberland, was the King's second living legitimate son. Hugh had never met the boy.

"Undoubtedly." Shrugg sank heavily into the chair behind the desk with his own teacup. "He's never caused us problems before. Well"—he waved a hand dismissively—"mistresses and the like, but nothing out of the ordinary for a lad his age. Now this."

Hugh frowned. "How old is he now?"

"Twenty, and just bought a commission as colonel of the First Regiment of Foot Guards," Shrugg said. "He's always liked everything martial."

Hugh looked at him intently. "Then you have no idea what it could be about?"

Shrugg was silent a moment, twisting his teacup in his hands. "There were rumors—only rumors, mind. About a secret society."

Hugh snorted and stood, stretching. "Tell me you didn't drag me out of bed for a bloody secret society, Shrugg. Every boy who ever went to Cambridge or Oxford—or any London coffeehouse, for that matter—is a member of what he thinks is a secret society."

But Shrugg's old lined face was grave. "No, Your Grace. This was different. The members were older. They called themselves the Lords of Chaos. It's said that each member actually had a tattoo of a dolphin somewhere on their person and the things they did..." He grimaced, looking away.

"What?"

Shrugg turned back to him. "Children. There were children involved."

For a moment Hugh didn't say anything. Kit and Peter were safely in their beds, somewhere at home, Kit with his foot hanging out of the covers and little Peter clutching a kerchief that had belonged to his mother.

He took a breath, making sure his voice was flat and matter-of-fact. "You're saying Prince William might've done something with these Lords of Chaos. Something with children?"

"I don't *know*," Shrugg said. "That's why I asked you to come. We need you to find what Montgomery has. To find it and take it and make sure it's destroyed. Permanently."

Chapter Two

When this king was born the royal physician peered into his eyes and mouth and ears and pronounced them all good, but when he laid his head upon the baby's tiny breast he heard… nothing….

—From *King Heartless*

Bridget's chatelaine jingled at her waist as she strode into the kitchens a little after ten o' clock the next morning. The servants had been up since five of the clock and the entire lower floor was cleaned and aired. In fact most of the staff were just finishing their morning tea.

"Good morning, Mrs. Bram," she greeted the cook, a sensible woman of middling years with graying frizzy hair.

"Mrs. Crumb." The cook glanced up alertly. "I understand His Grace is in residence."

"Indeed he is," Bridget said briskly, ignoring the slight twinge of anxiety even his name caused. "I trust you'll be able to prepare both his meals today even on such short notice?"

"I'll have no problem," Mrs. Bram replied. "Got a lovely roast in just this morning that'll do for supper and I've a fish pie in the oven for his luncheon, should he call for it."

"Excellent." Bridget nodded her approval, though she'd never doubted Mrs. Bram. She'd seldom worked with such a competent cook.

Bridget crossed the kitchen as the maids and footmen rose to resume their duties. By the back door to the kitchen was a table and on it was a tin plate with another inverted over it. Bridget picked it up without pausing and opened the back door, stepping outside and closing the door behind her.

She felt her shoulders relax just the tiniest bit.

She stood in a small, square bricked well, for the kitchen was naturally below ground. A short flight of stairs led up to the garden and a path and thence to the mews behind Hermes House, but that wasn't what interested Bridget at the moment.

A small brownish-gray terrier had been sitting on the brick, but he hopped to his feet as soon as he saw Bridget and gave one sharp emphatic bark.

"Now hush," she said to him—not that he seemed to care. She set the tin plate down and uncovered it, revealing the scraps that Mrs. Bram had saved for her.

The terrier immediately began gobbling the food as if he was starving which, sadly, he might be.

"You'll choke," Bridget said sternly. The terrier didn't listen. He never did, no matter how businesslike she made her voice. Grown men—footmen—might jump to obey her, but this scrawny waif defied her.

Bridget bit her lip. If she was forced to leave Hermes House, who would feed the terrier? Mrs. Bram might—if she remembered to do so—but the cook was a busy woman with other matters on her mind.

The dog finished his meal and licked the plate so enthusiastically that he overturned it with a clatter.

Bridget tutted and bent to pick it up.

The dog thrust his short snout under her hand as she did so and she found herself stroking his head. His fur was wiry rather than silky, almost greasy, but the dog had liquid brown eyes and seemed to smile as his mouth hung open, tongue lolling out. He was very, very sweet. She'd never been allowed a pet dog as a child. Her foster father was a shepherd and had considered dogs farm animals. A pet dog wasn't even to be thought of, especially for her, the *cuckoo.*

Housekeepers, and indeed servants of any kind, weren't allowed pets. Sometimes a cat might be kept to catch mice in the kitchens, but it was a working animal. Dogs were dirty things and required food and space that, technically, she didn't own.

Bridget stood and frowned down at the dog. "Shoo now."

The dog sat and slowly wagged his tail, sweeping the bricks. One of his triangular ears stood up while the other lay down.

She wished—

Behind her someone opened the door to the kitchens. "Mrs. Crumb?"

She turned at once. "Yes, I'm coming."

Bridget hurried into the kitchen without a glance back.

Bob, one of the footmen, was staring at her anxiously. "'E wants a word with you."

Was he summoning her to dismiss her in the light of morning?

Bridget straightened, smoothing down her apron.

"His Grace wants a word with me," she gently corrected. She never let the servants in her command descend into disrespectful language toward their employer or employers, even belowstairs.

"His Grace." Bob blushed violently. Though well over six feet, he couldn't be more than twenty years of age and was fresh from the country. "But ma'am... that is..."

"Yes?"

"Well, the duke isn't alone."

"Ah." So that was what had the boy so bothered. Poor lad. He'd soon enough become inured to the carnal excesses of the aristocracy. "I know, dear."

Behind them came a snort and Bridget whirled.

Cal, the most handsome of the footmen—and thus one who *hadn't* been sent up with the bath the night before—had his upper lip curled. "He's a rutting devil, born and bred."

"That's enough." Bridget didn't raise her voice, but then she didn't have to—the entire kitchen had gone quiet at her reprimand. "The duke is our master and we will speak of him respectfully. Anyone who does not is most welcome to seek employment elsewhere. Is that clear?"

She glanced about the kitchen, meeting everyone's gaze for a second.

Then she nodded once and swiftly exited the kitchen.

That might have been her last command as housekeeper, but she wouldn't leave a house with the servants in disorder.

Not even *his* house.

Bridget made her way through a back hall and up the servants' stairs to the upper floor, aware, vaguely, that her hands were trembling. She didn't like change. Didn't like always having to find another place to call home—though none, of course, were truly *her* home—but that was the nature of her work. She'd chosen this life and she was proud of what she'd accomplished. How far she'd come. The position she'd achieved.

There. Her hands had stopped shaking.

And really, had Bob thought she wasn't aware that George, one of the older footmen, had procured a pair of courtesans for the duke's entertainment last night? A good housekeeper—and Bridget considered herself the best—knew *everything* that happened within her domain.

No matter how sordid.

The duke's bedroom door was shut so she tapped once before entering. "Good morning, Your Grace."

The duke was sprawled, entirely naked, as far as she could see, between two equally bare women. Well, *one* woman was visible at least. A petite blonde broke off her embrace of the duke and glanced curiously at Bridget in the doorway. The other—a thin brunette—soon emerged from under the sumptuous sky-blue velvet coverlet, wiping her mouth discreetly.

"Pardon," the brunette murmured, as if she'd belched at the dinner table.

Bridget took no note. It wasn't the *courtesan's* fault that Bridget was witnessing her dishabille.

His Grace slowly opened his azure eyes. The bedroom overlooked the back gardens and a previous servant had already drawn the curtains. In the morning sunlight, reddish-gold stubble glinting on his chin, and the curling hair about his shoulders, he really was quite beautiful. Like an ancient Greek god taking his leisure. One almost felt he deserved his wealth, his status, and all the things he'd accrued, merely by the accident of his birth.

Almost.

"Mrs. Crumb," he purred, "What a lovely day, don't you think?"

"Indeed, Your Grace."

"And with such lovely companions," he continued, slinging his arms about his bedfellows.

She hoped she needn't comment on *that* statement—although one never knew. She'd once been invited in rather crude terms to join an elderly baronet and one of the maids in his bed. She'd declined with the vigorous application of a bed warmer and packed her bags before the next morning.

It'd been one of her shorter positions of employment.

"I was told you had need of me, Your Grace," she reminded him, folding her hands at her waist to hide the trembling that had begun again. She'd been in *demand* before this position. Duchesses and lionesses of society had wanted her.

"So practical," he mused, tilting his golden head back to gaze, presumably, at the gaudy sky-blue velvet canopy of his bed. She'd always thought it rather vulgar, actually.

"I suppose that would be considered a good thing in a housekeeper."

"It's generally considered so, Your Grace."

"And yet, I find it somewhat..."—he raised his naked arm straight up above his head and twirled his hand as he thought—"*irksome*."

"I am sorry, Your Grace," Bridget said as pleasantly as she could, which, sadly, was not very.

"Oh, don't be," the duke murmured silkily. "One can't help one's nature, no matter how irritating it is to others."

His azure eyes suddenly dropped to pin her, hard and merciless, and she lost her breath as she fell into his predator's stare. It was like looking into the eyes of something inhuman, almost otherworldly. Her chest ached as she stared at him, the air still locked within her, but at the same time the place between her legs ached as well. She was suddenly made very aware that beneath the starch of her apron, the wool of her dress, and the bone of her stays, she had soft nipples that had tightened into points.

Then she inhaled, filling her lungs with sweet air, as he watched her still, his eyes half-lidded, and she felt an odd exhilaration, as if a gauntlet had been thrown down. As if they were adversaries, equal on the field.

Which was completely ridiculous.

Possibly she shouldn't have indulged in that third cup of tea this morning.

"I wonder whom you work for, Mrs. Crumb?" he whispered.

"Why, for you, Your Grace," she replied, holding his gaze.

He snorted.

She felt a bead of perspiration trail down her spine.

"Now away with you, my temptations!" the duke cried, suddenly animated.

He leaped from the bed and, catching up a purse lying carelessly on a table, poured a shocking amount of gold into the giggling women's hands. He bundled them, still nude and laughing, clutching their clothes and shoes, out the door.

Bridget quietly stepped to the door and beckoned to a wide-eyed footman. She gave the man—Bob again—instructions to escort the women to the servants' door when they were properly attired.

When she returned to the duke's bedroom he was watching her, an ironic light in his eyes. "What an officious woman you are, Mrs. Crumb."

"You'll thank me when none of your possessions go missing, Your Grace," she replied.

"Will I, though?" He strode, nude, to his desk, and, bending over it, afforded her a quite scandalous view of his muscular bottom. He seemed to have a dark mark of some kind on the left cheek. Good God, it looked like a *tattoo*. What—? "I have the most lamentable taste sometimes. It probably would be *better* if a few of my things disappeared. Why, Mrs. Crumb," he drawled, and she snapped her gaze belatedly up to find that he'd turned back to her—*damn it*! "Were you ogling my arse?"

She opened her mouth and then wasn't sure, exactly, what to say. *Was* he about to dismiss her or not? "I... I—"

"Ye-es?" He took one long stride toward her.

She was suddenly, overwhelmingly aware of what she'd until now successfully ignored: He. Was. *Nude*.

His shoulders were wide, his chest highlighted by

pale-pink nipples drawn tight, with but a few curling golden hairs between. His torso narrowed in a perfect V to a slim waist and a shallow belly button. A thin line of slightly darker hair led to his genitals.

During his supposed absence Bridget had had plenty of time to study the life-size nude portrait of the duke hanging next to his bed. She'd long thought the dimensions of his manhood exaggerated.

They were not.

His cock swayed, ruddy and healthy, between muscled thighs. His testicles were lightly furred and comely—if such things could be *called* comely—and his legs were downright beautiful. Even his feet—his *feet*—were oddly lovely, long-toed and high-arched.

Those toes brushed her skirts and she hastily glanced up to find him standing far too close to her, a wicked smile playing about his mouth.

"Oh, Mrs. Crumb, such a look," he murmured, his voice a deep purr, his bare chest brushing against her snowy white apron. "Why, I don't know whether to guard my bollocks . . ."—his gaze dropped to her mouth—"or to kiss you."

"You mustn't embrace me," she said quickly, her voice far more breathless than it should be.

His head cocked, his dark eyebrows rose, a corner of his mouth curled teasingly, and he leaned closer still as if considering the idea. "Mustn't I?"

His hot breath whispered across her lips and she realized that she'd *closed her eyes*. Oh, God, she—

Someone squeaked, and Bridget was almost certain it wasn't she.

Bridget opened her eyes, scurrying backward in a sadly undignified manner.

A slender youth stood in the doorway. He wore a proper brown coat, waistcoat, and breeches, but he had a red-and-yellow printed cloth wrapped about his head.

"Ah, Mehmed, there you are," the duke said, as if he were used to being disturbed nearly embracing a woman while nude and—*Good God*—in a state of excitement.

Bridget hastily averted her gaze from the duke's endowment, which had chosen to flaunt itself. Her face was hot and she clasped her hands before her to keep herself from pressing the backs of her fingers to her cheeks.

The boy at the door looked as embarrassed as she felt. He held a steaming pitcher of water, but he began to back out again. "You with whore, Duke. I go."

Behind the boy, the duke's valet, Attwell, appeared, looking not a little startled.

The Duke of Montgomery—the only person *not* embarrassed—burst out laughing. "No, no, Mehmed. Whores—at least *mine*—wear much more ornamental clothing than *this*."

And he waved rather insultingly at Bridget's dress.

Her lips pursed as her brain once again was engaged. "Who is this?"

"Mehmed, as I said." Both Mehmed and Attwell entered the bedroom. The boy carefully set down his pitcher of water and Attwell crossed to the dressing room. "Mehmed is a follower of the prophet Mohammed and no doubt destined for hell, if the Christian philosophers are to be believed. Of course *his* people think that *we'll* all end in hell, so I suppose in the end everyone will meet in a jolly sort of molten Babel. I ordered both Mehmed and Attwell to come to Hermes House from the inn they've been staying at."

"But..." Bridget frowned. She'd met Attwell before, and indeed had seen him just this morning in the kitchen.

The duke glanced at her and then glanced again, a slow smile forming on his lips—a smile she did not like. "You didn't realize Mehmed was in the house, did you?"

"I—"

"And you don't *like* not knowing." He grinned as he casually held out an arm and Attwell—at last, thank *God*—helped him into a garish purple silk banyan with a gold-and-green embroidered dragon on the back.

"It's my job to be apprised of all that goes on within Hermes House," Bridget replied. "Your Grace."

"But you didn't know he was here, did you?" the duke said in a very grating singsong voice. "Do you know, you've never told me your Christian name."

"No, I haven't," she said, rallying. The man was the Devil in the flesh, but she wasn't known as the best housekeeper in London for nothing. "When did you take Mehmed on?"

"He came with me when I returned to England from my travels abroad last year," the duke said carelessly. "But then he was taken ill crossing the Channel, so I left him at my house in Bath to convalesce. Attwell fetched him to London in September."

Bridget pursed her lips. The boy looked healthy enough now. "Will Mehmed be living at Hermes House, Your Grace?"

"Oh, I think so," the duke said, widening his eyes in pretend innocence. "How else will he serve as my catamite?"

Attwell, arranging the duke's apparel for the day on a chair, choked.

Bridget could not blame the valet. She herself merely narrowed her eyes at the duke.

He smiled at her angelically.

"What is *catamite*?" Mehmed asked. He was a very lovely boy with a dewy complexion, large brown eyes, and white teeth. At the moment he was busy assembling the tools for shaving on a small table.

"A person who likes cats," Montgomery replied, drawing out a chair and seating himself in the middle of the room.

"I like cats," Mehmed said promptly.

He poured hot water from the pitcher into a basin, wet a cloth, wrung it, and tenderly draped it over the lower half of the duke's face.

Bridget cleared her throat. She had no idea why the duke had originally asked her here—if not to let her go—but she had work to do. "Mehmed, I am Mrs. Crumb, the housekeeper. When you are—"

"How do you do!" She was interrupted by Mehmed stepping smartly forward and bowing, his upper body completely parallel to the floor, his arms plastered to his sides.

"Erm." Bridget blinked as he straightened, smiling at her. "Yes. How do you do. I—"

"I am good!" Mehmed said, very loudly, and Bridget couldn't help noticing that the duke appeared to be laughing under his damp cloth.

Attwell, for his part, was ignoring the proceedings. She'd found the duke's valet an exceedingly phlegmatic man.

"I'm glad," she said gently, but firmly. "When you are done helping the duke dress, please come to the kitchens and I will discuss with you your place in this house."

She turned to go.

"Not so fast, Mrs. Crumb," her blasted employer said, having snatched the cloth from his face. "I'm not done with you yet."

She took a deep breath. Then another.

And *another.*

Then she turned with a small, polite smile pasted quite firmly to her face. "How might I help you, Your Grace?"

"Take a look at those," said the maddening man, pointing straight-armed at his desk.

Bridget looked and noticed for the first time—well, there *had* been quite a bit of male nudity about previously—that there was a pile of jewels on his desk. She shot a questioning glance at the duke, now being lathered by Mehmed.

His blue eyes glittered back at her. "Go on. They won't bite, I assure you."

She humphed under her breath and stalked over to the desk. There were two necklaces lying there, both incredibly opulent. They were things that a duchess or princess or queen would wear. A lady's maid might touch a necklace like one of these to put it around her mistress's neck, but otherwise someone of Bridget's station would never in a thousand years have cause to handle such wondrous things. The first necklace was made of diamonds and sapphires, tangled in a heap. The other seemed to be of rubies and huge, baroque pearls, interlaced with opals and other, smaller gemstones. She stared at them, wondering rather whimsically where the stones had come from. Far-off India? Some Persian mine? And the pearls? What exotic seas had they seen? Had pirates fought for them?

"Which do you like better?" came the duke's voice from behind her, interrupting her silly musings. "I ask because I'm to present one to my fiancée."

She looked up at that. "You're to be married?"

He'd had his eyes closed as Mehmed carefully shaved him, but he opened them now. "Oh, yes."

"But to whom?" she blurted.

What sort of woman would he chose as his consort? An aristocrat, obviously, but beyond that? She couldn't imagine. Would he want a lady easily led? A woman renowned for her beauty or her wit? Or did he not care about such things at all?

"Now, now, I haven't informed the bride yet and I *do* think she should know before my housekeeper, don't you?"

Was he teasing her? He must be. No one, not even mad aristocrats, conducted his affairs in this manner.

"Well?" He was still watching her, lazily, like a well-fed cat, too sleepy to bat a mouse.

She blinked. "I'm sorry?"

"Which do you like, Mrs. Crumb?" he said slowly—as if *she* were the one who was acting odd here.

Bridget could've said that it was *quite* inappropriate for a housekeeper to be picking out a duchess's jewelry—if he was indeed speaking the truth—but what would be the point?

Instead she bent closer, carefully examining the pieces.

"You can touch them," he said. "Hold them up, if you wish."

She ignored him, but straightened each necklace. The ruby one was much gaudier, with several tiers of pearls and jewels.

She picked up the slightly more sedate sapphires. "These."

"Good," he said. "I'll have the sapphires returned to the jewelers right away and keep the rubies for my future wife."

She stared at him.

He waited, smiling, but she'd learned patience and to bite her tongue—*hard*—from an early age.

Slowly she put the necklace back on the desk. "If that is all, Your Grace?"

"Oh, fine. Run and scrub the front steps or whatever it is you do."

She swallowed an irrationally irritated retort—he was *not* good for her self-possession—and turned. The chatelaine at her waist made a faint tinkle.

"Was it a lover?"

She stopped and looked at him—very, *very* careful to keep still.

He nodded at the chatelaine. "The one who gave you that incredibly practical piece of ornamentation? Couldn't he at least have afforded a ring or a locket to hang between your breasts? I'd wager you have lovely breasts under all that wool and boning."

She stared down at her chatelaine. It was made of sturdy steel, but the central piece was a pretty blue-and-red-enameled disk. From it hung four chains, each with smaller enameled disks matching the main one. Suspended on the chains were a ring of keys, a tiny pair of scissors, a very small, very sharp folding knife, and her watch. Not all housekeepers had chatelaines, but many did. Though few had one as pretty as hers.

And he was right: it had been a gift.

She met his gaze, her own, she hoped, showing nothing. "If that is all, Your Grace? I'm afraid I must be about my work."

Behind her the door opened. "Your Grace, a letter."

Bob hurried past her with the letter, which the duke immediately tore open.

And then he said something in another language that made Mehmed jump back from him.

The duke looked up, though he did not seem to see her or anyone else in the room. "My sister is marrying a bloody, goddamned *commoner*."

VAL PULLED HIS tricorne lower as the sedan chair jolted and swayed through the London streets. A risk to be on the streets in broad daylight before the King had submitted to his terms, but needs must. He simply couldn't let darling Eve marry Asa Makepeace. The man was a mountebank, the owner of Harte's Folly, a pleasure garden that Val had chosen to underwrite for reasons of his own, and of all ghastly things, a beer brewer's son.

Val had put his half sister, Eve, in charge of the finances when he'd supposedly left town.

In hindsight that had been an obvious mistake.

Eve was a shy woman. A woman who had spent years hidden away from the world, traumatized by their shared past. True, she was also stubborn as a mule when she wanted to be, but he never should've put her in the position of facing off against Makepeace. He'd obviously proved too overwhelming for her. God only knew what the pleasure garden owner had done to Eve to make her agree to marry him.

Val growled under his breath as his chairmen turned into a quiet street and then down the side of a house. He climbed out of the chair and rapped smartly at a side door with his cane.

A tall man of African descent, wearing livery and a snowy-white wig, answered it. His name was Jean-Marie Pépin and he'd been hired by Val himself to guard Eve.

"Your Grace," Jean-Marie intoned in a bass voice, his face curiously expressionless. For a moment Val had the oddest feeling that Jean-Marie wasn't going to let him in the house.

He raised a ducal eyebrow.

The footman bowed his head and silently backed in, opening the door. "She is in 'er sitting room."

Val nodded curtly and bounded up the stairs, bursting through the door and into Eve's inner sanctum as he said, "Whatever possessed you, dear girl to—bloody *hell*, what is that?"

For on his entrance a massive—and massively ugly—dog had risen to its feet in a not entirely welcoming manner.

"That's my dog, Henry," said Eve from behind her

desk, as blithely as if she were announcing that it was a sunny day.

Val glared at her. The last he'd heard she'd been deathly afraid of dogs. "You don't *have* a dog."

Eve raised her eyebrows. Despite their blood relation and their father's golden hair and blue eyes, she was a plain woman, her face dominated by her mother's overlong nose. "I do now."

He stepped around the beast, keeping his eye on it. "And that's not all you have—or so I've heard."

She looked wary. "When did you return from the Continent, Val? I had no word that you intended to return. In fact, I thought to journey there myself to find you."

"Before or after you married Asa Makepeace?" Val shot back.

"After, actually."

He stared at her. She didn't *act* like a damsel bullied into marriage by a rogue gold digger, but he knew his sister's history. Eve simply *wouldn't* willingly marry a man as randy as Makepeace.

"Is he forcing you?"

She actually looked shocked. "No, of course not. Why would you think such a thing?"

"Because you're the daughter of a duke—even if a bastard—and he's a common ruffian." Val flung out his palm. "If marriage is what you want, darling, I can find you someone much better. Someone *titled* at the very least."

"I don't *want* someone whom *you* consider better," Eve said, and her voice actually rose. Her cheeks had bloomed pink as well. Perhaps Makepeace had drugged her in some way? Val had heard in his travels to the Levant tales of drugs that could be used to persuade. "Val! Are you even listening to me?"

"Yes, yes," he said distractedly. "Where is this paragon of a pleasure garden owner?"

"Here."

Val swung around at the male voice.

Asa Makepeace stood in the doorway, big and burly, in breeches and shirt, but *not* waistcoat, coat, shoes, or stockings. He'd quite obviously come from bed.

Eve's bed.

Val saw red.

He had his left hand inside his waistcoat, his right one raised, gripping his cane, and was advancing toward Makepeace when he felt a small palm on his breast.

He looked down.

Eve peered up at him. "Whatever you were about to do, *don't*."

He stared into her eyes—the same blue eyes as his own—watching, searching. "He was in your bed."

"Yes," she said, unwavering, though that blush bloomed again. "He was. But he didn't hurt me. He never hurt me, Val." She took a breath. "Quite the opposite, in fact."

He held her gaze a moment more, making sure, and then he raised his eyes to look at the man his sister had taken as her lover.

Makepeace stood still in the doorway. Smart. Makepeace might outweigh him, but had Val continued his trajectory, the other man would've lain bleeding on the floor.

"Why?" Val growled at him.

"I love her."

Val squinted at Makepeace. Cocked his head. And then shook it.

Of all the possible answers, he'd never considered that one. It made no sense at all. Love . . . didn't matter. Love—as he understood the term—wasn't a reason for marriage.

He looked at Eve.

And saw sadness lurking in her eyes. "It's true. He loves me, Val. As I love him."

"So . . . ," he said cautiously, feeling his way, "you'll . . . marry him."

"Yes."

"Ah." He tried to think of something to say to that—perhaps something wise and elder-brotherly, but for the life of him, he couldn't think of a thing. "Do you still have that dove?"

"Val," Eve said, ignoring his perfectly civil query. "You should come to the wedding."

He winced. "Must I?" He glanced at Makepeace, sure the other man didn't want him there.

But it seemed all were arrayed against him today.

"Yes," Makepeace said, and he didn't even look to be under duress.

Was the world mad?

"Are you mad?" Val asked, just to make sure.

Makepeace snorted.

But Eve was still looking grave. "*Did* you ever leave England? Because Asa only proposed to me last night at Harte's Folly. I'm sure the news swept London, for he did it in front of a crowd, but even so, there's no way you could've come from the Continent so fast."

"Of course I left England, darling Eve," he replied,

staring straight into her eyes, never blinking, letting his habitual smile play about his mouth. "I arrived just last night and heard the news this morning."

The corners of her mouth drooped and he felt an odd panicked twinge somewhere in that empty space where a heart might dwell in other people.

"The trouble," Eve said, "is that I've never been able to tell when you're lying to me and when you're not. It wouldn't matter, I suppose, but that you don't *care* if you lie to me or not. And I do. I used to not. Or maybe I used to tell myself I didn't care. But Val," she said softly, looking at him with his own eyes, "now I do."

She turned and, taking Makepeace's arm, very quietly left the room with her fiancé.

And it was a very good thing, Val thought, that he hadn't a heart.

Because it might've broken then.

BRIDGET CAUTIOUSLY PRESSED open the hidden door in the duke's bedroom and held high her candlestick. She didn't know how long the duke would be gone—he'd simply hared off to see his sister—but she couldn't let the opportunity to investigate his hidden lair slip away.

The space revealed by her candle's flickering flame was narrow, naturally, but bigger than she'd expected, perhaps five feet by at least ten. A small table, crowded with a treasure trove of bejeweled objects, was set up directly next to the door with a stool stowed neatly under it. Over the table was a single shelf, jammed with books. Just past the table was a cot with rumpled bedding. And beyond the cot was more corridor—too long to be illuminated by her candle's small light. Dear Lord. Just how extensive were his hidden passages in Hermes House?

She set the candle down and looked cautiously around. The room was comfortable after a fashion, but it was very Spartan for a duke—especially for the Duke of Montgomery. She couldn't imagine him spending one night here, let alone *months*.

Unless, of course, he wasn't entirely the man she thought him.

The notion disturbed her. She'd worked in the duke's house for over three months now, and even though he'd been supposedly absent for all but two weeks of those three months, she'd been complacent in the idea that she knew the man. The Duke of Montgomery was a wicked, vain blackmailer. Evil and duplicitous. Not a man who should merit a second thought from her beyond her duties.

And yet she had thought about him quite a lot since this morning. That muscled bottom, those knowing predator's eyes, and the way the corner of his mouth had curled just before he'd bent as if to kiss her...

Bridget pressed her lips together and set her mind firmly to her task, reminding herself she might have very little time.

She pulled out the stool and sat, noticing as she did so a small wooden disk affixed to the wall with a nail at the upper edge. She touched it and the disk swiveled aside, revealing a peephole. Bridget paused a moment and then leaned forward to put her eye to the hole. She could clearly see the far end of the duke's bedroom, including his enormous bed and his desk.

Damn! She sat back, remembering with some consternation when she'd picked the lock on that very desk. She'd thought she heard a chuckle at the time, but had disregarded it as the sound of a mouse.

He must think her a fool.

Well. There was nothing for it but to outwit the Prince of Schemes and Diabolical Plots. Bridget examined the treasures on the narrow table without touching them. A ship took up most of the space, as long as her forearm. It was a fanciful—and no doubt expensive—thing, with mother-of-pearl sails, a gold hull, and tiny enameled sailors manning the glossy deck. A key projected from one end of the ship. Perhaps it had a secret compartment. Bridget turned the key.

Immediately there was a *click* and a soft whirring sound.

Bridget raised her hands in alarm.

What—?

On the ship's deck, a miniature trumpeter set his instrument to his lips and tinkling music played as the sailors marched around, the captain saluted with his sword, tiny cannons projected from the sides of the ship, and—oh, Lord!—the ship began *sailing* forward.

The cannons suddenly exploded with miniature *bangs!* and billows of smoke. Bridget squeaked as she just caught the gold ship before it sailed itself off the table. She held it cradled in her arms, gasping, as the captain seemed to give her a little bow.

A monkey ran up a rope ladder and exposed its buttocks to her.

Bridget scowled at the little enameled beast. It slid back down to its starting position and the ship went quiet.

Gingerly she placed the clockwork ship back on the table, half-afraid it was going to go off again, but nothing happened.

She took a relieved breath and noticed a very small pair of copper tweezers lying on the table. Beside the tweezers was a small dish with infinitesimally tiny cogs and wheels. Surely he hadn't been tinkering with the golden ship? She couldn't even begin to imagine the sort of skill—and money—it would take to build such a thing. The little ship was completely frivolous, like the duke himself, and yet...she touched the tiny captain. It was also amazing and wonderful...and *beautiful*. If *she* were as rich as a duke, with money to spend on anything she wished in the entire world, why...she might spend it on such a thing as the golden ship herself.

Bridget jerked back her hand as if it had been burned.

Silly thought.

She turned determinedly to the rest of the table. There were four jeweled snuffboxes—two of them with *quite* scandalous pictures on the insides of the lids. None of them held snuff. Three were empty and one contained a sort of perfumed unguent. Bridget frowned over that a moment and then set the snuffbox aside. Three gold watches were piled together, along with a jeweled magnifying glass and a little penknife. One of the watches was completely in pieces and she imagined the duke sitting here, taking the thing apart, inspecting the pieces with inquisitive azure eyes, and then putting it back together.

Had he been bored waiting to emerge from his walls? Impatient? Stifled?

She shook her head and resumed her inventory. A

scatter of broken quills and a small glass-and-gold ink bottle—stoppered—attested to the duke's having written letters in his little hideaway hole, but as far as she could tell, there were none here.

She looked up at the bookshelf and couldn't prevent a small smile.

The volumes ranged in size, shape, age, and degree of wear. Some were small and gilded, perfectly beautiful. Some cracked and with the pages falling out. She ran her finger across the spines reverently and then took them down one by one and shook them out gently to look for papers hidden in the pages. Here was a tiny illustrated volume with men in turbans charging across a flower-strewn field. Another book—quite old—was in Latin and held a skull and crossbones on the title page. She was oddly surprised by a volume of poetry by John Donne, not at all by Machiavelli's *The Prince* in the original Italian. One of the larger volumes opened naturally to an engraving of men in classical dress standing to either side of a map of the Greek isles.

Bridget stilled, looking down at the illustration. Oh... she traced with her finger, finding Athens and Corinth and Thebes and the Aegean Sea. Such exotic names. Such *wonderful* names.

She stared for a moment more and then mechanically went through the book. There was no letter hidden within its pages.

Carefully she replaced Thucydides's *History of the Peloponnesian War* on the shelf with the other volumes. As she did so, her knee brushed against the table and she heard something rustle to the floor.

Bridget picked up the candle and peered under the table. A sheet of paper was lying there. She glanced at the underside of the table. Two thin strips of wood were fixed against the underside. They were just big enough to have held the paper.

She picked up the paper and tilted it so the light shone upon it and felt her heart shudder to a stop.

It was her reference—the reference that Lady Amelia Caire had given Bridget. The one she'd shown the duke's man of business, along with her other letters of reference.

Without thinking, she touched her mobcap, but it was in place. Her hair was covered.

Bridget looked up, examining the room without moving, like a startled hare. Everything seemed nearly the same as when she'd come in. She straightened the ship, pushed the stool under the table, and, taking both her candle and the paper, quickly left the hiding hole.

Her breath was coming too fast, but she made an effort to walk sedately out of his bedroom and down the hall. Mustn't let the other servants see her in emotional disarray. She hurried down the grand staircase, through the back hallway, and into the kitchens, nodding at Mrs. Bram and one of the footmen as she passed.

To the side of the kitchens was her own tiny room and she gratefully shut the door behind her, leaning back against it. Here was her single bed, neatly made, a chair, a row of hooks to hold her shawl and hat, and a small chest of drawers. On top of the drawers were a washbasin and pitcher.

She crossed to the chest of drawers and, using one of the keys at her waist, opened the top drawer. Inside were her most valuable possessions—all she had in the world, really. A small purse of money. An illustrated *Gulliver's Travels.* And her letters of reference, neatly stacked. He must've picked the lock on her dresser, just as she'd picked the lock on his desk.

She laid the letter from Lady Caire atop the others and stared at it. Why take that one? Was it mere coincidence? Or did he know?

She closed and locked the dresser drawer and went to the small round looking glass beside the door. Slowly she raised her hands and drew off her mobcap. Underneath, her hair was tightly twisted into a knot at the back of her head. It was black, save for a pure white streak that started just over her left eye. She stared for a moment at her very distinctive hair. The white threads had started only a few years ago, when she'd turned three and twenty, but she knew already that in another ten years her head would be entirely white.

As her mother's was.

Bridget tucked a few loose strands back into place and replaced her cap. She made sure her skirts and apron were properly aligned, properly neat.

Then she straightened her shoulders and opened her door. She left behind any foolish dreams of Grecian isles or golden clockwork ships and walked out of her barren room as the housekeeper.

Nothing more.

Chapter Three

The baby's mother wept and his father (the old king) stomped and roared, but the physician merely shrugged. There was simply no way to replace a missing heart. And that was that....

—From *King Heartless*

"And here are the kitchens again," Bridget said briskly that evening as she led Mehmed on the last stage of her tour of Hermes House.

She had started Mehmed's tour later than she'd originally planned due to the unfortunate dismissal of one of the footmen that afternoon. She'd discovered George in the duke's study, bent over his desk and holding a gold snuffbox, and really there wasn't much poor George could say after that, particularly since he wasn't supposed to even be on the upper floor at that time of day.

A sad task and one that made her feel something of a hypocrite considering she'd rifled that same desk only weeks before, but there it was. She couldn't have a thief on her staff.

She turned to the boy. "We take breakfast promptly at six of the clock, have tea at ten, luncheon at two, tea again at five, and supper after His Grace has eaten. Mrs. Bram is in charge of the kitchen and you will address her as ma'am or Mrs. Bram or Cook. Is that clear?"

Mehmed, looking slightly overwhelmed, nodded.

Bridget permitted herself to unbend enough to give him a very small smile. It was hard enough for an English boy to come to a first position in London—the pace was faster, the accents and people new and different. What must it be like for a lad from a different country altogether? She wondered in that moment why the duke had chosen Mehmed for his second valet. Was it merely a whim to take the boy from his home so far away?

She'd found—to her relief—that the boy was a little older than she'd first thought him. He was sixteen rather than the thirteen or fourteen she'd originally placed him at.

Still.

If the duke *hadn't* been joking when he'd called Mehmed his catamite…

She pushed the thought aside. What her employers chose to do in their bedrooms was not her concern until and if they decided to include her or another servant who did not wish to participate.

As far as she could tell Mehmed seemed happy at Hermes House.

"You'll do fine," she murmured quietly to Mehmed. "The duke likes you and that, after all, is what matters most in the end."

Mehmed gave her a shy smile, but darted a nervous look at Mrs. Bram.

The cook, who was putting the finishing touches on her roast, gave him a skeptical side-eye. Mrs. Bram had been none too pleased to discover, early in the tour, that the boy didn't eat pork of any kind—not ham or sausage or even bacon. Bridget had hastily led the boy away, leaving Mrs. Bram muttering about "heathenish" ways. She'd hoped that the cook would've forgiven the boy's dietary oddities in their absence, but such was obviously not the case.

Bridget cleared her throat, raising her voice to address the servants in the kitchen. "Mehmed will be the duke's second valet, serving under Mr. Attwell and sleeping in His Grace's dressing room. You will accord him the respect of a second valet."

She made sure to glance about the room slowly, letting her words sink in. Londoners in general were fairly sophisticated folk, used to exotic foreigners from all corners of the world. London was, after all, a port city. Still, it never hurt to place a new servant firmly within the ranks. A valet was in a rather nice position—above the footmen and below only the butler, had there been one.

There was not. The butler at Hermes House had retired very soon after Bridget had been hired and she'd never seen the need to find a replacement. Why hire a man who might think it his right to order *her* about, after all?

In any case, she wanted to make sure Mehmed would find acceptance at Hermes House. Attwell seemed to treat him with a sort of benign indifference that she supposed was better than hostility, but not by much.

Bridget nodded briskly. "Good. Now, Mehmed, if you

would like to attend to Mr. Attwell and your duties in the duke's—"

"Ma'am."

She turned, irritated at the interruption. It was Cal, lounging in the doorway to the kitchens, his handsome face marred by the sneer on his lips. "Yes?"

"He—I mean, *His Grace*—wants you." His emphasis on the honorific was almost an insult.

Bridget eyed the footman a moment, but decided to let the matter go. Cal had been in the Montgomery employ for years—ever since he'd been a youth, in fact. For all she knew there was some sort of fondness or loyalty between him and the duke. Better to find out first before making any moves.

Too, she was already a footman short after this afternoon.

Therefore she simply asked, "Where is His Grace?"

Cal jerked his head behind him. "In the dining room."

"Thank you," she replied drily, and swept past him.

She hadn't crossed paths with the duke since this morning's odd reception. She found her pulse beginning to quicken as she neared the dining room, wondering what he'd called her for, what strange question or request he'd put to her. Or had he tired of her after this morning? Would he simply dismiss her finally?

He couldn't.

She'd spent three months searching for her mother's letter—and the miniature she'd found last night. The miniature belonged to a friend of her mother's, Miss Hippolyta Royle, a wealthy heiress, whom her mother had asked Bridget to help. But with the duke's "return" she'd had only a few minutes this morning in his hiding hole and less than that this afternoon to search one of the lesser-used salons. She needed more *time*. Specifically, she needed more time spent with *him*.

Bridget paused before the dining room door.

It might take weeks more—*months* more—to find all the duke's hiding places. But if she were to talk to him, *observe* him, might not she discover his secrets simply by catching him unawares? Perhaps she needed to… well, not *seduce* him—*he* was the one for seduction—but engage him more in discussion? Let herself… loosen? He might give himself away when he was talking on and on, thinking he was the cleverest person in the room.

She raised her hand to check that her mobcap was straight and orderly, then caught herself. She balled her hand and let it drop.

Instead she threw back her shoulders.

And strode into the dining room.

VAL WATCHED AS his housekeeper walked toward him down the length of his dining room. It was quite a long length, actually, for he sat at the end of the table nearest the lit fire, but she didn't seem cowed by either his silence or his stare. She held her head high and she met him stare for stare, her eyes dark and intense and oddly arousing.

Really, she was very self-possessed for a housekeeper when one came to think about it.

And rather young, too.

"Have you ever thought about taking off that incredibly ugly mobcap?" he asked as she drew near.

Was that a flicker of fear in her dark martyr's eyes?

He watched in interest as he popped a date in his mouth and chewed.

"No, Your Grace," she replied boringly.

For a moment he considered sending her away again. He was in a strangely melancholy mood after this morning's meeting with Eve. He'd thought Mrs. Crumb might provide a distraction, but perhaps he had been wrong. Perhaps he should call for Cal instead and have a veiled sparring match over which of them his mother had treated worse all those years ago.

But then he licked his lips and her gaze flickered—for just a second—to his mouth and he made his decision. "Come sit, Mrs. Crumb. You'll give me a crick in the neck, standing there."

He waited as she pulled out a chair and sat so close to the edge he feared she might tip herself over and land on her nose.

His lips curling at the thought, he asked, "Do you have brothers or sisters?"

She looked at him while he selected another date, waiting.

Finally she seemed to sigh without making any sound at all and said, "Yes, Your Grace. I have two brothers and a sister."

"Really?" He widened his eyes. "I'd thought you entirely solitary, like a mushroom sprung up alone in the dark. Who are they? What are their names?"

"My brothers are Ian and Tom, my sister is Moira. She is married to the blacksmith in our village. Tom is a farmer. Ian is—"

She stopped because he'd waved his hand hastily at

her. *This* was *too* much information—and very tedious at that. He told her as much, and got in return a glare. She might try to hide it but he'd lay odds that his housekeeper frankly loathed him.

He felt a sudden fondness for her.

"No, no, no," he explained. "Not this dull stuff. I want to know which one you don't talk to, which one is jealous of you, and which one hit you as a child. Oh, and if any of them stole from you or killed your cat or dog when you were but a wee thing."

This time she outright stared at him for some reason. "I..." Her voice trailed away and stopped. She appeared to think for several minutes, her brows knit over her dark eyes.

Val ate two dates and drank some wine. It was French and quite good.

"Did you see your sister when you were out?" she asked eventually, which didn't answer his question at all.

"Yes." He laid his chin in his palm. "Have you ever kissed one of your brothers?"

"No," she said rather loudly, looking appalled. "Have you kissed your sister?"

"No." He shrugged. "Well, on the cheek."

"Is that what you meant?" she asked weakly. She looked a bit flustered, he was pleased to note. It brought some color to her severe alabaster face. This morning her cheeks had burned rose red and he'd wanted to lick them.

And then bite her mouth.

"Not at all," he said gently. "I meant exactly what you thought—the worst. I'm not entirely sure why you're surprised. People often do do the worst, you know."

"Yes," she said, "I do know."

And that was the most interesting thing she'd said so far.

He leaned a little forward, but the doors to the dining room opened and a swarm of footmen came in bearing his supper.

She started to rise.

"Sit," he commanded, and then to Cal, who had swanned in among the rest, "Bring another setting for Mrs. Crumb. She'll be joining me for supper."

Her face flamed scarlet—and not becomingly, either. "I can't join you, Your Grace," she hissed—strangely without moving her lips—"I'm your *housekeeper*."

"So you are," Val agreed. "And as such you're supposed to do whatever I command of you."

"Within reason," she amended, as if she were negotiating—and still through immobile lips. What a lovely trick!

He arched his eyebrows, amused. "Really?"

"Yes, really."

"Well, I can't see"—he half stood in his chair to look over to the last dish being brought in—"how roast beef, while rather dull, is without reason, so perhaps you'll stay."

He sat back down and waited to see if she'd argue the point. He couldn't remember when last he'd had an opponent whose response he couldn't predict. It was rather refreshing, actually.

She merely nodded and folded her hands in her lap and it came to Val that his housekeeper with her ugly mobcap and plain black woolen dress was as proud in her own way as any duchess.

Cal sailed back in, placing a plate and silverware in front of Mrs. Crumb with lingering care. Val remembered once, long ago, that same lingering care bestowed upon his mother. Did the footman know Mrs. Crumb's Christian name? Did she have a lover belowstairs? He found he didn't entirely like the thought.

Val leaned back in his chair and met the footman's eyes. He lifted his eyebrow slowly and waited, still staring, until the other flushed, bowed, and backed hastily out of the room.

One of the other footmen nervously began to serve the beef, but Val had had enough. He waved his hand. "Begone, the lot of you."

They nearly dashed from the room.

"You needn't be rude," chastised his housekeeper, taking up the carving knife and fork. She neatly sliced two pieces and transferred them to his plate along with carrots and peas and other miscellanea. He filled her wineglass whilst she did so.

She hesitated, then gave herself a meager slice of beef.

He smirked into his wineglass. Did she think she sat at a table of Sodom? Or was it simply her sense of class and their disparate rank that had so outraged her sense of decorum?

He set his glass down at this reminder. "My sister is engaged to the owner of Harte's Folly."

She paused in the act of cutting her meat. "Yes, Your Grace."

He grimaced. "That's right—you were there this morning when I received the letter. Do you know my sister?"

"She often came to Hermes House to look at your

accounting books, Your Grace." She hesitated, and then said circumspectly, "Miss Dinwoody seems a very nice lady."

He moodily pushed the carrots off his plate and onto the table. Carrots were always so very *orange*. Now peas he rather liked—round and green. He picked one up with his fingers and popped it between his teeth. "Do you like carrots?"

"Yes, Your Grace," she said, eating one neatly.

He frowned at her, but she didn't seem to mind. "She says she *loves* him."

She looked at him and he noticed that her lips were wet and red, an erotic contrast to her immaculate saint's eyes. What would they look like, those lips, those eyes, were she to take his cock into her mouth?

He threw down his knife and fork with a clatter. "Explain it to me, this thing, *love*. Why would a perfectly intelligent girl want to marry a man so beneath her? She could take him as a lover if she wanted—*I* certainly wouldn't care. Why marry the fellow?"

Mrs. Crumb carefully placed her fork and knife upon her plate and folded her hands in her lap. She turned to face him. "Love is the best of all human emotion. It separates us from the beasts and brings us closer to God and to heaven. There is no greater gift than love between a man and a woman."

He looked at her a moment, studying her earnest expression, and then grinned. "You've never loved a man, have you?"

She pursed her lips, looking not a little irritated. "No."

He took up his knife and fork again, feeling more cheerful. "A woman?"

"Pardon, Your Grace?"

He waved his knife, a bit of the beef skewered on the end. "Have you ever loved a woman?"

She pursed her lips and for a moment he thought they'd have another round of tedious prevarication. Then she sighed—audibly this time. "I was fond of my mother but I doubt that is what you mean. I've never loved another woman romantically."

He smiled and ate the bite of beef. She came from the country. Yet she was rather more sophisticated than he'd first thought her.

"Then..." She stared at him very seriously, almost shyly. "You've never loved another?"

"Good God, no."

"Not even your intended fiancée?"

He threw back his head and laughed at the very thought. "No. *Oh, no.* I think that one must have some essential part to love."

She knit her black brows again, quite severely, and the resemblance to some stern saint was very strong. "What part?"

He shrugged, twirling his fork in the air as he thought. "I don't know? A belief in goodness and God? Or maybe godliness? Perhaps innocence?" He smiled and looked at her. "In any case, whatever that essential thing is, I don't have it in me. I never had it."

Her brows were level. Her dark eyes intent on him. He might be the only man in the world to her right now. Oh, heady, erotic thought. "Never? Not even when you were a child?"

He shook his head slowly, aware of the soul-deep

blackness that had seeped into his skin, been driven through his muscles, and embedded in his very bones. "Not even in the womb."

He rarely told the truth—why bother? It was so dull—but when he did, most mistook it for jest.

She did not.

She looked at him soberly, and despite her martyr's eyes, she seemed to make no judgment of him, which, if nothing else, was refreshing.

He leaned a little forward and took her chin, her skin soft and warm under his fingers. Alive. Human. Womanly.

Her dark eyes widened.

"Now, you, Mrs. Crumb, you aren't like me at all. You have that part, whatever it is. You *can* love, which raises the question: Why *haven't* you?"

She made a movement, like a mare trying to shake a bridle, but he held her, squeezing her face tightly. Perhaps he even left bruises.

He enjoyed that thought, imprinting his fingertips on her face for all to see.

"Why, my gentle housekeeper?"

Her nostrils flared and she stilled, glaring at him. "I like my job. I like doing as I please. Falling in love with a man would inconvenience me, Your Grace."

He caught his breath in admiration. "How very practical of you, Mrs. Crumb."

He drew her forward, making her half rise, his gaze fixed on that wet, reddened mouth and her angry dark eyes, his cock beating, bold and insistent, against the placket of his breeches. Perhaps he'd mark her further. Perhaps he'd see to what depths a saint could fall.

The doors to the dining room opened and he turned in irritation to see who it was, opening his mouth to send them away again.

But then he saw it was Alf and changed his mind.

He let go of Mrs. Crumb and sat back. "What have you for me?"

"A letter," the girl said with a sideways glance at Mrs. Crumb. The housekeeper had resumed her seat breathless and stony-faced. "From that toff you sent me to th' first time. In a right rage 'e was."

She gained his side and proffered the missive.

He took it, broke the seal with a bread knife, and, holding it in his right hand, read it while sipping from his wineglass. It was indeed from Mr. Shrugg, who appeared to be quite flustered and begged for more time, et cetera, et cetera.

Val flipped the letter to the table and yawned. Amazing how predictable people were.

Mrs. Crumb made to rise.

He slapped his hand over her arm. "Stay." Then looked at her and smiled. "*If* you don't mind?"

Her eyes narrowed, but really, she *was* a housekeeper.

She sat.

"Thank you." And to Alf, "Bring me pen and paper and sand from that cupboard there." He pointed out the pertinent piece of furniture to Alf.

The girl brought over the accouterments of letter writing and he bent to his task under the watchful eye of his housekeeper.

"I thought you were left-handed, Your Grace?" she asked, her tone abrupt. Oh, she hadn't forgiven him, had she? How delightful.

He smiled and continued to write, gracefully and deftly. "You are sharp-eyed, Mrs. Crumb. My father thought being left-handed an unpardonable fault. Perhaps he considered it too sinister."

He waited, wondering if she'd ask the question, probe into *how* he was made properly right-handed in his writing, but he was apparently to be disappointed.

Five minutes later he sealed the second of two letters and held it out to Alf. "Please deliver this letter to Mr. Ferguson, the proprietor of the *Daily Review*, and *this* one to Mr. Shrugg."

Alf, who had been gazing longingly at the roast beef, took the letters and the guinea he gave her as well. "Yes, Your Grace."

"And Alf?"

"Aye?"

He smiled gently. "Mind you don't peek."

The girl paled and backed quickly from the room.

He looked at Mrs. Crumb and realized that she'd been reading the letter from Shrugg, which had landed face-up. How very rude.

She glanced up at him, her expression appalled. "You're blackmailing the *King*?"

HUGH HAD FORGOTTEN how cold London's nights were. He'd seen more snow in the Colonies and in the Alps, but the air itself was damp here. Damp and chill, so that the wind seemed to carry the cold through the layers of leather, wool, and linen he wore, to penetrate to his very bones.

He pulled his cloak closer about his chin, keeping his eyes on the house. He stood in the mews, behind the great house, mostly deserted now that the stable hands were at their dinners. A carriage rumbled by now and again, summoned by the residents of the other, smaller houses on the square.

There.

The boy slid silently from the gate that led from the back garden into the mews, a slim shadow. Hugh would've missed him had he not been watching for him for the last half hour.

"Boy," he called in a low voice, meaning to offer coin for information—messengers were usually ripe for bribery—but the lad immediately took to his heels.

Hugh cursed and raced after him. He had a longer stride but the urchin was swift and small. If he lost sight of him in the dark mews he'd never find the lad again.

He was gaining on the lad when the boy darted around a corner. There was a cry and a curse. Hugh rounded the corner to see, in the light of a nearby shop lantern, the boy cowering before a large man in a bloodstained leather apron. The butcher held the boy by one arm and had his fist drawn back.

Hugh stepped forward and caught the massive fist.

The butcher swung around when he felt the impediment, his reddened, doughy face twisted in a scowl. "Wotcher?"

Hugh smiled. "That's my boy you've got there."

At the sound of his accent—or perhaps because of his size—the butcher lowered his fist with a curse, spit, and walked away.

Fortunately Hugh had taken the precaution of securing the boy first.

He turned to examine his prize, such as it was.

The top of the boy's battered hat came only to Hugh's shoulder. He wore a threadbare coat and waistcoat and patched hose. His breeches were dirty. The lad made no move to pull away, but he looked at Hugh with such open defiance in his huge brown eyes that Hugh knew that if he let go of the boy he'd be out of sight within seconds.

He sighed. "Hungry?"

The boy scowled and for a moment Hugh thought he wouldn't answer. Then the boy nodded once and said gruffly, "Yes."

"Come with me, then." Hugh turned but found a dead weight at the end of his arm. He looked back, eyebrows raised.

"Where we goin'?"

Ah. So that was the problem. Hugh mentally winced. The boy had obviously grown up on the streets and knew well the dangers posed by grown men.

But all he said was, "There's an alehouse not far from here. The White Hare."

A specific, public destination seemed to relieve the boy a bit and they set off. Hugh was sure to keep a firm grip on his charge, though. He'd already lost one gamble—a footman named George who had turned out to be a singularly inept spy. The man had been caught and dismissed his first time searching for the blackmail evidence—and then had the effrontery to demand payment from Hugh without anything to show for it. That left him only one contact within Hermes House—a figure too low for Hugh's peace of mind.

They made their way rapidly through the streets, not

talking, though Hugh looked at his charge several times, assessing the boy.

Finally, as they neared the White Hare, he asked, "What's your name?"

The boy in turn gave him a look. "Alf. What's yours, then?"

A corner of Hugh's mouth kicked up at the cocky tone. "You may call me Kyle."

The boy grinned, flashing surprisingly white and even teeth. "Right you are, guv."

Hugh pushed open the alehouse door and the warmth of the inner room rushed out. The place was loud and swarmed with the smells of beer and roasted meat. He shouldered his way through the crowd and found a small table in a corner. It wasn't near the fire, but it offered a bit of privacy, which was better under the circumstances.

A woman with a pockmarked face and stained leather stays over red flannel petticoats swung their way. "What'll ye 'ave, luv?"

Hugh deliberately roughened his accent. "Beer for my friend an' me, an' some o' yer beef with all the fixin's."

"Right away, luv."

He waited until the wench left before turning to Alf.

The boy was eyeing him speculatively and Hugh realized that he was still holding his wrist under the table.

He raised an eyebrow. "If I let go of you will you run off?"

Alf raised his own eyebrow, mimicking him. "Not till after that food arrives at least."

Hugh sat back on a grunt of laugher and released the delicate wrist. "I suppose I ought to be glad you're honest."

The boy tilted up his chin. "S'pose you oughter."

"Then I'll be honest with you as well," Hugh said. "I need information on the duke."

The boy's lips flattened. "'Is Grace ain't a man t' cross."

Hugh leaned forward and lowered his voice. "He's blackmailing the King."

"Aww, poor Georgie. I'm that worried o'er th' old sod," Alf drawled.

Hugh mentally amended his estimation of Alf's age up several years. "Even if—"

The barmaid returned with a tray heaped with two beer mugs and two plates full of steaming beef and vegetables, generously splashed with gravy. She plonked the offerings down and set her brawny arms on her hips. "Anything else?"

"This'll do," Hugh replied.

He watched the woman retreat and then turned back to the table to discover Alf shoveling food into his mouth as if he hadn't eaten in days.

Perhaps he hadn't.

Hugh picked up his beer and took a long drink as he watched the boy demolish potatoes and beef. Surely the duke paid him well?

He shook his head, glancing down at his own plate. None of his concern. "Listen. You may not care for the King, but surely you care for the country, and the King *is* the country. What the duke is doing is treason."

Alf glanced up, a smudge of gravy at the corner of his lips. "Treason?"

"Treason," Hugh said solemnly, relieved that he might

have finally gotten to the boy. "But if you help me find the papers the duke is using to blackmail the King you will be stopping this treasonous activity."

"An' I won't get in trouble?" Alf asked anxiously. He slipped two pieces of bread into his pocket.

"No," Hugh said, leaning over the table. "I just need to know where—"

He was interrupted by Alf upending the entire table, beer mugs, plates of beef and gravy and all, straight into his lap.

Hugh shouted and scrambled back.

The nearby patrons looked around, some standing, some exclaiming.

Alf ducked and ran with a dexterity that Hugh couldn't help but admire—even covered in beer and bits of carrots and beef. The lad slid under the tables through the alehouse patrons and around the barmaid—who was carrying four mugs of beer, which she raised with an oath—and straight out the door. He paused only a moment in the doorway to glance back and give Hugh a wink and a jaunty salute.

And then Alf was gone.

Chapter Four

The baby grew. When he did awful things like drowning moths in his milk or locking the palace cat in the dungeons, his father sighed, his mother wept, and the courtiers whispered. But all agreed: no one could teach a boy with no heart right from wrong. . . .

—From *King Heartless*

The woman who sat across from Bridget had given birth to her and yet the very thought of calling her *mother* was ludicrous in the extreme.

Lady Amelia Caire was aristocratic elegance personified. The daughter of a viscount, she'd been a celebrated beauty in her youth. Now, in her seventh decade, she was still captivatingly lovely.

Bridget looked nothing like her.

Well, except in one small, but very significant, regard.

Lady Caire wore a midnight-blue sack gown trimmed with tiny rows of black and silver lace. Her hair was snowy white—due not to age, but to an odd familial trait. Both she and her only son, Lord Caire, had gone white in their early years. She wore her hair pulled close to her head and adorned with an almost medieval triangular cap of black lace.

Bridget was sure Lady Caire knew how well the black lace contrasted with the white of her hair.

"A pity he's returned," Lady Caire mused, a faint line between her brows. "And to actually blackmail the King." She shuddered. "Did you see the *Daily Review* this morning? All this business about a Dolphin Society. Absolute rubbish, but they did make mention of a royal connection—and now you tell me Montgomery is behind the whole thing. The man is the absolute Devil. He has no shame."

There wasn't much to say to that so Bridget said nothing. She stood in Lady Caire's salon—a room nearly as elaborate as one of the duke's, though no one could truly touch his overblown taste in furnishings. White Corinthian columns guarded the doorway, the capitals picked out in gold. Dainty settees painted in greens and pinks were scattered about the room. Overhead a beautiful blue sky was painted on the ceiling, with cherubs playing hide-and-seek among fluffy clouds.

Once, when Bridget had newly entered service at the age of twelve, she had returned to her foster home, filled with the wonders of the upper crust and its profligate spending. Her foster mother—a woman she'd affectionately called Mam—who had been listening and stirring a pot of peas porridge, had turned and laughed and said that the aristocracy would put gold on a cat's whiskers if they could.

She wondered now what Mam would have made of Lady Caire's salon.

Bridget lowered her gaze from the ceiling to find Lady Caire watching her impatiently. She straightened hastily, feeling like a scullery maid caught napping.

"Do you think you can still find the letters now that he's back in the house?" Lady Caire asked.

"I can try, my lady," Bridget said cautiously. "But it's a very big house with many places to hide such a small thing, and the duke is very clever. And now that he *knows* I'm looking..." She shrugged.

Lady Caire made a moue.

"Has he..." Bridget cleared her throat. "That is... has he asked you to do anything else?" Several months before, the duke had forced Lady Caire to introduce his sister to the Ladies' Syndicate for the Benefit of the Home for Unfortunate Infants and Foundling Children, a charitable group made up of some of the most influential ladies in London society, including Miss Hippolyta Royle, the miniature's owner.

"No," Lady Caire replied. "But he might do so at any moment." She smiled very stiffly. "It's just that my son—Lord Caire—I wouldn't like him to find out. To know the very worst about me."

Bridget nodded, glancing down. She couldn't help but feel a twinge of hurt, though, even if it was silly. For of course *she* was the result of the worst thing about Lady Caire.

"I'll do my best," she promised.

"Bridget?"

She met her mother's gaze, startled by the use of her given name. "Yes, my lady?"

Lady Caire hesitated. "Is he a danger to you?"

Bridget thought of his strange, insistent teasing.

Of the way he'd gripped her face tight last night. Forced her to rise from her chair. Drawn her across the table and toward his mouth. Of how hard and angrily her heart had beaten.

And of how a small, renegade part of her had yearned impatiently for his lips.

She looked straight into the eyes of the woman who had birthed her. Who had made sure she'd had a home and a foster mother to bring her up. Who had given her references when she'd made her way to London, enabling Bridget to reach the heights of her profession at the young age of six and twenty. "No, my lady."

The older woman's face softened in relief. "Good. Then continue as you are. But, please, if you feel at all worried, leave Hermes House at once. The Duke of Montgomery is a dangerous man, as I think you know. Promise me this."

"I will, my lady," Bridget said, feeling a shy sense of warmth because the lady had expressed worry for her safety. "Thank you."

Lady Caire looked away. "'Tis I who should, no doubt, be thanking you," she said rather formally.

Bridget glanced down at her hands, noting absently that she was digging her fingernails into her palms. She took a deep breath. She owed this lady her life, her loyalty... and nothing else. "If I might go, my lady? I have duties to perform yet this afternoon."

"Of course, of course." Lady Caire waved an elegant hand in dismissal.

Bridget curtsied and quietly walked from the room.

She nodded to the butler and left by the servants' entrance, wrapping her black shawl tightly about her shoulders as a gust of wind swept up her skirts. The sky was dark gray and ominous, fat drops of rain spitting in her face as she hurried through London. She passed a tiny woman singing sweetly on a corner, a baby slung on her back, another held in her arms, and fumbled out a penny to drop into the beggar's outstretched palm. Then she crossed the street, watching both for the big dray horses pulling carts and for the odiferous piles they left behind. She made the opposite side only to be stopped abruptly by two chairmen trotting by and bawling, "Make way! Make way!" as they passed.

The occupant of the sedan chair—a rotund man—turned his head and stared at her as he went by, his expression as bored as if she were a dog.

Bridget had a sudden urge to make a very rude gesture at the man's back. Aristocrats treated commoners as if they were rubbish, having neither feelings nor wants. Desires nor dreams. Servants were simply there to bring the masters their food and clothing, take away their dirty plates and full piss-pots. They might as well be monkeys in aprons and mobcaps. No, worse—wooden puppets with painted-on smiles, hinged at the neck and waist to nod and bow.

Oh! Bridget swiped at her streaming eyes. She didn't know what had put her into such a bitter disposition. It must be the cold. She quite loathed chilly weather.

She continued on her way, dodging hawkers of oranges and fish, apprentices playing dice in a doorway, an old man in a full-bottomed wig and black velvet suit, and two sailors who made quite inappropriate comments to her.

By the time she arrived at the mews that ran behind Hermes House, Bridget's nose was cold and, she suspected, red, and she was still in a grumpy mood.

Her mood wasn't helped, either, when she heard the loud, excited shouts of boys from the mews. Lord only knew what they were up to back there. Bridget pulled her shawl tighter and marched down the mews, wondering where the stable hands had gone. Usually they were quick to drive any loiterers off.

But it wasn't until she heard a yip and a whine that her heart tripped over itself.

Bridget picked up her skirts and broke into a run.

Around back of the stables she saw a group of boys surrounding something on the ground. As she gasped, a boy—a great big fellow, nearly as big as a man—drew back his leg and kicked.

The thing on the ground yelped.

"No!" Bridget shouted, but she was drowned out by a gunshot.

She turned to see the Duke of Montgomery, standing in his shirt-sleeves and pink embroidered waistcoat and breeches, hip cocked, a smoking pistol held almost negligently aloft in his left hand.

He smiled, as sweetly as an adder baring its fangs, at the boys. "Won't you please vacate this area?"

The boys seemed frozen by surprise—or stark fear.

The duke tilted his head and his smile dropped from his face, leaving it blank—and somehow much more frightening. "*Now.*"

There was a mad scramble and then the mews was deserted save for her and the duke.

Bridget blinked and hurried to her little terrier, tied quite disgracefully by a cord around his neck to a stake in the ground. He lay on his side in the mud, but his tail thumped against the dirt when he saw her. He jumped to his feet, shaking himself, and tried to limp toward her, but was stopped by the cord.

She knelt in the mud and tried to pull the cord from his neck, but it had been tied terribly tight and her hands were trembling.

She felt the duke crouch behind her, his arms reaching around her, warm and hard, and felt a moment's confusion before he leaned forward and murmured in her ear, "Here."

He placed her opened chatelaine knife in her hands.

She took it gratefully. "Thank you."

Carefully she cut the cord and picked up the little dog, his body warm and rather smelly in her arms.

The terrier immediately began licking her chin.

Bridget inhaled on a sob, even as she felt the brush of the duke's tongue at the corner of her eye.

"Your tears taste like salvation." His voice was deep, resonating against her back, and he almost sounded puzzled.

She shuddered, gasping, but didn't dare look around, and then he was gone.

Biting her lips, she smoothed her hands over the dog's small, wriggling body, trying to feel for broken bones. As far as she could tell, the terrier was bruised, but fine, although he had a bit of blood over one eye. He gazed up at her adoringly and it came to her all at once that his name was Pip.

Pip.

She looked up.

The duke was still there, watching her in the gloaming, his beautiful golden hair ablaze in the setting sun.

She cleared her throat. "I…thank you. For saving him."

It was hard to tell his expression in the dim light, but she thought he smiled.

She still held Pip, loath to let him go. Would the boys find him again, perhaps kill him this time? "I…er…I didn't know you liked dogs?"

"I don't." He shrugged. "But you do." He turned toward the gate, calling over his shoulder, "Bring him in the house if you want."

"I can't do that," she said, appalled.

He stopped and looked back. "Why not?"

"I'm a servant in your house. We don't keep pets. There are *rules*."

She saw him cock his head quite clearly and he laughed softly, as the snake in the garden must have at the beginning of time. "Fuck the rules, Mrs. Crumb."

A CLOCK CHIMED three in the morning as Hugh crept up the master staircase of Hermes House. He'd entered via a door left unlocked by his paid inside man. Too bad he didn't trust that same man to do this work tonight, but some things must be done by oneself if they were to be done well. Which was why Hugh now moved by memory alone—having earlier memorized a sketched map of the interior of the house. He daren't chance a light. Not yet. Already he'd passed a footman in the hallway—

fortunately dozing. He eased up the stairs on the balls of his feet, carefully judging each step, pausing and listening as he went. All was quiet, but many people lived in a great house, any of whom might by happenstance decide to go for a midnight stroll.

The upper floor was silky black. A movement. Hugh jerked back—and then felt a fool. It was his own reflection in a mirror along the upper hall. He made his way down the hall and to the door at the end. According to the sketched map, this was Montgomery's library.

The door creaked when he opened it.

He blew out a breath and closed the door behind him quickly.

Inside he found a candle and, taking flint and steel from his pocket, lit it. The library was huge—it must run across almost the entire back of the house—and it was filled with books. The papers he was looking for might be in any of them.

But Hugh was beginning to know his quarry by now. Montgomery didn't like the obvious. He was a clever man—perhaps too clever for his own good. And Hugh's informant had told him Montgomery was frequently to be found in front of the fireplace—at the far end of the room.

Hugh strode the length of the room.

The fireplace itself was black tile but the mantel and surround were white marble, magnificently sculpted and gilded. Winged cherubs held aloft a central oval medallion. Behind that was a huge baroque mirror. Around the fireplace was wood paneling, painted a light green.

Hugh set the candle down and began running his hands over the paneling, gently feeling and pressing with his blunt fingertips. This sort of thing took patience and an iron control of one's nerves. He knew that the longer he stayed in Hermes House the more certain it was that he would be discovered. But if he rushed his search he ran the risk of missing what he'd come for.

Patience and attention to detail were paramount for success.

And he had to succeed. Already Montgomery had sent letters to a broadsheet hinting at the damnable secret society and the King's son's, Prince William's, link to it. Montgomery obviously wasn't afraid to use his blackmail material. Discreet enquiries had in fact borne this out: only a year previously Montgomery had ruined a wealthy tobacco importer who had kept a second wife in the country. The man had apparently refused to yield to whatever Montgomery's demands had been and as a result the duke had released his blackmail material. The man had been forced to flee England when the truth of his bigamy had been revealed.

Therefore Hugh took a deep breath and began searching a new section of the fireplace. Half an hour later his back was beginning to stiffen when he heard a distinct *click.* Oddly it was on one of the cherub's wings, not on the wood paneling itself. At first he couldn't figure out the mechanism. The marble wing didn't seem to swivel or tilt, but when he pressed *inward*, something gave and the wing shifted aside to reveal a cavity in the cherub's back. He peered inside. The space was no bigger than a child's fist.

And it was empty.

Behind him someone tutted, and the hairs stood up on Hugh's neck.

He turned.

In the dim light of the single candle, Montgomery's patrician good looks took on near-satanic aspects as he smiled. "Now, *that* must be very disappointing."

A POUNDING ON her door jolted Bridget awake.

Pip, who had insisted on sleeping at her feet on top of the bed, leaped up and began a frantic barking.

Bridget staggered upright, dragging a wrapper about her. She had the wits to check in the little mirror beside the door that her nightcap was tied firmly beneath her chin, and then she flung it open.

Outside, Bob, in only breeches and shirt, barefoot and holding a candle aloft, was white-faced. Behind him stood several maids and Cook, wearing a voluminous yellow-and-orange-printed wrapper.

"There be a burglar in th' duke's library!" Bob exclaimed, his country accent suddenly broad.

"Call the watch and throw him out," Bridget snapped. She disliked intensely having her sleep interrupted. The terrier was busy investigating everyone's toes.

"He won't let us," Bob replied.

"Who won't?"

"The duke," Bob said. "He's in there wi' the burglar and he's like to kill 'im, last I saw."

"Oh, good Lord," Bridget muttered. "Where are the other footmen?"

"Bill and Cal are up in th' library," Bob said. "Bill was the one on duty by the front door and gave th' alarm when he 'eard th' shouting. Sam and Will came wi' me to tell you."

"Very well." Bridget nodded. "Mrs. Bram, would you be so kind as to take the maidservants back to the kitchens and start a pot of tea. I'm sure everyone will need some when this is all over."

"Right you are." The cook nodded and shooed the disappointed maids before her.

"The rest of you"—Bridget addressed the footmen—"please follow me."

She lit a candle from Bob's candle and strode briskly into the hall, leading a procession consisting of the three footmen and Pip to the front of the house and up the grand staircase. Bob had said that shouting had caused Bill to raise the alarm, but she could hear nothing now from above, which made her quicken her step to a near run.

If the duke had killed a burglar it might be *hours* before she had that tea.

She made the upper floor and hurried down the hall. As she neared the library she could see that the two footmen stood outside the room, peering inside like timid children too afraid to enter. *Idiots.* She pushed past them both and sailed into the room.

And then stopped short. The sight that met her eyes really was rather extraordinary.

Of all the ostentatious rooms in Hermes House, the library was far and away the most extravagant. The paneled walls were painted a seafoam green. Paired columns of black marble with gold Corinthian capitals marched down both walls of the library, supporting arches, and within the arches were exotic-wood bookcases holding thousands of books. The floor was black-and-pink checkerboarded marble. The ceiling was painted with scenes from various myths of the god Hermes—in all of which he was nude and looking remarkably like the Duke of Montgomery himself.

And in the center of the library stood the duke and another man.

The Duke of Montgomery was dressed in his purple banyan—the one with a huge gold-and-green dragon embroidered on the back. He was barefoot and his curling hair was loose about his shoulders.

He appeared to be engaged in a sort of duel with an exceptionally large man dressed all in black, wearing a tricorne hat, and with a black scarf wrapped about the lower half of his face. The duke and the stranger circled each other and Bridget was appalled to realize that they each held a knife.

The duke's was a small pocket knife, grasped almost negligently in his left hand, his gold thumb ring winking in the candlelight. The man in black gripped some sort of dagger.

The duke couldn't win against such a large man. Not armed with a damned *pocket knife*. Whatever was he thinking?

She had started forward, intending to intervene *somehow*, when the big man lunged, caught the duke about his middle and slammed him violently against one of the bookshelves. There was a terrific crash and books rained down on the both of them.

Pip gave one sharp bark at her feet, as if expressing his disapproval of the proceedings.

Both combatants slid to the floor in a tangle of limbs, the stranger on top, his broad back straining as he tried to control the duke's arms. The duke made a quick snakelike strike. There was a metallic click—the man in black just managed to block the duke's knife thrust with his own knife. The force of the parry flipped the little knife out of the duke's hand.

It skittered across the marble floor.

And then she heard it: the duke was *laughing*, a lock of his shining hair caught in his lips.

It was a low, affable chuckle, as if he were sharing a joke with a friend rather than fighting for what looked like his life in his own library. Fighting—*and losing.*

"Give it up, Montgomery," growled the stranger, his left forearm thrust firmly against the duke's throat.

"Oh, I don't think so," the duke gasped. "Not when you've come into *my* house, *my* library, *my* sanctum sanctorum. I'm going to cut out your tongue and shove it down your blasted throat before I send you back to your masters."

"What are you talking about?" the black-clad man asked, sounding much the more reasonable of the two. "You've *lost*."

Bridget couldn't help but agree. The bigger man all but hid the duke's flamboyant purple silk form beneath his bulk. The duke must give up.

She bit her lip. Was the stranger a blackmail victim? If so—

"Have I?" A flash, and then a wickedly curving gold-hilted dagger pressed hard against the stranger's throat where it was exposed beneath the scarf, cutting the flesh. The duke's upper lip curled in a feral snarl. "Get. *Off.* Me."

And Bridget saw that the duke held the second dagger in his *right* hand.

A trail of blood trickled down the stranger's bared throat.

The man in black seemed equally stunned. He opened his fist, his dagger clattering to the floor. "Easy."

He moved back very slowly, the pressure of the blade at his neck unrelenting, keeping his head held unnaturally high, until both men were kneeling. "I thought you were left-handed."

The duke grinned—a mere exposure of his teeth and hardly reassuring. "I find committing to one side leaves out a world of possibilities."

With a swift movement he reached forward and snatched the scarf from the other man's face. The man revealed had a pugilist's features with a heavy forehead and cheekbones, and a large nose with a rather prominent bump on it. His hat and wig had been knocked off in the fight, exposing black hair trimmed close to his skull. He was handsome in a brutish sort of way—his thick lips especially might've belonged to a dissolute Italian angel.

Beside the Duke of Montgomery, though, he looked like a plow horse next to an Arabian stallion.

"Oh, it's the royal rough-jobs man," the duke breathed, finally taking the knife away from the other man's throat. He got to his feet, motioning to the stranger to do so as well. Without taking his eyes from his captive, he waved his hand at the door. "You may all go, excepting you, Mrs. Crumb. Oh, and your small dog. I may need you both for protection. Or witnesses."

The three footmen shuffled away.

"Close the door and come here, Mrs. Crumb," the duke called.

Bridget did as he commanded, picking up her candle and snapping her fingers to draw Pip's attention away from a statue in the shape of a golden elephant. She had the sudden realization that the terrier had not visited the garden since his bath before bed and she hoped fervently that he wouldn't embarrass her in the duke's library.

"Have you ever met a member of the royal family?" the duke asked her as she neared.

"No, Your Grace," she said cautiously.

"Then you're in luck. May I present Hugh Fitzroy, the Duke of Kyle, although I suppose he's not a proper royal as such, hence the Fitz in his Roy." The Duke of Montgomery smiled that snaky smile—the one Bridget was beginning to loathe—at the impassive Duke of Kyle. "My housekeeper, Mrs. Crumb. I can't supply you with her Christian name as she won't tell me it, though I've begun to think I should simply give her one of my own choosing. What do you think, hmm? Shall I name her Annis, chaste and pure? Or Félicité because she's so very happy?"

He glanced sideways at Bridget and though she tried to make her expression blank, a little of her outrage at his taunts might've shown through.

He chuckled, looking back at Kyle. "No, you're quite right. Neither does her justice. Oh, but what an odd duck this fellow is," he continued, now apparently back to addressing Bridget. "Neither fish nor foul nor bonny, bonny prince. For you see, though His Grace was born of the most royal spunk that ever spurted from kingly pud, his mother was but an actress." He swung suddenly to Bridget. "*Have* you ever heard of Judith Dwyer? No? Well, she wasn't very—"

He was cut off by a guttural growl. "*Montgomery.*"

The curved knife was back at Kyle's throat before Bridget could blink. For a moment she didn't breathe, for she very much feared that Montgomery would actually slit the other man's throat.

Then the duke lowered his arm and she inhaled softly—so softly.

"Be careful," Montgomery whispered, and the sound sent shivers along Bridget's nerves. "You've frightened my housekeeper with your thoughtlessness. Never forget: you're here without invitation in *my* domain. I might do anything to you here." He smiled gently. "Anything at all."

Kyle must have very steady nerves indeed, for he didn't even blink. "There would be repercussions should I not return."

Montgomery's eyes widened, blue and guileless. "You see, this is the difference between you and me. When you make a statement like that, you think it will sway me. It doesn't. I. Don't. *Care.* I could kill you as easily as stepping on an ant and with *far* less remorse. Perhaps I'd face your repercussions on the morrow. Perhaps not. But that is for the sunrise. Tonight the shadows reign and the blood is singing in my veins. My very muscles tremble with the urge to carve the meat from your bones. Tell me"—he swept wide his arms—"who in this whole dissolute world is to dissuade me from my pleasures?"

Standing barefoot in his purple silk banyan, books scattered at his feet in the flickering light of a few candles, still holding that jeweled, curving dagger, he might've been some druidic priest, born before history was written.

Before men knew human sacrifice was forbidden.

Bridget found herself with her hand on his arm. How it had happened she could hardly think. Had it been daylight, had she been better rested, been better prepared, had at least one cup of tea inside her, she would've had better control over herself.

As it was, she was left with the act already done and the duke staring at her with his dangerous, mad eyes.

She swallowed, her lips trembling, and lifted her chin. "Don't. Please."

He cocked his head as though hearing a new song. Or a sound he'd never heard before at all. Something alien and strange.

He took her hand and, holding it, looked at Kyle. "Go. Tell your masters that you have failed and I tire of waiting. Tell them that I want the King in Hyde Park tomorrow at one. That if he doesn't acknowledge me in front of witnesses I'll have everything to the newspapers by three. Do you comprehend?"

She looked at the royal bastard, hardly believing her simple words had persuaded her master. She was very aware that Montgomery still held her hand.

A muscle flexed in Kyle's jaw, but he merely bowed his head.

He picked up his hat, wig, and knife and strode to the door of the library.

The duke brought her hand to his mouth and, his azure eyes glittering in the candlelight, pressed a kiss to the inside of her wrist.

And then the edge of his teeth.

She felt the warm softness of his lips, the prickle of

stubble against tender skin, and a sort of shock seemed to go straight through the center of her body.

He let her go and her wrist felt the cold of night. "Séraphine. The burning one. I should've known. Now I think you and your little dog had better see that Kyle makes it to the door. It'd be a sad thing indeed if he started rifling through the rest of the house on his way out, hmm?"

Chapter Five

The heartless prince grew into a brawny youth, tall and broad and with arms like oak trees. When he sparred with the other boys of the court he knocked them down like bowling pins.
And they soon learned not to get up again. . . .
—From *King Heartless*

Bridget fought to catch her breath, still dizzy from proximity to Montgomery, as she hurried after the Duke of Kyle, Pip panting happily by her heels. The terrier at least seemed to think they were on an exciting nocturnal adventure.

She caught sight of the Duke of Kyle at the end of the upper hallway and called after him, "Your Grace."

He halted and half turned, watching her with grave eyes as she walked toward him.

"The duke asked that I show you the way to the door, Your Grace," she said as diplomatically as possible, for she had never before been required to escort an aristocratic burglar from the house.

He inclined his head.

She hesitated, eyeing the cut on his neck. It really was quite nasty-looking and still seeping blood. That made up her mind.

She straightened, smoothing her wrapper—well, as much as possible. "Follow me, please."

Bridget took the main staircase, both the little dog and the very large duke following her. Bob was by the front door, alert now that the house had already been broken into. She nodded at him and led the duke back to the kitchens.

As she'd expected, everyone else was gathered here, having what was probably a lovely gossip around the kitchen table.

Cook rose on her entrance. "Mrs. Crumb."

Bridget nodded. "Mrs. Bram. Will you be so kind as to send Alice to the small drawing room with some hot water and the bag of clean linen cloths? Oh, and a pot of tea as well."

She didn't wait for a reply, but led the duke to the aforementioned room. It was painted lavender, lined with white pilaster columns linked with gilt swags, and small only in that the rose drawing room was larger.

She gestured to one of the purple-and-gold settees, which had a low, marble-topped table before it. "I hope you don't mind, Your Grace. I thought you wouldn't like to be introduced to the other servants."

He'd just lowered himself to the settee when there was a knock on the door.

Alice, a very pretty, but rather slow, maid, shouldered the door open. She held a tray with a jug of steaming water as well as the teapot and cups, and the linen bag was over her arm. She stood there, gaping at the Duke of Kyle, eyes wide.

"Put the tray on the table, please, Alice," Bridget said briskly. Pip had trotted in after them and was now investigating the far side of the room where a group of chairs were arranged.

Alice carefully lowered the tray and handed her the bag, but then stood there, still gawping at Kyle.

"You may go," Bridget said, long used to having to tell Alice exactly what she must do.

The maid meekly left.

Bridget poured two cups of tea. "Do you take sugar or milk, Your Grace?"

"Neither," Kyle murmured, at last speaking, and then, as she handed him the cup, "Thank you, both for the tea and for what you did upstairs." He met her gaze and she saw for the first time that his eyes were a warm brown and heavily lashed like a girl's. They were almost pretty on his rough face. "I know it takes great courage for a woman in your position to come between a master and his desires."

She blinked, uncertain of what to say. To acknowledge his thanks was to agree that the duke, her employer, had been in the wrong, which would be rather disloyal.

He seemed to understand her dilemma. He smiled lopsidedly—and very charmingly. "That's all right. I just wanted to thank you. I don't know what would've happened if you hadn't spoken up."

She remembered Montgomery standing like some mad warlock...and that kiss afterward. Her wrist almost burned at the memory.

"Yes, well..." She cleared her throat and took a sip of

her tea before setting the cup down and reaching for the jug of hot water. "I thought we should see to your throat, Your Grace, before you leave." She wet a cloth from the bag. "With your permission?"

He nodded.

She bent and gently pressed the cloth against the cut on his neck.

He hissed softly.

The cut wasn't terribly wide, but it was deeper than she'd initially thought. The blade the duke had used must've been very sharp—and he'd wielded it with awful precision.

Unless, of course, Montgomery hadn't cared if he killed his opponent.

Bridget shivered at the thought, hastily drawing away to find an appropriate length of cloth in the bag. The wound had begun to bleed again, gentle as she'd tried to be, and she needed a piece of linen to make into a pad.

Finding what she wanted at last, she turned back to him, carefully placing the pad against the wound. "Hold that there, Your Grace."

He did as she asked and then she began winding a long length of cloth around his neck. She was so intent upon the chore that she didn't notice how close she was to the big man until she glanced up when she was almost done.

He was watching her with those long-lashed eyes and her fingers faltered.

"He's a villain, you know," Kyle said matter-of-factly, "your master. He's blackmailing the King, as I think you understand."

She swallowed and looked away, concentrating on tying the bandage at his throat.

But she couldn't shut out his calm voice. "You seem a sensible woman. A good woman. I know you can't approve of what your master is doing."

She made no comment at that, simply rising and gathering the debris of her work.

"Mrs. Crumb." He caught her arm and she stilled, looking at him. "I understand that you probably fear for your position, but please believe me, if you are ever in need of employment, I promise I can supply you with a position every bit as good as this one. I only ask that if you are aware of information—*any* information—that might help your king, you will bring it to me."

"But you've already agreed to his terms, Your Grace," Bridget said, frowning uneasily. "Will you renege?"

"No." He smiled bitterly. "I have no doubt at all that Montgomery would indeed do as he threatens and damn the consequences."

"Then how can I help you after that?"

"He'll keep something back," Kyle said. "Blackmailers always do. I have some experience with the breed. Montgomery was right: I am sort of a...a..." He made a self-deprecating grimace. "Well, I suppose *rough-jobs man* is as good a description as any. I work for the King in secret to clean up messes that can't see the light of day. What Montgomery has is such a thing. He would destabilize the monarchy and perhaps throw this land into chaos if it is published. The last time that happened we had a civil war that lasted over a decade, with thousands killed and families torn apart." He looked at her, his brown eyes soft. "I know you don't want that."

Instead of replying directly, she opened the door to the small drawing room. "This way, Your Grace."

He sighed, but moved past her.

Pip came running over and trotted briskly out the door.

Bridget ushered the duke to the front door and watched as he descended the steps. London was still dark—there was no moon tonight. In the blackness the Duke of Kyle called a good-night and disappeared. Bridget stood shivering as Pip did his business, and then hurried inside.

She returned to the kitchens.

A few of the servants had retired back to bed, but most were still up.

She looked around at her small company. "I know it's been an eventful night, but we've barely an hour before our day begins. I suggest we all take to our beds to spend that hour getting what sleep we can."

She could tell by the slumping of shoulders and a few mutters that this wasn't a particularly popular suggestion, but it *was* practical.

And in any case, she was quite tired.

Bridget marched to her little room, shut the door firmly behind her, and shed her wrapper. She climbed gratefully into her bed and pulled the coverlet over her shoulders, shivering a little. The fire had always died down a bit by the early hours of morning, but she usually slept through this time.

She felt the jolt as Pip leaped on the bed just behind her hip. He turned about several times and then settled, curled in a tight ball.

As she pulled the covers over her cold nose, Bridget wondered sleepily why she hadn't simply agreed to help the Duke of Kyle in whatever way she could. He was obviously working for good and Montgomery... well, he worked only for himself, didn't he? He was on the side of evil. Why hadn't she betrayed him when she was given the opportunity? She thought about the way he'd touched her—the way it had made her feel like a woman. Had she sold her own honor for a handful of kisses, a bite, and a lick?

Or was it because of his gaze when he'd told her to *fuck the rules*, when he'd turned aside from threatening Kyle at her touch, when he'd called her a ridiculous, exotic name?

When he'd looked at her and seen her as a person, not just a servant?

As if to echo her conflicted thoughts, the terrier gave a heavy sigh.

VAL EXAMINED HIS pocket watch as he rode into Hyde Park the next afternoon. On the inside of the gold cover was a quite risqué scene of a pale-pink Venus sucking the cock of Mars—or possibly Vulcan. Whoever the male was, he was so swarthy he was rendered red. Or perhaps that was his reaction to the performance of the goddess. In any case the opposite side of the watch more prosaically showed the hour, twelve forty-five. Which meant he was exactly on time to ride to the south side of the park and Rotten Row, where society liked to parade.

He snapped the watch closed and tucked it into his waistcoat, turning his gray gelding's head to the south. His gold watch reminded him of Mrs. Crumb. Most women when surprised from bed emerged in some state of dishabille. Hair artfully tumbled. Shoulders bared. Breasts delightfully revealed by drooping chemises.

Not his housekeeper. Oh, no.

Mrs. Crumb had worn a nightcap even more hideous than her daytime monstrosity—and with enormous flaps that tied under her chin. Perhaps she was bald. Was that a possibility? Did he have a bald female housekeeper? The thought intrigued. *Had* he ever seen her hair at all? But no, certainly he'd seen a wisp of a dark lock before.

Hadn't he?

And then the wrapper.

Val mused on the voluminous wrapper she'd worn. So plain—white printed with tiny gray…somethings. So concealing—there had been yards and yards of it. He hadn't even gotten a glimpse of her toes!

Now, had *he* the dressing of her—and why should he not?—he would put her in reds—rose and scarlet and deep, sensual crimson. Those dark inquisitor's eyes would *burn* from a foil of crimson cloth, mysterious, feminine. Beautiful.

He was startled at the thought. Plain Mrs. Crumb beautiful? Well, most might not think her so, but oh, if she burned—

"Montgomery."

The uncouth growl came from his right and had he not been daydreaming about houri housekeepers he would not have been taken unawares by it.

As it was, though, he was rather unprepared to see the Duke of Wakefield glaring at him from an open carriage.

"What the *hell* are you doing in London?" demanded the man.

A couple riding side by side were dawdling nearby and another carriage slowed.

Wakefield was tall and patrician and his habitual expression, now that Val thought about it, was a glare. Wakefield's family was just as old as Val's but there any similarity ended. Wakefield had obviously had his ducal duties drummed into his infant head, for he was a pillar of parliament, a scion of society, a confidant of the King, et cetera and boring et cetera. The man was tedious in the extreme and Val rather loathed him.

Beside the duke was a plain woman with an intelligent face and striking gray eyes. Unless Wakefield had suddenly decided to overthrow convention and acquire an unlovely mistress, this must be the duchess.

Actually, the eyes were *very* fine indeed.

Val smiled slowly and bowed, ignoring Wakefield entirely. "Your Grace, I don't believe I've had the pleasure of an introduction. I am Montgomery."

"I know," she said in a lovely contralto. "You kidnapped my sister-in-law, whom I'm quite fond of."

Val winced. "It was rather bad of me, I confess."

"It was *criminal*," Wakefield growled. "You gave your word to me as a gentleman that you'd leave England forever."

"*Did* I?" Val asked, eyes wide. "I don't seem to *remember* such a conversation—"

"There are rules about such things and—"

"*Fuck* your rules," Val snarled, fast and low.

Wakefield's head reared back. "I can have you before the courts if that is what you truly wish."

"*Can* you, though?" Val's blood was racing, his

head pounding in time, his vision narrowed to the man before him.

Wakefield was clenching and unclenching his fists.

Val undid two buttons of his waistcoat. He had his dagger against his breast inside, ready to slip out if need be.

His lips curved. "Your sister is a very pretty girl—and newly married, if I'm not mistaken. Felicitations are in order, I think, though as I understand it the nuptials had to be hurried due to the scandal from the kidnapping. Scandal is such a horrible thing. Tainting, don't you think?"

The low, guttural sound coming from Wakefield's throat was quite animal. The duchess had her hand on her husband's upper arm, obviously restraining him. There was a bit of a crowd now around them, drawn to the prospect of scandal like flies to shit. What would it take, he wondered, listening to the thunder of his blood, to make Wakefield break the bonds of social acceptability? Another few words? A sly smile at the wife?

He slid his hand into his waistcoat, feeling the hilt of his dagger.

Feeling the razor's edge of danger and life itself.

Slow hoofbeats, the creak of carriage wheels, and a certain murmuring rustle.

Val looked around.

Just as the King's carriage passed.

The man himself sat beside his queen, staring straight ahead without expression, but as the royal carriage drew abreast he nodded quite clearly, once to Wakefield, and again.

To Val.

And then the carriage was past.

Val straightened from his own deep bow with the knowledge that he'd won quite decisively over Wakefield and the potential for war was over.

As he slid his hand from his waistcoat he strove not to feel disappointment.

"SIT." BRIDGET SPOKE the command clearly and firmly late that afternoon in the garden.

Pip stood at her feet, his eyes alert, one ear up and one ear down, as he looked from her to the bit of piecrust in her hand.

Tentatively he wagged his tail.

He did not, however, sit.

Beside her Mehmed giggled. "This cur does not know the trick of 'sit,' I think."

Bridget sighed. Apparently in the land where Mehmed came from dogs were not regularly kept as pets. Because of this he seemed curious about the terrier, treating him with wary fascination, as if he were a wild tiger brought to heel.

"Yes, well," she replied patiently, "he hasn't much practice, has he?" *Nor have I*, she added mentally.

She'd never had a dog before. She cleared her throat and tried again. "Sit."

At that moment—most likely by pure chance—Pip lowered his bottom to the ground.

"Oh!" Bridget immediately dropped the piecrust, which Pip lost no time in gobbling up, and Mehmed shouted with glee.

This had the unfortunate effect of making the terrier jump up and bark excitedly while leaping about their feet, which Bridget thought might very well negate the entire exercise. She glanced at Mehmed's grinning face, though, as he chattered in his native tongue to the happy dog, and decided not to voice her views. Instead she tilted her face back to feel the autumn sun on it. It was rare to have such a lovely London day so late in the year and rarer still that she was outside to enjoy it. But after last night she thought she might be permitted a half hour's respite. The Hermes House garden had several small pollarded trees turning colors against a deep-red brick wall, a lovely sight next to the rows of neatly trimmed evergreen box hedges.

Bridget bit her lip as she lowered her gaze. Perhaps the duke's anarchical disregard for rules had rubbed off on her.

The kitchen door opened and Alf came hurrying out.

Bridget's eyebrows drew together. Now what had the duke wanted with Alf?

The messenger gave a cocky wave and disappeared out into the mews.

Bridget smoothed her skirts. "Come, we should return to our duties."

Mehmed sobered and obediently fell into step with her, though Pip was less willing to give up his play. Every few steps he leaped up and nipped at the boy's coat.

"This is nice palace," Mehmed said as they walked. "Although very cold."

Bridget smiled at that, wondering how the boy would fare when winter and snow came. "Did you live in a very big house in your homeland?"

"Not so big as this," he said. "But nice with a fountain in the garden that was cool on very hot days. My father was a spice merchant, a rich man with two wives. I am his third son and his favorite." He grinned at her.

Bridget frowned. She'd stopped walking as she listened to the boy. Things might be very different in heathen lands, but presumably not so different that the son of a rich man who could afford two wives and a nice house became a servant. "How did you come to be in the service of the duke, then, Mehmed?"

The smile fell from his merry face and she was almost sorry she'd asked. "My father, he had bad argument with the *vezir-i azam*." He must have seen the puzzlement in her expression, for he tried to explain. "*Vezir-i azam* is very great man. Is like king, but not king. Maybe big friend to king."

She thought a moment. "Perhaps the prime minister?"

"What is this?"

She explained who Sir Robert Walpole was and his relationship to both the King and the government of England as concisely as possible as Mehmed listened attentively. The boy was very quick to pick up the rather complicated concepts, even with the language differences.

"Perhaps like this, yes." He brightened a little at the new words, repeating, "Prime minister. Prime minister" to himself under his breath several times before continuing his tale. "The *vezir-i azam* liked a horse very much and he wanted to buy it. But my father did not know this and he bought it instead. When the *vezir-i azam* found this out he was very angry. He said my father must give him the horse. My father of course did this and with many apologies, but it was too late, such was his fate."

"But why?" asked Bridget, confused.

"The horse," Mehmed said, growing animated. "We like horses that like to fight. This kind of horse is very strong, very fast, very beautiful. The horse my father had bought, that the *vezir-i azam* had wanted, was such a horse. But the horse had fought the boys in the stables and injured itself very badly against the stall. Because of these injuries my father was forced to cut off the horse's man-parts." Here Mehmed made an extremely graphic gesture, which made Bridget wish she had averted her eyes in time. "The horse could not have daughters and sons. The *vezir-i azam* was very, very angry."

"What happened?" Bridget asked, caught up in the story. Pip had wandered off and now had his upper half under one of the hedges. She hoped he hadn't found anything too terrible under there.

Mehmed shrugged. "The *vezir-i azam* demanded payment for his debt. Man-parts for man-parts."

Bridget's mouth opened and then stayed open. "But what does that mean?"

Mehmed sighed, sounding far too weary, far too cynical for his years. "It mean he wanted man-parts from my father's family. My father already had sons. My elder brothers already had sons. But me?" He shrugged again. "I am young and no sons. Like the horse. The *vezir-i azam* said I was to be made eunuch and sold into slavery to pay my father's debt to him."

"But... but..." Bridget found herself floundering. This was barbaric—though she knew aristocrats who had done worse here in her homeland. It seemed the ones in power did as they liked the world over. She asked delicately, "Did... ?"

A lovely wide smile spread over his gleaming face. "The duke, he visiting the *vezir-i azam*. He see me and he like me. He show the *vezir-i azam* a ruby this big." He held his forefinger and thumb two inches apart. "And the duke say, 'I give you this for Mehmed *and* his man-parts.' And the *vezir-i azam* say, 'Very good!' so I come away with the duke!" Mehmed beamed at the triumphal end of his tale and then added, only a little wistfully, "But sometimes I miss my mother."

"Of course you do," Bridget murmured sympathetically, for she remembered missing Mam when first she entered service.

This cast an entirely different light on the duke, though. He'd actually *saved* Mehmed from a terrible fate—at quite an extravagant price, too. That didn't align with her idea of him as pure evil, did it? And whyever would the duke save Mehmed? Had he done it on a whim—or had he had another reason?

Bridget cleared her throat. "And now you help the duke shave and dress. Is that erm . . . *all* you do for the duke?"

"No!" Mehmed said proudly, and her heart sank. If the duke truly was using this sweet, intelligent boy as a courtesan she was going to strangle him. "I also teach the duke how to write my language and I play the tambour and sing. I have beautiful voice," he added without any show of modesty at all, and she could've kissed him.

"Yes, well, I'm sure you do," Bridget said briskly, allowing herself a small smile for the boy. "Thank you for telling me your tale, Mehmed, and I suppose you'd best find out if the duke wishes to see you now."

But as it turned out it wasn't Mehmed the duke wanted to see.

"Séraphine!" he exclaimed when she entered his bedchambers. He thrust a bare arm in the air in a sort of salutation because, *of course*, he was in the bath.

"Your Grace," Bridget replied gravely. Briefly she considered pointing out that her name was not, in fact, Séraphine, but then decided there was simply no point. "I was told you wished to see me."

"Did I?" he asked the ceiling. "I believe I did. Please. Pull a chair closer. You might as well be comfortable. Here, now." He scowled at Pip, who had placed his front paws on the rim of the copper tub and was curiously sniffing the water. "I don't believe we're well enough acquainted for you to join me."

The duke flicked the surface of his bath, sending droplets of water into Pip's face.

The terrier sneezed and dropped down from the bathtub. He sneezed again, shaking his head, and trotted purposefully over to the duke's bed to explore underneath it.

Bridget found a chair and set it a safe distance, several feet, from the bathtub.

He still gazed at the ceiling, but a corner of his mouth twisted up. "Cowardice, Mrs. Crumb? Tut-tut."

Bridget cleared her throat, determined to keep this audience as businesslike as humanly possible, considering with whom she was speaking and that he was *nude* once again. "What did you wish to see me about, Your Grace?"

"We-ell," he drawled, throwing both arms into the air with a splash and proceeding to weave them about one another as if he were conjuring magic only he could see. "I could have called you to discuss the revolution of the spheres. Are they singing up there as they make their way among the stars? A song we can't quite hear though we build ever more mighty telescopes, peering, peering through the blackness?" He cocked his head, his arms suddenly still. "The Italian heretic says no, that there is no song but the sun's, and grave Newton nods his head and agrees. But I put it to you, if this is so, that we center on the sun, then why do all the pope's men disagree? Is God dead? Or does he play celestial billiards with the planets?" He pointed his finger at her, his azure eyes blazing madly. "And tell me, burning housekeeper, if Newton and his ilk are correct, why haven't we all crashed into the sun in a fiery implosion of nothingness?"

There was a small silence.

Then Bridget cleared her throat. "As I understand it, it's because of the Earth's momentum."

The duke dropped his hands. "What did you say?"

She could feel heat moving up her cheeks. "That's what you were talking about, weren't you? Mr. Galileo's theory that the Earth moves about the sun, and the disgraceful way he was imprisoned by the pope, and Mr. Newton's discovery of gravity, and then you asked why the Earth didn't fall into the sun and I answered that it was because of the momentum the Earth has as it orbits the sun. At least," she faltered, "I believe that is what Mr. Kepler wrote."

He folded his arms on the bath and laid his chin on them and simply stared at her, a gloriously nude man—a *duke*—his entire attention upon her, Bridget Crumb. His shoulders gleamed like alabaster in the candlelight and his golden hair curled damply about his neck.

"You," he murmured finally, "are an indecipherable puzzle. When did you read Kepler?"

"When I was a maid in a country house there was a library that had been neglected. The worms had gotten to some of the books and the mistress said they were to be burned. I took them to read before they were destroyed. It wasn't theft," she added hastily. "I *did* burn them afterward."

"What else?" he whispered. "Besides Kepler?"

She shrugged. "A history of the Roman Empire. A book on the fishes and aquatic animals of England. A book of cookery. And Shakespeare's tragedies."

"How very eclectic."

"They were the only things I had to read." If he made fun of her now, she'd walk out and damn the consequences.

"So you read them—all of them?" he asked as if he was fascinated.

"Yes."

"Every word? Even the bits about newts?"

"Yes."

"Oh, my Séraphine," he breathed, and what was strange was that he didn't sound amused.

He sounded admiring.

"Well," he said, sitting upright on a great splash. "No more shall you go bookless, Mrs. Crumb. From this day henceforth you have free run of my library with my compliments."

She stared. "I—"

He grinned, looking not a little wicked. "Have you looked at my books? Glanced at my titles? Fondled my spines?"

The heat in her cheeks returned, for of course she *had.*

There were enormous volumes with gilded pages, tiny, delicate books with writing that looked like lace. There was shelf upon shelf of books that were shining new and books so old they looked ready to crumble at a single touch.

The duke's library was simply *wonderful*.

"Thank you, Your Grace," she said, meaning the words sincerely. "You're most kind."

"No, Mrs. Crumb," he said. "I am many, many things, but kind is not one of them."

She looked at him and knew she couldn't refute his words. "Even so."

"Even so." He clapped his hands, startling Pip, who came rushing out from under the bed, barking, his tail adorned with a ball of dust. "Hush, you," said the duke, and the dog sat down.

Bridget frowned at him.

"And now the reason I asked for you, Mrs. Crumb," the duke said, and her gaze immediately returned to him to find his eyes sparkling mischievously. "My plots have come to fruition, my foes are vanquished, I've had a nod from the King himself, and in return I've sent him his son's letters—and because of all this I've decided to hold a victory ball to celebrate my return to London."

Bridget immediately came to attention. A ball on the scale that the duke would probably want would involve a month's worth of planning and work.

His smile widened into a grin. "And I'll be holding it in two weeks' time."

Chapter Six

In time the old king died and King Heartless took his place. The new king decided his kingdom was too small, so he invaded his neighbors' kingdoms, riding into battle clad in golden armor. And because he had no heart, he gave no quarter to the armies who fought him. . . .

—From *King Heartless*

Two weeks later Val paused a moment in the corner of his ballroom and drank in the sweet, heady liqueur of his success. Every person of import in London was here—some very much against their will, for he'd had to make gentle and not-so-gentle insinuations about the repercussions were they to refuse his invitations. Here was an elderly roué, tottering in heels, his macabre rouged face peering beneath a high periwig. The man had once whispered secrets into the ears of kings and queens and now was rumored to be dying of the dread disease. There the canny young wife of a member of parliament, much smarter than her husband, and the reason he'd been elected at all. She came from a prominent Whig family—her father and both brothers were members of Parliament—and she was rather interestingly too close to her sister-in-law. And in the corner, a French aristocrat watching carefully from behind a painted fan. He sold secrets to his own government—and to any other willing to meet his price.

Val smiled and inhaled, breathing potential, breathing power. Oh, this was lovely. His ballroom was massed with pink and white hothouse roses, hundreds of them, making the air heavy with their perfume. Swaths of gold cloth were draped at the windows and tied at the tables placed here and there along the walls. The colors were repeated in the livery of the footmen, dozens of them, most hired especially for the ball.

This. This was *his*.

Val grinned and, employing his gold walking stick, stepped out into what he had caused to be created.

He nodded ironically to the Duke of Kyle, drinking a glass of wine and maintaining a look of wary alertness.

It was a popular expression tonight.

Val exchanged pleasantries with a member of the royal family and then crossed paths with Leonard de Chartres, the Duke of Dyemore. The duke was a tall man, broad-shouldered when he'd been younger, but now beginning to stoop. He wore an elegant bag wig that only highlighted the wrinkled dissipation of the face beneath.

Val swept Dyemore, a contemporary of his father's, an elaborate bow and upon straightening found the elder man smiling at him, revealing long, coffee-stained teeth.

Dyemore laid a liver-spotted hand on Val's sleeve. "Montgomery! You've grown if anything more beautiful. I'm most pleased to find you've taken your rightful place in London society finally. You were gone so many years from our shores." The last was said with a sort of sly twist of Dyemore's purple lips.

"Thank you, sir," Val murmured. "I sailed near round the world, I vow, and returned to find everything changed, everyone aged, almost decayed some would say."

Dyemore's smile didn't falter at the admittedly unsubtle jab, but the corners of his mouth crimped, deepening the wrinkles there. "Have you decided to assume your rightful place in other areas as well? Your father, I know, would've wished it."

Dyemore moved his big arthritic hand from Val's sleeve to his shoulder.

Val stilled, glancing at the duke's hand, and noticed that his sleeve had fallen back, revealing a tiny tattoo on the inside of the old man's wrist. It was in the shape of a dolphin. "Indeed? I had thought the... club defunct by now?"

"Oh, no, oh, no!" Dyemore chuckled. "As vital as it ever was—perhaps more so even than in your father's time. We have a great many members. We just lack a new heir for when I decide to retire from my leadership."

Val glanced up into Dyemore's eyes—a bright, bloodshot green. He remembered, long, long ago, seeing those same eyes glittering from behind a wolf's-head mask. Yet what the duke referred to *was* after all just another means to power, was it not? And what power it would be—to hold dozens of England's aristocrats in thrall...

Val's blood rose at just the thought, but he kept his smile serene. "Under certain circumstances, I might be amenable, Your Grace."

The smile this time was frankly satisfied, like that of a man who had just orgasmed down the mouth of a particularly pretty woman... or boy. "Then we should have a chat. Perhaps you'll visit me for tea?"

"Perhaps I will, sir." Val bowed again with a flourish and continued on his way, wondering if he should nip upstairs for a quick bath first.

The sight of Lady Ann Herrick, strolling arm in arm with another lady, one he'd not been introduced to yet, diverted him, however. Lady Herrick was a wealthy widow with whom he'd had a liaison last spring. By the moue she shot him she wouldn't mind a re-acquaintance, but he'd already swum those waters. Now, her friend was another matter. A petite, buxom redhead—probably hennaed—she had the look of a woman who knew her way around a cock. He arched his eyebrow at her and Lady Herrick's smile abruptly dimmed, although her friend's face brightened in almost exactly inverse proportion.

He wondered what Mrs. Crumb's face would look like should she find him abed on the morrow with the faux redhead. The lovely disapproval, carefully hidden. The exasperation, less well concealed. The sharp comments, meant to cut and reprimand. Oh, he would have a wonderful bickering argument with her and her cheeks would bloom that hot red as her temper rose.

He'd lay his palms against her cheeks to feel the heat. To absorb her emotion.

"Val."

The voice was Eve's so naturally he turned, a half smile still playing about his mouth.

His sister's face was grave, though, as she paced toward

him, *that* man on her arm. "Val, how did you do this? How did you reestablish yourself in London society?"

But he had other, more important matters on his mind as he stared at her, horrified. "*What* are you wearing?"

She glanced down at the . . . well, he supposed one must call it a gown. It did, after all, drape her form, covering her adequately if not suitably.

She looked a little hurt. "Don't you like my new dress?"

"It's . . ." He swallowed and turned his head, for his eyes really could not take the sight. "*Yellow.*"

The man beside her made a restless movement. "So help me, Montgomery—"

"We have the same coloring, you and I," Val pleaded with his sister. Surely she wasn't entirely lost to reason? Good God, was this what love did to a person? "We have golden hair, fair skin, blue eyes."

"Yes, I know," she said, sounding puzzled.

"*Blues,*" he said simply, because perhaps her brain was so befogged she couldn't take in more complex words. "We look good in shades of *blue.*"

He spread wide his arms, showing her the pale silvery-blue suit that he wore tonight as a demonstration.

"You see?"

Makepeace wrinkled his nose as if an odd thought had entered his brain. "But you're always prancing about in pink."

"Yes, yes," Val said impatiently, waving him off. "I look good in everything, really. But to be safe, blue, *not* yellow, darling Eve."

"She looks wonderful," Makepeace said intensely, which only went to prove that he had lost his mind over this love thing, because Val might adore his sister, but no one could call her beautiful. "The dress is perfect on her."

"Thank you, Asa," Eve said. "But I have something much more important to discuss with Val." He opened his mouth to disagree—very few things trumped one's toilet, after all—but she continued without pause. "How did you get into the King's good graces?"

He closed his mouth slowly and smiled. "Why, Eve, whyever *wouldn't* I be in His Majesty's favor?"

"Because," she said sadly, "you're a liar and a blackmailer and, for all I know, far worse."

He blinked, a little... startled. Yes, startled. He'd been called much filthier things before, but never by his sister.

Never by Eve.

"Darling," he said gruffly.

"You can't keep doing this," she said. "You can't keep hurting people. People I like. People who are my friends."

"I hardly think you're bosom bows with His Majesty," he said, smiling, but his words seemed to fall flat.

"No, Val," she said, her face stern. "*No.*"

She used to be so frightened when they were young. Like a pale little ghost, slipping into the shadows, hiding from their vicious elders, trying not to be noticed.

He'd saved her once. Swept her away like a prince in a fairy tale, but that was long ago and far away and perhaps no longer mattered. How were such things counted among normal people?

For she'd thawed. He could see that now. She was no longer that frozen, scared little girl afraid to be noticed. Afraid to live. He supposed he should thank Makepeace for that. For taking his Eve, his sister, and blowing warm life into her. But all he could think was that in doing so, Makepeace had shattered Val's last link to her.

Leaving him alone in the frozen cold.

He actually shivered, there in the overheated ballroom.

"I love you," she said quietly. "I always will. But this must stop. *You* must stop."

And she took Makepeace's arm and walked away from him.

He turned, a bit blindly. The room was bright and chattering and he was the king of London. He was. *He was.*

And yet he felt as if he might be bleeding to death here in his crowded ballroom, all the warmth trickling from his body.

Where was his bloody housekeeper anyway? It was *her* job to keep him warm. Probably gliding unnoticed in the back hallways, wearing black always, like the inquisitor she was. She would tell him that he'd deserved it. That his sister was right. And then her dark burning eyes would drop to his mouth and widen a bit and he'd think about throwing up her skirts, tearing through staid wool and linen, and finding out if her cunt was as hot and molten as those eyes.

He started for the door, thinking of crimson velvet and burning eyes—and a woman's face swam into view.

Ah. A quarry. A victim of his plots and of his villainy.

He diverted his course, intercepting the woman. She was on the arm of an older man, her father.

Val swept her an abrupt bow. "Miss Royle. Sir."

Hippolyta Royle was the only daughter of Sir George Royle, who had gone to the East Indies to make his fortune and had done quite a good job indeed. The result was that Miss Royle had a dowry with few rivals in England.

"Your Grace." The lady's face, oval and proud and naturally olive-complexioned, paled at the sight of him.

Actually, he was rather used to that sort of reaction to his sudden appearance.

Blackmailer, and all.

He took her hand and brought it to his lips, peering over her knuckles. Her fingers were trembling. "Might I have the pleasure of this next dance, Miss Royle?"

Oh, she wanted to deny him, he could tell. Her full berry-red lips were pressed together, her dark brows gathered. The lady did not look entirely happy.

A state of affairs that didn't escape her father. "My dear?"

She patted the elderly man's hand. "It's nothing, Papa. It's just so hot in here."

"Then perhaps if we venture close to the windows—"

"Oh, but I insist on a turn on the floor," Val purred, his pulse racing, his nostrils flared. If she darted for cover he'd spring and sink his teeth into her. She was prey—*his* prey, and he'd not let her go. She was a prize and he'd parade her before all. "*If* you please."

The old man frowned as if to object, but she drew a deep breath and nodded. "Certainly, Your Grace."

"Splendid." He held out his hand.

She placed hers in his and he glanced around to see who was looking, who was taking note. He frowned for just a second, irritated, for the one he truly wanted to take note wasn't even in the damned room. Such a shame housekeepers didn't frequent balls.

He led her to the dance floor where he performed the steps much more gracefully than she, but that was all right. He could hire dance masters to teach her better later.

As he brought her back to her waiting parent he lowered his head to hers and said, "I'll call on you next week, shall I?"

The hand on his arm jerked, but she kept her composure. "I beg your pardon, Your Grace?"

"I intend to court you," he informed her kindly, and then added to make it perfectly clear, "and make you my wife."

She swallowed. "Oh, no."

He smiled. "Oh, yes."

She stopped dead and turned to face him, her fine dark eyes large and her delicate nostrils flared. "I don't like you. Doesn't that matter to you at all?"

"No." He smiled kindly at her, his chest still and frozen. "No one likes me."

BRIDGET STRODE THROUGH the bustling Hermes House kitchens, surveying her army of footmen and maidservants. What looked like total chaos at first glance turned to concentrated work on closer inspection. Two footmen hurried past her, bearing silver trays of filled wineglasses on their shoulders, no doubt bound for the gentlemen's gaming room. A row of kitchen maids assembled plate after plate of salmon pâté in a golden jelly. On another table three footmen were making punch in an enormous silver bowl under the watchful eye of a hired butler.

Bridget nodded to herself. After two weeks of near sleeplessness she'd brought off the almost impossible: a successful ball with no advance warning and no mistress of the house to hostess the event. A pity there was no history of housekeepers, for had there been, this night might have been made into legend to be told and retold through the ages, she mused rather whimsically.

She really *did* need some sleep—and she thought longingly of her little room where no doubt Pip was already curled up on her bed.

But she couldn't rest yet.

Right now she had to make sure the ball finished as grandly as it had begun.

She motioned to Peg, one of the Hermes House maidservants. "Set a tray of wine for the musicians with some bread, cheese, and meat." Bridget pointed to two of the hired footmen. "You'll bring the trays to the musicians with my compliments for the excellent music."

"Yes, ma'am," the elder of the two men said, nodding.

"And Peg?"

"Ma'am?" Peg looked up alertly.

"Be sure to water the wine well. They still have hours yet to play."

Bridget turned without waiting for Peg's reply, heading for Mrs. Bram, when one of the hired footmen came running into the kitchens near breathless. "Gentlemen come t' blows in th' hall. Shattered a vase and there's blood all about. I think someone heaved up."

He was white-faced.

Bob tutted. "Anyone dead?"

The hired footman turned to him, wide-eyed. "No?"

"Then best we clean up," Bob said briskly. "You an' me can help th' gentlemen an' the maids will do the washing, yeah?"

Bridget caught Bob's eye and nodded approvingly before continuing on her way to Mrs. Bram.

The cook was bent, her reddened face gleaming, over a platter of tiny, delicate white candies. On each she was piping a minuscule pink rose.

Bridget kept her voice low as she asked, "You have enough food, you think?"

"Enough and just a bit more to be safe," Mrs. Bram said with satisfaction. "But it were close."

It had been *very* close. Simply acquiring and preparing all the food and drink needed for the midnight supper tonight had been no easy task and Bridget knew the cook had worked just as hard as she.

"Mrs. Bram, you are to be commended on an excellent job well done," Bridget said.

"An' you, Mrs. Crumb, an' you," replied the cook.

For a moment Bridget shared a weary smile with the other woman.

And then one of the maidservants touched her shoulder. "There's a lady asking to speak to you, ma'am."

Bridget looked at the girl, one of the servants hired for the night. "Me? She asked for me by name?"

The maidservant nodded. "Mrs. Crumb. That's what she said."

"Thank you," Bridget said, and, nodding to Mrs. Bram, made her way to the door of the kitchens.

At first the hallway—admittedly ill lit—seemed crowded only with rushing servants.

But then an elegant figure in a cream-and-gold dress stepped forward. "Mrs. Crumb."

Bridget recognized Miss Hippolyta Royle at once.

Bridget hurried to her. "Ma'am, this way, please."

She took the lead silently, hoping that she looked as if she were helping a lady guest with a feminine need of some sort. At the end of the hallway, instead of turning right and taking the stairs up to the main floor, she headed left into a smaller hall. There were several doors here and she used her key ring to unlock one, glancing quickly over her shoulder to make sure they weren't seen before ushering Miss Royle into a storage closet. Shelves lined the walls, stacked with cheeses, liqueurs, pickles, medicinal herbs and ointments, wax, oils, and vinegars.

There was a small window high on the wall, with shutters on the inside. Bridget opened the shutters to let in a little light from the carriage lanterns on the street before turning to her guest. "What did you need to see me about, ma'am?"

Miss Royle closed her eyes a moment, taking a deep breath. Her face was oval and quite beautiful, her complexion almost olive in the low light, her dark mahogany hair pulled back into intricate loops at the back of her head.

When she opened her eyes they looked desperate. "Oh, Mrs. Crumb, he told me tonight that he'll be calling on me. That he means to *wed* me."

Bridget stared, for she knew at once that Miss Royle was correct. She must be the mysterious fiancée that the duke had talked about. For some reason Bridget had never dreamed it would be someone she already knew. An unfamiliar emotion entered her breast, something akin to rage. She was too overworked, too exhausted from lack of sleep. This news shouldn't affect her so.

The aristocracy married all the time and rarely for anything as mundane as affection. *Of course* the duke would blackmail Miss Royle—the most sought-after heiress in England—into marriage. Just because he'd saved Pip for Bridget, just because he'd rescued Mehmed from slavery and worse, just because he'd offered her the use of his library in such a lovely way didn't mean he wasn't essentially the same as he'd ever been.

Evil. Vain. Self-serving.

And any other consideration—any other emotion Bridget might have on the matter? Well, that simply wasn't to be heeded.

Her feelings didn't pertain.

She straightened, pulling her wandering thoughts together. "I take it that His Grace's suit does not appeal?"

"No." Miss Royle pressed her hand to her mouth for a moment before letting it drop again. "*No*, not at all."

Bridget nodded. She did understand. The duke was a very mercurial creature—although that was somewhat balanced by great wealth, overwhelming handsomeness, and a magnificent library she hadn't yet found the time to explore. Also, she secretly found his conversation amusing. Sometimes, at any rate.

Still. *She* wasn't the one being blackmailed into a marriage she didn't want.

Miss Royle took her hands. "You must find the miniature, you *must*, Mrs. Crumb. I cannot marry the Duke of Montgomery. He is a loathsome man. The mere thought of sharing a marital bed with him..."

She swallowed, closing her eyes.

Bridget squeezed the other woman's hands. Miss Royle

might be wealthy and far above a mere housekeeper in station, but at the moment Bridget felt sorry for her.

"I'll do my best, ma'am, truly I will." She hesitated, debating. She didn't think telling Miss Royle that she'd actually had the miniature in her hands at one point would comfort the other woman—quite the opposite. Instead she said, "He isn't really as awful as he makes himself out to be."

Miss Royle frowned, withdrawing her hands. "What do you mean?"

Bridget blinked, feeling awkward. She shouldn't have spoken so impulsively. "Just that he likes shocking people, I think. If you talk to him about something that truly interests him..."

She trailed away, for Miss Royle was looking at her rather oddly.

Naturally. How would a housekeeper know about conversing with a duke?

Bridget cleared her throat, folding her hands at her waist and saying more formally, "Yes, well. I had better return to my tasks and you to the ball, ma'am. Rest assured I shall look for your miniature."

"Thank you." Miss Royle took a breath as if bracing herself. "I feel as if you're my only hope, you know. It's as if I'm being stalked by some predator." She flashed a not-very-convincing smile. "Wouldn't want to be luncheon."

Bridget smiled bracingly and opened the door for Miss Royle, watching as she disappeared down the corridor.

Then she closed the shutters of the window and locked the door behind her before leaving as well. No one seemed to particularly notice when she reemerged into the servants' hallway.

Bridget eyed the hurried flow of maids and footmen and made a decision. She turned back down the hallway, and then took another passage. She walked along it alone, listening to the sounds of the revelries, took another turn, and came to a servants' hall that ran behind the ballroom. There was a small door here and she turned the handle, opening it and slipping through.

She emerged in an obscure corner—this was a servants' entrance, after all, meant for such as she. The musicians were directly to her right, a grouping of statuary and vases half shielding the door.

The ballroom was stiflingly hot—so many bodies massed together with innumerable flaming candles made it almost a natural inferno. Bright silks and velvets drifted slowly past. No one could move particularly swiftly due to the crush. She saw him at once, despite the fact that there must be hundreds of people present.

The Duke of Montgomery would always be the center of attention, after all.

He stood in a small group of gentlemen. An aristocrat in a complicated two-tailed wig was talking earnestly at his elbow as the duke surveyed the room. Montgomery wore a pale-blue suit especially made for the ball—she knew since she'd overheard the poor tailor being berated for the last two weeks. It really was a magnificent creation, with silver embroidery at cuffs and pockets and along the edges. His golden hair was tied back with a wide black ribbon and he held a gold walking stick in his left hand.

This was the man who had blackmailed the king of the land. Who had blackmailed her own mother—and still held the means to blackmail her in the future. Who aimed to blackmail Miss Royle into marriage.

He was a terrible, evil man, and most likely mad to boot. She knew that.

And yet.

As if he could hear her thoughts, his head turned and his eyes met hers.

She should've ducked before he could see her. That would've been the sensible thing to do—the *smart* thing to do. Instead she lifted her chin and stared back as if she were equal to a duke.

Without acknowledging the gentleman still talking to him, the duke pivoted and walked toward her.

Through that crowded ballroom, as if nothing stood between him and her. And all those people parted as if he were a ship cleaving the waves. Why shouldn't they? He was the Duke of Montgomery. Nothing stood in his way. He made sure of that.

He made her side and took her hand and simply said, "Come."

VAL CUT THROUGH his guests, something animal beating at his chest. He was dragging his housekeeper behind him, and if he received an odd look now and again he simply stared back, teeth bared. He took a glass of wine from a passing footman—his fourth of the night—and then he made the French doors that led out onto one of the balconies.

He let go of her hand only long enough to shove aside

the gold draperies, open the doors, and pull her outside before shutting the doors again behind them.

It was too late in the season and too cold to open the doors for the ball. That was what they had decided. Or rather what *she* had decided. He, as he remembered the discussion, had been distracted by his tailor's egregiously horrible placement of the buttons on his cuffs.

In any case, the result was that the balcony was deserted.

"It's cold out here, Your Grace," she said.

"Not with the warmth from the windows," he replied, which was at least partially true. "Look."

He turned her to face the garden and all that lay beyond.

"Oh," she murmured. "The moon is full."

"Yes." He leaned his shoulders against the cold stone of his house, let his head fall back, and gazed over her crown at the celestial body. It seemed to hang, pale and glowing and monstrously large, over the rooftops of London. He took a sip of wine. It was tart and rich on his tongue. "I knew a girl once who liked to wish upon the moon."

"What did she wish for?" Mrs. Crumb asked, her voice low. She had a lovely voice, he realized absently, here in the near dark. Feminine and grave. A voice to whisper secrets. A voice to console and give absolution.

He shrugged, though she couldn't see. "I don't remember. Girlish things, I think. I'd take her to the top of the widow's tower at Ainsdale Castle, late at night, and we'd watch the moon rise. The widow's tower was very high but she wasn't afraid. Sometimes I'd steal a pie from the kitchens and we'd picnic up there. I brought up a blanket, too, so she wouldn't have to sit on the bare stone floor."

Mrs. Crumb made an aborted movement, as if she'd meant to turn to face him and then changed her mind.

He let the wineglass dangle by his side. "I told her a rabbit lived on the moon and she believed me. She believed everything I told her then."

"What rabbit?"

"There." He roused himself, straightening.

He drew her back, fitting her against his chest and setting his chin on her shoulder. She smelled of tea and housekeeperly things, and she was warm, so warm. He caught up her right hand in his and traced the moon with it. "D'you see? There the long ears, there the tail, there the forepaws, there the back."

"I see," she whispered.

"I told her the rabbit had lavender fur and ate pink moon clover up there." His mouth twisted, as he remembered. "She'd watch me with big blue eyes, her mouth half-open, a bit of piecrust on her dress. She hung on every word."

He could hear her breath, could feel the tremble of her limbs. Did she fear him?

"D'you believe me?" he asked against her ear, his lips wet with wine. She was a housekeeper and housekeepers didn't matter in the grand schemes of kings and dukes and little girls who wished upon rabbit moons.

But she was silent, damnable housekeeper.

They breathed together for a moment, there in the night air, London twinkling before them, overhung by a pagan moon.

At last she stirred and asked, "What happened to the girl?"

He broke away from her, draining his glass of wine. "She grew up and knew me for a liar."

He drew his hand across his face and pushed open the doors to his ballroom, striding in without looking back at her.

The heat was dizzying. The voices a grating cacophony. The stink of bodies, perfumed and sweating, nauseating.

Cal the bastard footman emerged from the crowd, a glass of wine in his hand. "Wine, Your Grace?"

Val took the wine and downed it in one gulp. "Get out of my sight."

For some reason that made Cal smile.

Val shook his head and unhooked his gold walking stick from the loop at his waist. Then he lifted his head and grinned. He was the Duke of Montgomery. He'd successfully blackmailed the King. He was about to blackmail himself a wife. No one loved him.

And that was the way he liked it.

Chapter Seven

Soon King Heartless had merely to show himself in his shining golden armor for the opposing commander to turn tail and run and the enemy army to lay down their weapons. He didn't even have to raise his sword.

And after that? Well, really, there was no one to gainsay him. . . .

—From *King Heartless*

Why did gentlemen always cast up their accounts in hidden corners? Bridget pondered this eternal housekeeperly question late the next afternoon as the maids found a belated mess in one of the drawing rooms off the ballroom. She saw to it that Alice and another maid had the cleaning well in hand and then made her way to the ballroom to check on the progress of putting everything to rights there. Pip trotted along busily beside her.

She—and most of the household staff—had had barely four hours' sleep before they'd begun work this morning. The last carriage had pulled away as the sun was just beginning to rise over London.

She was overseeing Bob, on a very tall ladder, carefully taking down a swag of gold cloth from a crystal chandelier when Mehmed came into the ballroom. "Mrs. Crumb, I have need of you, please."

She watched as the chandelier swayed ominously and Bill, holding the ladder steady, swore under his breath. "Just a moment, Mehmed."

"It cannot wait, I think. It is the duke."

She glanced swiftly at the boy and saw that his eyes were wide and solemn and fixed on her with a desperate pleading.

She motioned to a third footman. "John, please help Bill steady this ladder."

"Yes, ma'am."

She drew the boy aside. "What is wrong with the duke?"

"I do not know," Mehmed said mournfully. "He will not answer his door."

"Well, where is Mr. Attwell?"

Mehmed shrugged. "This I do not know."

"Cannot you get in to His Grace's bedroom from the dressing room?"

"There is a lock on the door there, too."

Bridget fought to suppress a sigh and an impending headache. "Mehmed, sometimes Englishmen like to drink to excess and then they lie abed for a *very* long time the next day. You needn't worry. Aside from a headache and a foul temper, His Grace will be fine."

She turned to resume her work, but felt a light touch on her sleeve.

Mehmed snatched back his hand as if touching her had

burned him. "Lady, please." There were tears in his big brown eyes. "Please. I hear a groan from room and sound like duke not well. *Please.* You must help."

Well, sounds of being sick would only be the natural result of overindulging. Bridget and her minions had spent the morning being quite aware of *that.* This information only bolstered her case.

Still.

Despite her pragmatic, practical reasoning, her body had already turned toward the door, had already started striding toward the stairs. What if he was truly ill?

Oh, he was going to laugh at her! When she opened his door and she saw him abed with two or three ladies of the night, all golden curls and pink nipples—theirs or his. He'd give her that cocky, sly smile, call her Mrs. Crumb or burning Séraphine, and flaunt his gorgeous nude body as she tried to usher his whores out the door. She'd become quite cross with him and he'd make her very flustered and everything would be all right.

She'd made the upper floor by this time, Mehmed at her heels, Pip racing ahead. She strode down the empty hall, the chatelaine jingling at her waist, until she reached the duke's rooms.

Bridget knocked briskly. "Your Grace?"

There was no response.

She laid her ear against the painted wood and listened. All was silence and then she thought she heard a faint, dry wheeze.

She drew back, staring at the door.

"What is it?" whispered Mehmed.

"I don't know."

She picked up her chatelaine, quickly flipping through the keys until she found the proper one. She inserted the key in the lock, turned it, and pushed open the duke's bedroom door.

The room smelled foul.

That was her first thought. It was dark, the drapes still pulled against the day, the fire cold. He'd been sick, that much was obvious, and more than once, by the stink.

She made her way cautiously to the bed. "Pull the drapes, please, Mehmed."

Behind her Mehmed grunted and a bright bolt of sunlight hit the bed.

"Dear God in heaven," she choked.

The duke was sprawled sideways on the bed, half on, half off. He wore his breeches from the night before and a sodden, filthy shirt, hanging from his shoulders. His hair was dark with sweat or some other matter and clung to his face and neck in damp ringlets. His face—*dear God*—his face was gray, his eyes closed and sunken, his mouth open, his lips pale and crusted, and she thought for a moment—a *dreadful* moment—that he was already dead.

Then she saw his chest, oily with sweat, move.

"Mehmed!" Her voice was high and shrill, but she couldn't help it, she was panicking. "Run for a doctor now!"

"*No.*" Somehow the duke's hand shot up and he gripped her with surprising strength—perhaps his last strength. "You send for no one, d'you hear me, Séraphine? *No one.*"

"But you're *ill.*"

He opened his eyes and she gasped. Blood vessels had

burst in both his eyes, making them look as if they were bleeding. "I've been poisoned."

He coughed and began heaving and she realized that he hadn't the strength to raise himself.

"Bring a basin, Mehmed."

She gripped his shoulders and with great effort turned him so he was over the basin Mehmed held. Though all he brought up was a terrible greenish-brown bile. When he was done he lay back, gasping for breath, his eyes once again closed.

"Listen to me, Séraphine. My enemies have poisoned me. I cannot trust anyone. Let no one in. Just you and Mehmed."

She was already shaking her head. "If you're poisoned, even more reason to send for a doctor." She met Mehmed's gaze. The boy's eyes were wide and scared. She probably looked much the same. "We can't nurse you alone. You'll *die*, Your Grace."

"Val."

She blinked. Was he delirious? "What?"

He opened those ghastly bloody eyes again and smiled with cracked lips, a parody of his usual beautiful smile. "If I'm to die, then I'd like the last person to tend me to address me by my given name. Call me Val."

She threw up her hands. "You're insane!"

"Yes." He closed his eyes again. "But not so mad as to allow my murderers into my bedchambers. Promise me, Séraphine."

"Dear God."

He opened his eyes again, simply looking at her. "Promise me on your chatelaine, Séraphine."

She pressed her lips together. "Very well. I promise you on my chatelaine that I won't let any other but Mehmed in here."

He nodded, then rolled his eyes to the boy and spoke in what was presumably the boy's native tongue. The boy replied with tears in his eyes.

"Good." The duke closed his eyes. "I apologize. For... the condition of..." She waited, but the next sound from his lips was a rather concerning rattling snore.

Bridget straightened, staring down at the duke. The panic was rising again. He looked so frail, lying there, and he'd put her and a teenage boy entirely in charge of his welfare.

If he died, she might very well be charged with the murder of a duke. She might be hanged.

No.

No, she wouldn't think of that.

Right now she would think of how she was going to make the duke better.

Bridget straightened, smoothing her skirts.

She carefully pulled the coverlet over the duke. Pip jumped on the bed and settled against the sick man's side. She debated shooing the dog off—she doubted very much that the duke would want him there—but Pip might provide needed warmth.

She said, "Mehmed, please go to the kitchens and bring up a hot pitcher of water and some cloths. If anyone asks, you're simply bringing the things for His Grace's usual shave, nothing more. We won't, of course, be mentioning his illness." She looked at the boy. "To *anyone*."

Mehmed nodded vigorously and was out the door.

Bridget crossed the room to lock the door behind him.

Then she went to fireplace and stirred the ashes. There was a faint glow still. A bowl on the mantel held a few paper twists and she took a couple and lit them. As they flamed she added coals until she'd built a nice fire and the room began to heat.

She stood and looked around.

The room was a shambles. She could almost see what had happened in the early hours of this morning. The duke must've returned, perhaps already feeling ill. Here he had shed his coat and waistcoat, dropping them to the floor. There he'd first been ill, violently, before he could reach a pot. Here he'd staggered and overturned a chair and been ill again. One shoe was by the fire, the other…completely missing, as far as she could see. An overturned pitcher and damp carpet bespoke either thirst or an attempt at washing.

He'd been in extremis, suffering, and had never summoned aid.

I cannot trust anyone.

She gazed at his sleeping form for a moment in wonder. He truly couldn't, could he?

If Mehmed hadn't come to her, if she hadn't opened the door, he would have suffered and perhaps died alone without once calling for help.

She'd never known anyone so alone.

Anyone so lonely.

Bridget shook herself. Now wasn't the time for morbid thoughts.

She began by opening the windows just a crack. She knew that cold air was bad for the ill, but frankly she couldn't stand the stench of the room. The fresh air seemed to help a little and she started righting the furniture.

A gentle scrape at the door heralded Mehmed's return.

Between the two of them, they stripped the duke and sponged him clean as best they could.

Even in this he couldn't be polite and remain unconscious and instead woke at the most inopportune moment, when she was pressing a cloth to his lower belly.

"Oh, Séraphine," he rasped. "Are you making advances?"

"I'm wiping vomit and sweat from your body," she said with rather too much tartness. "Nothing more."

"Are you . . . sure?" And she thought she saw his lips twitch as if they tried for his usual smile.

She blinked hard. "Yes. This isn't a moment for flirtation, Your Grace."

". . . always a moment for flirtation," he whispered, the beginning of his sentence too low to understand. "Especially . . . when you're handling my cock."

"That's Mehmed."

"Pity. Though he has very soft hands."

"Humph."

"Have I offended your delicate . . . sensibilities?" He wheezed a laugh and then began hacking, unable to stop—or so it appeared.

Bridget threw down her cloth and helped him, still coughing and choking, to sit up.

"Water," he managed to gasp.

She reached for a glass sitting on the table beside his bed and then paused, staring at it. The glass had been there, half-full, when they'd entered the room.

She turned to Mehmed. "Is there any more water in the pitcher you brought up?"

"Yes, a little," the boy said, hurrying away to fetch it.

"Smart lass," the duke whispered. His eyes were half-closed and there were two spots of bright red in his cheeks.

Mehmed came back with the pitcher. "What shall he drink the water from?"

"Just hold the pitcher to his lips."

The duke swallowed twice slowly and she took the pitcher away from his mouth, watching him.

He leaned over and vomited the water back up into her lap.

"Sorry," he managed to say.

And then he began convulsing.

Will you use your right hand like a proper boy should? asked the Masked Duke and Val tried and tried, but the quill was too big and his hand hurt and so the Masked Duke took Pretty and squeezed her neck until Pretty hung limp, her green eyes half-closed. This is what happens when you disobey my rules said the Masked Duke.

Val was five.

"...tea, it's only beef tea," said burning Séraphine, her voice too loud, her eyes too bright, her hands painfully hard. "Can you drink some? Please, please, *please*, can you drink some, Your Grace?"

"Call me Val, if I'm to die," he replied, or thought he did, but then Séraphine was lost to murmurs and howls.

Only peasants and abnormals use their left hands declared the Masked Duke. Val held the quill but it skittered across the paper and made strange squiggles. The Masked Duke took Marmalade—soft, fluffy Marmalade—and Val wept and wept. But still the duke wrung her neck until she hung broken. This is what happens when you disobey my rules said the Masked Duke.

Val was seven.

"She's your *sister*, surely you can't believe your sister is one of your enemies," Séraphine argued, her voice hoarse as if she'd been arguing for days. Perhaps she had.

"No one," he said. Eve, gentle pure Eve who hated him now. "No one."

He opened his eyes and for a moment thought he'd gone blind. Then he turned his head and realized it was night. The fire was ablaze on the other side of the room. He stared at it. Such a huge blaze, overrunning the hearth, licking up the mantel, skipping over the carpet.

"I'm going to hell."

The flames blew suddenly high and hot, right into his face, and then he was ablaze, too.

You'll learn if I have to kill everything you love said the Masked Duke. Val drew very, very carefully, his hand steady, his quill upright. And still a drop of ink blotted the paper. The Masked Duke took Opal and snapped her neck and she was limp and dead, her white-and-black body swaying gently. Just like all the others. This is what happens when you disobey my rules said the Masked Duke.

Val was nine.

"Don't die. Don't die. Don't die." The whisper was soft and thready, and yet clearly audible in the otherwise quiet room.

Well, he was obviously dreaming now—or already dead—for no one prayed for him, not even burning Séraphine. That would be a sacrilege of terrible proportions. He tried to smile at the thought, but no muscle moved.

Ah, death, come at last.

He might very well welcome it if it weren't for…

The Masked Duke's boots sounded in the hall. Val continued to write out his lesson—right-handed, perfect, and in Latin. The footfalls stopped. Val set down his quill and gently blew upon his paper. What is this the Masked Duke asked. Val glanced up. The gray striped body swayed gently from a hook on the wall. Tiger he said and smiled at the Masked Duke. Fuck your rules, Father.

Val was eleven.

THE HANGING MAN wasn't nearly as nice an alehouse as the White Hare, but then Hugh's informant wasn't a young boy like Alf.

Not that Alf had turned out to be quite as young—or as innocent—as Hugh had first thought him.

Hugh sat in a dark corner, his back against the wall so that there'd be no surprises. The alehouse had only a few customers at this time of day—not yet five of the clock. Four soldiers gambled by the fire, while a solitary drinker hunched over a small cup of gin. On another bench a man in ragged clothing was snoring, either a regular or a beggar the barmaid had let in to sleep out of pity.

The barmaid herself sat behind a simple board propped on two chairs, her wares in back of her on a shelf. She seemed occupied at present with picking nits from her head and crushing them between her fingernails.

Hugh sipped his beer, a near-tasteless brew he suspected was watered, and let his head lean against the wall behind him, watching the room from beneath his tricorne.

He yawned widely, blinking. Peter had had another of his nightmares last night and waked crying for his dead mother. He'd been inconsolable, a red, weeping child who wasn't much more than a baby, really, only four and a half. He'd pushed Hugh away, hit the nurse, and seemed only a little comforted by his half-asleep elder brother, aged all of seven.

Hugh had spent the rest of the night watching his sons sleeping, curled together like abandoned puppies. He'd commanded armies and masterminded political intrigue, yet he was helpless in the face of his children's grief.

The outer door opened and a man in a battered wide-brimmed hat entered, his head ducked low, his shoulders hunched. The newcomer glanced quickly around, then descended the steps into the basement alehouse. He spoke to the barmaid and obtained from her a small tin cup of gin before crossing to Hugh.

"Took me near an hour to get here," Calvin Cartwright

said as he sat. "Why the bloody hell did you choose a meeting place so far away?"

Hugh eyed the nervous way his informant was tapping his fingernails against his tin cup. "You said you didn't want to be recognized."

"And so I don't." Cartwright took a gulp of his gin. He was a handsome man, his features classically even and entirely forgettable. He was a footman in the Duke of Montgomery's employ and more than happy to report on his master for money.

So happy, in fact, that his enthusiasm gave Hugh pause. In his experience most servants were contemptuous to one degree or another of their employers—they lived, after all, cheek by jowl with them. Few, however, actively loathed the person who gave them roof, sustenance, and wage.

From his first contact with Cartwright, however, it had been apparent that the footman was such a man.

Which left the question: Why? Montgomery might be a blackmailer and an all-around rogue, but he paid his servants rather well. Besides Cartwright, Hugh had been able to bribe only the unfortunate ham-handed footman caught rifling the duke's desk.

"Well?" Cartwright demanded now. "Have you the purse?"

"Yes," Hugh said calmly. "But I need your report first."

Cartwright snorted. "The report is everything's gone to bloody hell." He took another gulp of his gin. "Montgomery's been poisoned."

Hugh stilled. "*What?*"

The footman grinned rather nastily. "Night of the ball.

Took real sick. Won't let none but the housekeeper and that foreign boy in his rooms ever since."

Hugh narrowed his eyes at the handsome face across from him and decided he really didn't care much for Cartwright. The ball had been two nights before. If Montgomery had really been poisoned..."How do you know it wasn't overindulgence in food or drink or simply a bad meal that—"

But the footman was shaking his head. He leaned forward. "*Poison.* In his wine—or so I heard." For a moment he looked downright scared.

"*Whom* did you hear this from?"

Cartwright gulped the rest of his gin and started to stand. "I need that money."

Hugh hooked his foot around the other man's chair and pulled it back to the table, forcing him to sit back down. "Then you'll stay and answer my questions."

Hugh stared hard at the other man until Cartwright nodded grudgingly and relaxed.

"Is Montgomery still alive?" Hugh asked.

That got a twisted smile. "He's the Devil. Took that poison, swallowed it down, and still lives...for now, anyway."

"You're *sure*?" Hugh pressed. "You've seen him?"

"I haven't *seen* him," the footman said, "but I've *heard* him. Muttering away in his rooms. And that housekeeper and the boy going in and out, bringing him food and drink. Oh, he's alive all right. Doubt anything could kill him."

That was superstitious nonsense so Hugh disregarded it. "Who could've poisoned him?" he mused aloud.

Cartwright barked a laugh at that. "Anyone. He's the most hated man in London. You should see the people come begging for mercy from him. Highborn and low-. And he never shows them none. Never."

"You're talking about people who *want* him dead," Hugh said. "I speak of people who had the *opportunity* to poison him—a different thing entirely."

The footman's gaze slid sideways. "There were hundreds at that ball. Talk about *opportunities*. Hundreds. Could have been anyone. *Anyone*."

"Hmm." Hugh watched the man—his nervous, tapping fingers, his eyes unable to meet Hugh's own. Had someone else employed Cal to poison Montgomery? Who? And *why*? "You've never told me why you hate the duke so."

The fingers stilled for a moment and Cal's lip curled in something very like fear. "Grew up near Ainsdale Castle, the Montgomery seat. Like a pack of wolves they are. All of them. Mother, father, and the duke especially. They have the Devil in their blood. Always have. Everyone knows it who lives near Ainsdale."

Hugh raised his eyebrow. More superstition? Or did the man truly know something? In any case Cal was no longer successfully hiding his antipathy for his employer. Should Montgomery survive the attempt on his life, Cal might not be very safe at Hermes House.

Hugh sighed and took a small purse from his pocket and slid it to the other man. "Perhaps it would be best if you not return to Hermes House."

Cartwright met his gaze across the scarred wooden table, his eyes wide with fear.

Suddenly the footman bent low over the table, nearly lying on it, his handsome face twisted into something feral. "I will go back, and I'll tell you why: I know him like no one else does. I was a favorite of the old duchess's and she told me a secret. A secret that could hang the Duke of Montgomery. She wrote it down and made me a witness to it and put it into an ivory box. And when that box is found he'll hang. He'll hang like a common sodding *thief*."

For a split second Hugh merely stared, dumbfounded at the spitting footman.

Then Cartwright was up and running from the alehouse.

Hugh swore and lunged after him. "Cartwright!"

He ran up the steps and into the black evening. "Cartwright!"

He looked right and left, but all he saw was London, bustling home in the dark. Even so he shouted, "Damn it, Cartwright, what was the secret?"

Chapter Eight

For many years King Heartless ruled his kingdom with courtiers tiptoeing around him and his advisors startling if he coughed. Once he offered for the hand of a neighboring princess, but the girl cried so much when she arrived that the king sent her back home again. All agreed she was lucky to have been spared marriage to the king without a heart….

—From *King Heartless*

"Fuck your rules, Father," the Duke of Montgomery's voice rasped in the dark, odiferous bedchamber.

Bridget paused in the wearying task of attempting to get some sort of liquid down Val's throat. It wasn't the first time she'd heard the words in the last two days—by any means at all—but they were just as shocking each time.

She and Mehmed were taking turns nursing him in his rooms. They'd told the other servants that he'd decided on an Oriental course of fasting and hermitage. Mehmed said such things were sometimes done in his religion and it was just mad enough to be believable for the duke. For such a fast he was allowed only invalid foods such as beef tea, which he wanted brewed to a secret recipe. This of course had to be made by Bridget's own hand, which she explained with many apologies to Mrs. Bram.

So far the other servants had taken it as all part and parcel of the Duke of Montgomery's eccentricity. As for Mr. Attwell, he was still missing, which Bridget found very worrying.

She shook her head and brought the cup of broth to the duke's lips again. "Drink this, please, Your Grace."

"Grace is as grace does," he sang rustily, and his eyes opened, glancing around the room. "Hush. He's coming and we mustn't be caught here together. Back to the nursery with you."

He'd taken her for his sister again, Bridget thought tiredly. She'd been able to piece together some of his feverish mutterings.

They'd made her feel ill.

"It would be easier to feed you if you didn't talk so much," she murmured.

"But then you wouldn't like me as much, either," he said quite plainly, his azure gaze on her.

She nearly dropped the mug of beef tea. "Val?"

Oh, good Lord, she had to get out of the habit of thinking of him by his Christian name. Sadly it was almost impossible not to become overly familiar when taking care of a person's most basic needs.

"The very same." He smiled a ghost of his famous smile. "Now listen very carefully, Eve. Whatever you do, *don't* become a cat. You shouldn't like what Father does with cats."

"Oh, God." Bridget laughed, for she didn't know what else to do. She was caring in secret for a mad, dying duke who thought her his sister and she didn't—oh, she really, truly *didn't*—want him to die.

"Eve? *Eve?*" He sounded like a frightened little boy now and her heart nearly broke.

"I'm here."

"No, you're not," he replied, very seriously. "I sent you away from Ainsdale. To be safe. It's for the best, I think. And then I'll..."

He trailed away, clutching at her hand.

"You'll do what?" she whispered.

It was night and they were all alone. Poor Mehmed had staggered off to the dressing room to get some sleep. Pip slept, curled against the duke's hip. He hadn't seemed to notice the dog there—which was just as well.

"Shhh," the duke murmured. "Mustn't tell. Ever. Never, ever, ever." He smiled a sweet, boyish smile. "That's why I killed him. So he'd no longer have power over me."

She stared at Val in confusion and horror. "Killed who?"

"Tiger." His azure eyes slid half-closed. "If you love no one, Eve, then he can't hurt you. So you must kill the thing you love. Simple. Don't know why I didn't think of it sooner."

She sat back shakily. Had he really killed his beloved pet cat to stop his father from killing it instead? As a *child*? Did such depravity truly exist in the world?

She came from a small country village. Had been raised mostly by Mam, an affectionate woman. The rest of her foster family might not have been overly loving, but they hadn't been truly hateful either—not even her foster father, who had considered her a cuckoo in his nest. The worst punishment her foster father had ever given her was three swats on the bottom for poking her fingers in the Christmas pudding. She'd cried and cried and then wiped her eyes and apologized to Mam, who'd kissed her and given her a slice of the pudding.

Mam had always loved her.

How could a boy survive a childhood with so little love?

What would it do to his soul?

Well. She knew what it would do to him, didn't she? The result lay before her, rasping with every breath, a man who had fought his nightmares for the last two days. A man who trusted no one.

A man whom no one trusted.

Bridget put the mug of beef tea aside and went to the window. It was past midnight. That was the problem. It was a time of darkness, of despair and the loss of hope.

When the sun came up it would all be better.

She glanced back at the still man in the bed.

If he survived this night.

The terrible convulsions had stopped yesterday. The fever seemed to have peaked this morning. And yet he was still delirious. He was still weak.

And getting weaker.

If he died without seeing his sister, Bridget knew she would forever regret it. Not only for the duke, but also for Miss Eve Dinwoody, who was a good woman.

He loved his sister—no matter what he might say aloud. He *did* love Eve.

Bridget strode to the dressing room. She hated to do it, but needs must. She shook Mehmed awake.

The poor boy sat up, his black hair sticking out at all angles. "What is it?"

"You must go to the servants' quarters, Mehmed. You must wake Bob, the footman. Ask him to go to Miss Eve Dinwoody's house—the duke's sister—and deliver a note. Tell him it's important. Can you do that?"

"Yes. Yes." Mehmed stood swaying and looked around groggily.

Bridget left him to dress while she wrote a hurried note to the duke's sister.

By the time she was finished, Mehmed was dressed and looked much more wide-awake.

She handed the note to him. "Try not to wake any of the other servants. We still don't know who poisoned the duke."

He nodded soberly and quickly left on his errand.

She returned to the bedside and sank into the chair that had been placed there. For maybe half an hour she merely sat there and stared. Val was sleeping deeply. He'd lost weight in the last two days, unable to keep anything down. The flickering light of the fire gave the illusion that his skin was stretched directly over bone. If he died…

Bridget shuddered, looking away, and swiped at the tears running down her face with the back of her hand.

He would hate to be seen this way. Such a vain man.

She inhaled shakily, glancing at the bed. This big bed, where he'd caught her just three weeks before, with Miss Royle's miniature. It had been in the secret compartment just to the left of the swirl there.

Bridget stared at the swirl in the headboard a moment. She'd looked in all the other rooms since that night.

He *wouldn't* have…

In a second she'd kicked off her slippers and carefully climbed on the bed.

Pip rose and stretched, front paws outthrust, bottom in the air, as she lifted her skirts and crawled toward the headboard on her knees. She knelt and felt with her fingers. There was the small hole. Her finger slid in and…

The panel popped open. She looked inside and there was the miniature.

She reached in and picked it up. "You *devil*."

"You *saint*."

Bridget nearly dropped the miniature on Val's head at his words. She shoved it in her pocket instead and looked down to find him bemusedly eyeing her legs—her skirts were still hiked nearly to her hips. "Why are you in my bed, Séraphine?"

"I…"

His gaze lifted to her eyes, his lips curling slyly. "Oh, Mrs. Crumb, if you could see your face."

A knock came at the door.

Bridget nearly startled off the bed.

Pip started barking, stiff-legged, from his position beside Val.

The duke turned his head and raised an incredulous eyebrow at the dog.

Hastily Bridget got off the bed as gracefully as she could—which she had the feeling wasn't very gracefully at all—and went to the door. The dog sprang down from the bed and ran over to help.

Bridget opened the door to find Miss Dinwoody and Mr. Makepeace with Mehmed behind them.

"Where is he?" Miss Dinwoody said, stepping inside the room.

Bridget pointed mutely to the bed.

Tears ran down Miss Dinwoody's cheeks as she started toward the bed. "Oh, Val."

"I told you not to tell anyone, Séraphine!" he said, glaring accusingly from his pillows.

Bridget merely closed the door behind her and the dog.

And burst into tears of relief.

THREE DAYS LATER Bridget flung wide the curtains in Val's bedroom.

Behind her he said, "There is still a dog on my bed."

She turned to look.

The duke was sitting up in bed, looking much better than he had the night his sister had come to visit. His hair was clean and clubbed back with a black silk ribbon and he wore his purple banyan. He really was the vainest man she'd ever met, insisting upon a full toilet before he was truly well. He frowned down at Pip beside him, who in turn was staring at Val's breakfast of fried eggs and sausages. "I don't like dogs."

"Yes, Your Grace," Bridget said briskly, coming over to fluff his pillows. She might've done it a bit vigorously, since the duke, once he'd begun to feel better, had immediately become the world's worst patient.

"I like dogs!" Mehmed said cheerfully.

"Did you make this yourself?" the duke asked Bridget, and then, to Mehmed, "I thought you said you liked cats."

"Yes," Bridget said, as she said every time she brought up a meal.

She was beginning to worry that Mrs. Bram was never going to speak to her again, never mind that it was becoming increasingly hard to explain away the stuff she was making as some sort of fasting food. The problem was, the sorts of things she could make by herself and quickly *and* that the duke would eat made a very short list indeed.

Hence this morning's fried eggs and sausages. *Not* her idea of sickroom nutrition by any means, but the duke had proved to be a very stubborn man.

"I like cats *and* dogs," Mehmed clarified. "Do you?"

"I like neither."

For a moment Bridget felt a pang as she remembered Val's ravings. Of the pet cats he'd watched his awful father strangle as a boy. Of the one he'd strangled himself so his father would no longer have power over him. No, she wasn't surprised that he no longer liked cats—but it did make her mourn for the child who had once loved cats.

The duke ate a sausage and then switched his frown to the boy, who was perched on a chair by the fire and not doing anything useful at all. "You *can't* like both. It's an either-or proposition. You must chose: cats or dogs."

Mehmed looked confused. "What?"

"Don't listen to him, Mehmed," Bridget snapped. "His Grace is over-tired from being abed. You can like both cats and dogs."

There was a short silence.

Then Val smiled slowly, like the uncoiling of an adder.

"Oh, Séraphine. Tread carefully, my burning one, as if you danced on the shattered skulls of children, for I may lie abed, but I am a duke yet, and not just any duke, but the Duke of Montgomery, and my inheritance is death and mayhem."

She stared at him, her mouth gone dry. He should be ridiculous, lying there in his gaudy purple banyan, sharing a bed with a little terrier dog, and tray of eggs and sausages on his lap, but he wasn't.

He wasn't.

"Your pardon, Your Grace," she said, very formally, while a sort of storm began brewing in her breast. She'd nursed him for *days*, listened to his darkest secrets. She was no longer *just* a housekeeper to him.

He waved a hand, so elegant, so *aristocratic*.

That child who had loved cats was long dead and she was a fool for ever having felt a smidgen of sympathy for him—a *duke*.

"Do you like cats, Mrs. Crumb?" asked Mehmed innocently.

"Yes," Bridget said through gritted teeth as she gathered the remains of the previous meal, "I do."

She glanced at Val to see what he thought but he was ignoring her. The *swine*.

"Cats *and* dogs?" Mehmed questioned.

"Yes."

"That is very good."

"I think so, too." Bridget moved toward the door. "I need to run an errand this morning, Your Grace."

Val glanced up from his eggs. "What—?"

"Come." Bridget snapped her fingers at Pip.

The terrier snatched a sausage from the duke's plate and ran to the door.

There was a roar from the bed.

Bridget shut the door gently behind them.

She looked down at the dog as she strode down the hallway.

Pip had already gobbled the evidence.

"That was very bad of you," she said to him in sugary tones.

They made their way to her rooms, where she donned her shawl and hat and gloves. Then she and Pip left Hermes House via the kitchens and through the gardens.

The day was overcast and rather dreary, and she walked swiftly, the terrier trotting busily beside her, as they made their way down the street. A big brewer's cart rumbled past, loaded with barrels of beer, and a ragged band of boys made a dancing show with their brooms at the corner crossing. Bridget gave them several pennies to sweep the way clear for her. She hurried along the next lane and turned at the corner down a quiet street to find an unmarked carriage pulled to the side, waiting.

Bridget glanced behind her, and then tapped at the carriage door.

It opened to reveal Miss Royle, clad in a beautiful dove-gray velvet mantle lined with ermine fur. Bridget couldn't help but think that it looked very warm as she pulled her gray wool shawl closer about her shoulders to ward off the morning chill.

She climbed into the carriage and sat down across from the other lady. Pip hopped inside.

Miss Royle smiled down at the terrier. "Oh, what a sweet little dog!"

Pip wagged his tail and placed his front paws on Miss Royle's skirts for a pat and Bridget began to suspect he was a flirt.

The other woman looked up from the dog. "Do you have it?"

"Yes, of course." Bridget withdrew the miniature from her pocket and handed it over.

Miss Royle took it, gazing down for a moment at the little family: an English gentleman, an Indian lady, and their baby. She looked up and there were tears in her eyes. "Thank you. You don't know how much this means to me. Not only because of the blackmail, but because..."

Bridget nodded, glancing down at her hands. She didn't know much of Miss Royle's background, but she did know her mother was dead. The miniature in her hands might be the only portrait she had of her mother.

For a moment Bridget thought of her own father. Not her foster father, the man who had mostly ignored her, but that shadowy man who had contributed his seed to her making. He'd been a footman, but that was all she knew of him. She didn't know if he was fair or dark, tall or short, or even if he was still alive or long dead.

And with Lady Caire her only source of knowledge, she'd probably never know.

Bridget pushed the bitter thought aside and looked at Miss Royle. "I'm glad you have it again."

"As am I." Miss Royle placed the miniature carefully into a small box before glancing up. "May I recompense you for your time and effort?" She held out a small purse.

"Oh." For some reason Bridget hadn't expected this. "There's no need."

Miss Royle's smile was wry. "I think there is. It was a dangerous job. Please." She pressed the purse into Bridget's hand. "And please know that you have a position waiting in my father's household if you ever have need of it. I expect you'll be leaving the duke's service soon."

"Thank you," Bridget replied, "but no, I have no plans to leave His Grace's service."

"But you must." Miss Royle's brows had drawn together and she looked alarmed. "When the duke finds the miniature gone—and he will—he might suspect you, Mrs. Crumb. You'll be in terrible danger."

Miss Royle didn't know the half of it—Val most certainly *would* suspect her. But Bridget couldn't leave Hermes House without her mother's letters.

And there was another reason she was loath to leave—a reason she didn't wish the other woman to see.

So she gazed at Miss Royle with calm certainty. "There are others I still need to help. Others that the duke is blackmailing."

"You are a brave woman." Miss Royle shook her head. "And he is truly a wicked man."

"Yes, he is," Bridget replied. Unfortunately, Val's wickedness no longer seemed to be a deterrent to her.

Probably that should concern her.

She made her farewells and departed the carriage as circumspectly as she'd entered it, but as she made her way back to Hermes House, Pip by her side, she finally acknowledged it to herself:

Wicked or not, vain or not, *outrageous* or not, she was falling in love with the Duke of Montgomery.

BRIDGET HURRIED UP the stairs to Val's rooms that night, carrying a tray laden with an unopened bottle of wine and a beefsteak cooked to the best of her ability.

She eyed the beefsteak as she climbed. It looked rather... burnt. Well, she was a housekeeper, not a cook. It wasn't her fault that she was being forced to perform in areas that simply were not her responsibility.

As she made the upper floor she thought she heard a door close. Bridget peered down the hall. She couldn't be certain but it seemed the duke's bedroom door had just shut.

Her heart beat faster. What if it was the poisoner, returned to try to kill the duke? She'd left Mehmed in the room with Val, but they were both apt to fall asleep and Pip had been confined to her bedroom since this morning's theft of the sausage.

Bridget rushed down the corridor. "Mehmed! Mehmed, open the door!"

Oh, she was a fool. She set down the tray and reached for her chatelaine, rifling through the keys.

The door opened, revealing the Duke of Montgomery, clad in his purple silk banyan, his golden hair clubbed back neatly, and his face clean-shaven.

She drew a grateful breath at the sight of him, whole and unharmed, but then it strangled somewhere in her throat when she looked up into his azure eyes.

They swam with wild fury.

"You... you're out of bed," she said dumbly. "When—?"

He propped his arm against the doorjamb near his ear, his lips curving as he murmured intimately, "Ah, Mrs. Crumb. You're just in time. Do come in."

He held out his other hand. His left hand. The gold ring glinted on his thumb.

She looked down at it and even with the menace surrounding him like a shroud, all she could think of was the words he'd moaned in his delirium, his voice cracked and broken. His father's words. *Only peasants and abnormals use their left hands.*

She took his proffered hand.

He curled his long musician's fingers over hers, and drew her into his bedroom, shutting the door behind them.

Inside she saw Cal the footman, standing by the fireplace, looking partly defiant, partly scared out of his wits.

Mehmed wasn't in sight.

"Where is Mehmed?" she asked quietly as Val led her toward the fireplace.

This felt like a ceremony somehow.

He shrugged. "I sent him away to sup with the other servants tonight so that he could learn about the true depths of both English cookery and English prejudice. He's quite excited."

She frowned at that and then hissed, "This morning you told me you couldn't get out of bed. What are you doing, strolling about your room now?"

He stopped and turned to her, taking both her hands as he leaned very close and whispered hotly in her ear, "I may've lied to you."

She glared as he stepped away and winked before turning and gesturing to the footman. "You see I had reasons to conceal my health. Whilst I was ill my enemies grew complacent. If they thought me well again, they might flee."

She looked from him to the footman. "*Cal?* But what about... I thought... *Attwell* is the one who disappeared?"

Val tutted. "Attwell has a mistress called wine who entices him away from his duties every so often for a week or more. He slumbers in her arms who knows where and when he awakens comes stumbling back, shamefaced and empty of pocket. In short, he wouldn't hurt a fly, much less me."

He turned slowly, gesturing with outflung hand, the purple silk rippling from his arm. "Now Cal on the other hand doesn't mind hurting, do you, Cal?"

The footman seemed to try to throw back his shoulders, despite what looked like near-paralyzing fear. "*You're* the one who hurts, Montgomery. You're the Devil."

"I?" Val smiled, an angel fallen to walk the earth and tempt mere mortals. "But I wasn't the one who made you service an old woman."

Bridget's eyes widened in surprised comprehension.

Cal flushed a mottled red. "That's not true. I *loved* her. I—"

"You were fourteen when she first took you to her bed." Val tutted. "I doubt very much it was love when you saw her withered teats. Though why you should blame me for my mother's venal ways, I don't know. We were the same age. I could hardly have stopped her if my father didn't care to."

"You were jealous!" Cal shrieked, spittle flying.

Val arched an incredulous eyebrow. "Is that why you tried to kill me?"

Cal's lips drew back, baring his chalk-white teeth. "I'll not hang for you."

"Won't you?" asked Val gently. He might've been crooning to a tired child. "Poisoning a duke is considered quite bad, even by those who might not like said duke. They'll drag you to Tyburn through the baying crowds and hundreds will watch and cheer as you dance at the end of the rope. It'll be a very ugly death. Tell me, Cal. Did you poison me?"

Cal stared at him, his chest heaving.

Val smiled. "Did you pour something noxious in that glass of wine and take it, balancing it carefully through the crowd that night, until you found me, and offered me that glass of death? Did you, Cal?"

"It should've killed you," the footman said, low and viciously. "I put enough in there to fell a horse. You should've died in your own vomit and shit that very night. Only a witch or a demon could survive that glass of wine. Your mother knew what you were. She cursed the day you were born. She cursed *you*. She told me what you did. She told me—"

"*Enough*," Val roared over the string of spiteful words falling from Cal's mouth.

He flung open his banyan and let it fall. Naked, he advanced on the cowering footman and only as he reached the other man did Bridget see that he held the gold-hilted curved dagger in his left hand.

"No!" She started forward. "*No!*"

He moved swiftly, like a striking snake. Once. Twice. Thrice.

So fast his hand was blurred.

Blood spurted from the footman's side, but his eyes were still open.

Slowly he looked down at the mortal wounds.

And almost lazily Val slit his throat.

The thing that had been Cal thumped to the carpet.

Bridget gasped, her hands covering her mouth. *Oh, God!*

Val turned, still naked, still impossibly beautiful. Only the gore spattered on his belly, chest, and arm, marred his perfection.

He walked toward her and she couldn't help it. She backed away from him.

He smiled.

Sweetly. Like a boy. The dagger still in his left hand. And caught her arm with his right hand.

"This is who I am, Séraphine. Naked, with blade and blood. I am vengeance. I am hate. I am sin personified. Never mistake me for the hero of this tale, for I am not and shall never be. I am the villain."

And he laid his lips over hers and pushed his hot tongue into her mouth and kissed her until she couldn't breathe and it was only later that she found the bloodstains on her dress.

Chapter Nine

Now there came into King Heartless's kingdom a magician who claimed he could perform all matter of miracles and wonders, turning lead to gold and ink to wine, and making the most spotted complexion smooth and dewy. Except, as those who bought the magician's charms soon discovered, he could do none of these things. . . .

—From *King Heartless*

Her lips had been sweet, like ripe figs, her mouth a cavern of delight. But her eyes—those dark inquisitor's eyes—had held only horror and disgust.

Val sipped his China tea the next morning and gazed out the window. The sun shone on his garden, giving the illusion of warmth, though his empty chest was ice-cold.

He could have explained to her that a razor-sharp blade was kinder than a hangman's noose. That death delivered in seconds with a few thrusts was preferable to a laughing, jabbering mob, gleeful at the jerking, agonizing execution.

But those saint's eyes would've seen the hypocrisy.

A footman laid down a small stack of letters at his elbow and then slid away.

The servants were careful to keep at arm's length from him now. They all knew he'd killed Cal. He'd placed a knife in the dead man's hand and said it was a foiled assassination attempt, but still they looked at him with wary beasts' eyes.

Mrs. Crumb had agreed to the fiction, but with a troubled expression on her face. She hadn't liked it, his little martyr. It disturbed some balance of rights and wrongs within her.

Still, he did not doubt her. Had she not nursed him with her own hands? Had she not suckled his tongue so ardently? He'd give her time—a day or so only—and then he would invite her again to wait upon him. He'd slide close behind her, whisper scandalous words into her mobcap-sheltered ear, and remind her of all the things she tried so hard to hide beneath black wool and starched linen. And then... oh, and then, he'd see if his little housekeeper truly burned at her core.

Patience.

He could be patient when the occasion called for it, and this one certainly did.

She'd come back to him, even with his true face revealed.

She only needed time.

So.

He turned to his mail, leafing through the letters without interest until he came to one in a feminine hand. This one he picked up and slit open with his butter knife.

Val read the letter—and then read it again, incredulous. It was from Hippolyta Royle, informing him that she would not be receiving him today or at any time in the future.

He thrust the letter in the pocket of his coat and rose, striding toward the dining room doors. He caught the footmen outside the doors unawares and they scattered before him like startled geese. He took the stairs two at a time and arrived at his bedroom slightly out of breath—damn Cal and his poison to the fires of hell. A maid was doing something to the windows. She squeaked at the sight of him, and he waved her out of the room with a flick of his wrist, continuing his stride straight to the bed. He leaned over it, reaching for the headboard, and opened the concealed compartment.

Empty.

Oh.

Oh, *Séraphine.*

He felt the grin spread over his face, felt his cock throb and stiffen. Suddenly the day was bright, *singing* with vibrant colors and stratagems.

She'd outmaneuvered him.

And that? That hadn't happened in a very, *very* long time.

"SÉRAPHINE."

The whisper was in her dreams and Bridget whimpered and tried to bat it away. She needn't wake yet. It wasn't time to rise. She had hours still.

A soft chuckle and the brush of something soft on her cheek. "I would never have guessed you were such a deep sleeper, my practical housekeeper."

She had a terrible foreboding, an awful suspicion, even

in her dreams, and she fought valiantly through the sluggish waves.

Bridget opened her eyes, blinking, in the candlelight, to find azure eyes only inches from her own.

They crinkled at the corners. "There you are."

"What." She jerked her face back, looking around frantically. She was in her own little room in her own little bed. Even Pip was there, standing at her hip, wagging his tail at Val squatting by her head, the *traitor*. "What are you doing in my *room*?"

He grinned like a vicious imp of morning hell. "Waking you, of course." He reached out and tapped her nose. "Do you ever take off that thing on your head? Are you bald? I've been wondering."

"I... *what*?" She reached up, suddenly fearful that he might've disturbed her nightcap as she slept, but no, it was as firmly tied now as it had been when she'd lain down however many hours ago. She let her hands fall, and said plaintively, "What *time* is it?"

The duke cocked his head as if he could hear some unearthly clock no one else could. "Just gone half past three, I think." He smiled angelically down at her. "Now get up. We leave at four."

And he turned to the door.

She scrambled upright. "Leave for *where*?"

He'd already exited, but he poked his head around the doorjamb. "Ainsdale Castle. My estate in the country."

Then he was gone.

For a moment Bridget stared, dumbfounded, at the place his devilishly smiling face had been. Her poor brain wasn't used to working so early in the morning and especially without her usual two or three cups of tea, but this was highly irregular. Most houses had their own housekeepers. Surely Ainsdale Castle was fully staffed? Why then was he taking her? Was it merely for his own amusement—or was it for some other, more sinister reason?

After all, only two days before she'd seen him kill a footman in cold blood. Of course Cal had tried to kill the duke in a particularly awful and vicious way. But then afterward the duke had kissed her as she'd never been kissed in all her life. His tongue had tasted of wine and sin and she'd wanted to moan and rub herself against him as he'd tilted her back over his arm. She very much hoped that she hadn't actually done that…although she wasn't altogether certain that she *hadn't*. She'd been avoiding him ever since.

She was very muddled at the moment and she very much wanted some tea.

"Hurry, Séraphine!" His voice came from the kitchens as if he saw her sitting there on her bed, debating.

Bridget rolled her eyes and began dressing. She pulled a small soft bag out from under her bed and swiftly packed the few necessities she might need, and then she glanced at Pip.

He was sitting on the bed, watching her motions with interest, his head cocked.

"Oh, damn," she said under her breath.

Bridget stood and picked up the soft bag in one hand, snapping her fingers for the terrier with the other, and went into the kitchens.

Somehow the duke had roused most of the servants without her knowledge. Cook was busy supervising the packing of baskets of foodstuffs, maids were bundling together boxes, and footmen were marching in and out of the kitchen, laden with the materials the duke deemed necessary for a journey.

He whirled at her entrance and beckoned her impatiently with his fingers. "Come, come, Mrs. Crumb. We mustn't dally."

"But..." She looked down helplessly at Pip.

The duke actually rolled his eyes. "Oh, bring the mongrel as well, if you must. Just come."

So she was hustled out the door and into the garden, still black, for it wasn't even dawn yet. They crossed to the gate, the terrier trotting happily along, stopping only to water a hedge, and then they were in the mews and Bridget saw that the duke had had two carriages prepared. *Only* two. She'd seen some aristocrats travel with three or more. She sighed and started for the second one, wondering if she'd be able to sleep again on the bumpy roads, but Val caught her arm.

"No, not that one." He led her to the first carriage—his carriage. "You'll ride with me."

She looked at him mutely. Of course. Of course he wanted her—the *housekeeper*—to ride with him. Shaking her head, she allowed herself to be helped into the carriage.

Inside she found Mehmed, already sitting on one of the luxurious red leather seats. He grinned at her. "Mrs. Crumb! We travel to an English castle!"

"So I understand, Mehmed," she said wearily.

She began to sit next to Mehmed, but the duke guided her firmly to the seat opposite, and then took his own place directly beside her. She was conscious suddenly of his warmth and of the hard muscle of his thigh pressed against hers.

Pip climbed in the carriage and leaped onto the seat beside Mehmed.

A footman closed the door.

"And away we go, sailing north into peril and adventure!" shouted the duke, striking the ceiling with his stick.

"Huzzah!" cried Mehmed.

Pip barked.

And the carriage lurched into motion.

"Lord, I need a cup of tea," Bridget moaned to herself.

"Why didn't you say so earlier?" the duke asked in a more normal tone of voice. "Mehmed, the tea, please."

"Yes, Duke," Mehmed said, and jumped up from his seat. He gently pushed the terrier from the seat as well and raised it, revealing a storage compartment. From this he took a polished wooden rectangular box. He stood it on the seat and opened it like a book. On the right was a stoppered ceramic bottle, carefully fitted and strapped into the padded interior. On the left were teacups, spoons, and a smaller stoppered bottle containing sugar.

Swaying gracefully with the movement of the carriage, Mehmed proceeded to serve both Bridget and Val tea—gratifyingly hot. Then he dived back into the storage compartment and came back up with a hamper containing a small bottle of milk for the tea, a basket of peeled hard-boiled eggs, ham sliced so thin it was nearly transparent, crumbling sharp cheese, crusty bread, a cold raspberry tart, and several crisp apples, all served on China plates.

Val motioned with his fingers and Mehmed brought out a final basket, removing the top with a flourish.

The inside was crammed with books of all sizes and shapes.

"Oh!" Bridget gasped.

Val caught her eye and smiled. "I always like to travel with reading material. Please. Take your pick."

And as Bridget watched the sun rise she decided traveling with a duke might be quite interesting indeed.

LATE THAT AFTERNOON Val watched with half-closed eyes as the autumn fields passed outside the carriage. They were making good time, which was excellent because by now no doubt there would be a hue and cry. He'd taken the precaution of sending off two other diversionary caravans, going in different directions from Hermes House. Even so, his pursuers would not be fooled for long.

A corner of his mouth curved.

Which only made the game more fun.

The carriage rolled over a bump and Mrs. Crumb's head lolled on his shoulder. She, like both Mehmed and the dog, had been asleep for the last half hour. In that time she'd migrated from what she'd no doubt considered a safe distance up against the far end of the carriage to nestle against his side, lax and entirely defenseless.

He wondered what she would do when she discovered the countermove he'd made in their private game of chess. Oh, but he was looking forward to her reaction! The flare of indignation or anger or passion in those dark eyes. Would she assault his person?

He rather hoped she would.

He looked down at her sleeping form. Her hands lay like half-opened flowers on her lap, one cupped within the other. Such sturdy little hands, meant for practical work. Her fingers were rather plump. He smiled at the thought. He held his own hand over hers, comparing. His fingers, long and elegant, dwarfed hers, and yet he found he preferred hers.

He let his hand fall to his lap.

She wore that dreadful mobcap, hiding both her hair and her face from him, and he wanted to pluck it from her head.

But to do so would disturb her sleep.

He cocked his head, considering the conundrum. He found, on the whole, that he didn't wish to disturb his housekeeper's sleep. It felt...nice to have her lying so trustingly against him.

If he listened very intently he could hear her breaths.

After a bit he breathed with her.

In and out.

In...and then out.

A carriage wheel dipped rather violently into a hole in the road.

The jolt jerked her forward and only his arm kept her from a spill on the floor. "What?"

"It's all right," he said.

A glance showed that Mehmed and the dog were still somehow asleep, the dog within the circle of the boy's arms.

"Oh," she said, and then attempted to move away from him.

That he did *not* like.

He slung his arm across her shoulders. "Careful. The road's quite rough here."

"I don't think—"

"If you watch out the window, you might see blue cows."

She tilted her face up to see him, her expression extremely skeptical. He might be hurt if he were a man at all used to telling the truth. "Pardon?"

He smiled down at her. "The area's quite famous for them. A product, I believe, of a breeding program by a local landowner. Of course there are those that claim that the color is more properly described as purple—"

"That's the most ridiculous thing I've ever—"

"—than blue," he finished, unperturbed by her outraged outburst. "Do you always interrupt your masters?"

"Only those who try and tell me a load of codswallop," she muttered.

He was watching her face, so he saw the moment when she realized what she was saying…and more importantly, to whom. There was a flicker of fear and then her expression closed entirely.

"I do apologize, Your Grace."

He'd never been sorry for his rank—why should he be? It conferred wealth and deference, things he found very useful in the world. But now, for the very first time in his life, Valentine Napier, the Duke of Montgomery, wished that for five minutes he might be a common man.

For those five minutes only, mind—let that be clear.

But if he were to divest himself of his glory for a few short minutes, become a plain, boring man—perhaps with the name Jack—what would she reply to him then?

He gazed at her a little moodily.

She made another movement denoting an attempt to escape.

He tightened the arm about her. "Tell me of your upbringing."

She brought her brows together suspiciously. "You were bored last time I did that."

He waved his left hand. "I find I have renewed interest."

She sighed, slumping under his restraining arm, pliant again. Good. "I grew up in the North, almost on the border. My . . . father was a crofter with a bit of land and sheep."

"How did you learn to read and write?" he asked.

"My mam taught us at night," she replied. "Or rather me, for my brothers and sister are all older than me."

"How much older?"

She looked wary for some reason, and then shrugged. "Ian is forty this year, Moira will be eight and thirty next month, and Tom just turned six and thirty."

"How old are you?"

"Six and twenty," she replied very stiffly.

He smiled. "So you were a belated fancy of your parents."

She looked away. "I suppose."

"Mm." He leaned his elbow on the windowsill and his head against his knuckles the better to study her. "And was your childhood very bucolic? Describe it to me."

"There were heather-covered hills and it was windy and cold."

"You hated it," he decided.

"No." She frowned at him. "It was nice to sit by the fire at night with the wind outside and Mam knitting or telling me stories or singing to me."

He cocked his head. "She sang to you?"

"Yes." She looked at him as if he were quite strange—

which was actually a look he was used to. "Didn't anyone sing to you when you were a child?"

He thought of the drunken songs that had sometimes echoed through his father's halls when he was young. That was probably *not* what she meant. "No."

"Oh." She bit her lip. "I suppose duchesses don't sing to their children."

"No, they don't." He smiled kindly. "Particularly when they dislike the child in question intensely."

She blinked, looking shocked for a moment, and then cleared her throat. "Well. It's nice, truly. And I liked walking over the hills as a little girl. There are birds in the heather and hares and mice and...are you *sure* you're interested in this?"

"I wasn't, actually, when I first asked," he confessed. "But now I am. Go on."

She made a little humphing sound at that and settled more comfortably at his side. "When I was a little older, about twelve, I went to work at a nearby house. It was owned by old Mrs. Cromby and oh, I was so homesick! I cried myself to sleep for a fortnight it seemed, until it was my day off and I could go home to see Mam."

He frowned at this, not liking to think of his infant housekeeper in tears. "Why did they send you then if you were so upset?"

She gave him a look. "Because I needed to learn a trade, naturally. And it was a good position. Mrs. Cromby was very strict but I learned so much from her and her housekeeper, Mrs. Little. How to keep records and how to make wood polish and brass polish and silver polish. When to turn linen and how to store cheese. What cuts of beef are the cheapest and how to bargain down the butcher. How to judge when a fish is fresh and when to buy shellfish and when not to. How to keep moths from woolens and mice from the pantry. How to get wine stains out of white linen and how to dye faded cloth black again. All that and so much more."

She drew breath and he looked at her, deeply appalled. "That all sounds frightfully boring."

"And yet without that knowledge you'd live in dirty, messy, vermin-infested chaos," she said sweetly.

"Mm."

She was strangely alluring in her confidence in her own abilities. Women of his rank didn't have *jobs*, didn't have competence in . . . well, anything, really, aside from the odd musical talent. Embroidery. Dancing. His sister painted miniatures, but Eve was an eccentric. He *did* know of several ladies quite skilled at fellatio, but could that be called a *job*? Well, yes, if one were a whore, but the ladies in question didn't actually *sell* their skills, not unless one counted obtaining ever more influential men as lovers, but that wasn't *exactly* a quid pro quo, therefore . . .

He blinked and realized that Mrs. Crumb was watching him quizzically. "Yes?

"Sometimes," she said, "I wonder what you think about."

He ran through his latter train of thought, considered sharing his musings, glanced at her clever, competent, and yet in some ways naïve face, and discarded the idea. "Tell me why you came to London."

That bright, open face closed again. Curious. She shrugged, glancing away from him. "The same reason any servant comes to London: to find work. I'd worked in several houses by that time, but I wanted to be a housekeeper and there were no situations nearby, so I came to London."

He watched her, thinking that there was something missing from that simple recitation.

She glanced at him, her eyes dark and fathomless. "And Mam had died by then. There wasn't anything to keep me by the border, was there?"

Wasn't there? Not father or brothers or sister? Not heather-covered hills or warm hearth? Val cocked his head, studying her.

Wondering.

But she was glancing about the carriage. "Where is the book I was reading?"

"I placed it here," he said, taking up *The Most Noble and Famous Travels of Marco Polo*, which he'd stowed on the seat beside him so it wouldn't fall to the floor while she slept. "An interesting choice."

"You mean for a housekeeper," she muttered, taking the book from him.

He cocked his head, watching her. So fierce. "For anyone," he murmured gently.

She smoothed a dimpled thumb over the worn red leather of the book cover. "Have you ever been to China?"

"No, but I would like to go."

The carriage bumped and slowed and he glanced out the window to see that they were coming to an inn.

Mrs. Crumb straightened, regrettably pulling away from him. "Is this where we'll be stopping for the night?"

"Only for supper and to change the horses," he said

cheerfully as Mehmed and the dog at last awakened. He pretended not to see her stare.

"When will we be stopping for the night?"

"We won't." He turned to her. "We're traveling at haste—and straight through the night and tomorrow night as well."

The carriage stopped.

"What?"

He smiled into her astonished eyes. They were headed north to Yorkshire at breakneck speed, no expense spared, changing horses as often as possible.

It was quite a reckless, mad journey—even for him. "If all goes well we'll make Ainsdale Castle by nightfall three days hence."

Or, as he sometimes liked to call the place where he'd been born.

The place where he'd been raised.

The place where he'd lost both heart and soul:

Castle Death.

Chapter Ten

The magician was dragged before King Heartless, who didn't bother looking up from his supper before ordering the man whipped and banished. But the magician wasn't alone, for he had a daughter who always traveled with him. Her name was Prue and when she flung herself at the king's feet and begged for her father, the king looked. And looked again. . . .

—From *King Heartless*

It was near midnight three days later when the carriage pulled down a long, winding drive leading to a castle silhouetted against the waning moon. Watching out the window, Bridget couldn't help but shiver. One tower in particular, taller than the others, seemed quite ominous in the moonlight.

She let the curtain fall.

It had not escaped her notice that Val, usually such an irreverent, talkative, restless man, had become quieter the closer they'd driven toward his childhood home, until now that they'd arrived he was almost a pale statue, sitting in the corner.

Still and watchful.

He caught her eye. "Imposing, isn't it? My ancestor acquired it centuries ago by storming it, skewering the previous owner, killing his infant heir, and raping his widow over the banquet table before marrying her." He shrugged at the horrified look she gave him. "The castle was from her family. I suppose he was just making sure everything was legal."

"What is *skewering*?" Mehmed asked.

"To pierce with a sword," Val said very precisely, omitting his usual verbal flourishes.

Bridget had an odd urge to take his hand. Which was ridiculous. He was a *duke.*

The carriage came to a halt.

There was a small jolt as one of the footmen descended, and then the carriage door was opened.

Pip bounded down the steps and disappeared into the darkness, the boy not far behind.

In the distance a series of yips and then canine yodeling started. Nearby, the terrier answered to the best of his ability.

"What is that?" Bridget glanced curiously at Val.

He grimaced. "Foxhounds. My father kept a pack and I suppose they've been maintained. Filthy things."

Bridget's eyes narrowed. "You don't know?"

He shrugged. "I haven't been back to Ainsdale since I left England when I was nineteen and spent a decade traveling the world. It's been eleven years since I've seen this place."

He looked morosely at the open carriage door.

He'd not told her why they'd hurried away from London

so precipitously, but she'd decided on the long journey north that it must be that he was worried his enemies might poison him again. Watching him now, she thought the fear must be very great to drive him here.

Bridget hesitated, and then said gently, "Shall we get out?"

Val seemed to come to himself. "I suppose we must."

He gestured for her to precede him and she stepped down with the aid of Bob the footman. The second carriage had drawn up behind them and she eyed it thoughtfully. Yesterday evening she'd noticed that the servants who manned it were all strangers to her. And this morning, when they were stopped for a change of horses, she'd happened to stroll near the second carriage. Her way had been immediately blocked by one of the unfamiliar menservants.

He'd been rather a rough-looking fellow, too.

"Ah, the seat of my forefathers."

She turned at Val's murmured words to find him standing and gazing with what looked like frank distaste at Ainsdale Castle.

"Why did we come if you hate it so much?" she asked softly.

His eyes flared wide and then he smiled gently. "Oh, Séraphine. Some things can neither be outrun, buried, nor burned. One must bear them like a twisted, degraded limb, dragged behind, odiferous and loathsome, forever reminding one of the most horrible time in one's life." He shrugged. "And if this foul disgusting thing becomes useful once and again? Should I not then make use of it?"

Without waiting for her reply, he strode to the great

double doors to the castle. The footmen seemed to be having some trouble rousing the staff within.

Bridget followed more slowly, glancing around the dark drive. Tall trees were rattling their branches against the moon. The windows of the castle were dark and they were obviously not expected.

Pip came trotting up to her, his tongue hanging out of his agape mouth happily.

Mehmed looked less cheerful. "English castles are cold."

"There'll be a warm fire inside," Bridget assured him. At least she hoped so.

One of the doors opened with a screeching creak, revealing a tall, thin man in hastily donned breeches and coat over a nightshirt, a soft nightcap covering his head. Behind him was an elderly woman, a thin gray braid trailing from under her mobcap, a gray shawl thrown over her nightdress.

"Your Grace!" exclaimed the man at the sight of Val. "We hadn't expected you."

"Few do," replied the duke. "And yet here I am, weary and famished, and on the doorstep on a cold and dreary night. Oh, will you let me in, kind sir?"

The last was said with more than a touch of irony and the tall man, who must be a butler, flushed, looking very young. "Of course, Your Grace. Yes, of course, do come in."

At the same time, the elderly woman's face had darkened. She muttered, "No notice. Beds aren't made. Don't have meat nor bread laid by in the kitchen, don't know what we'll feed such a crowd."

But the younger man had already moved back, letting Val stroll in, followed by Mehmed and the dog.

The duke continued into the castle but when it was Bridget's turn to enter she stopped and smiled at the two confused servants. "I am Mrs. Crumb. How do you do?"

The man made to remove a hat, remembered he was wearing only a soft cap, and ended on an awkward bow. "Erm... how d'you do? I'm John Dwight. Th' butler?"

"A pleasure to meet you, Mr. Dwight," Bridget said, and turned to the elderly woman. "And you are?"

"Mrs. Ives," the woman grunted. "Housekeeper and aunt to this one." She tilted her head toward the butler.

"Splendid." Bridget gestured to the boy, standing and gawking up at what were admittedly rather sinister-looking carvings in the ceiling high above them. In the flickering candlelight they seemed to be writhing. "This is Mehmed, the duke's valet. And this is Bob, one of his footmen. We have a party of a dozen or so." She was still uncertain about how many men traveled in the second carriage. "What sort of food do you have on hand?"

If possible, the housekeeper looked even more disgruntled. "Just enough to keep castle staff together, body and soul."

"And how many are in the castle at the moment?" Bridget asked smoothly. She gestured for Mehmed and Bob to precede her.

"A skeleton staff." The housekeeper snorted. "Don't know what Himself will do w'out proper help. Half a dozen maids, four footmen, the cook, her two scullery maids, an' me and John. Course that don't count the outside help—the stablemen, the groundkeepers, an' such."

"You've done very—" Bridget had begun in a conciliatory tone when Val interrupted her.

"Come, Mrs. Crumb," he said, appearing suddenly by her side and catching her by the upper arm. "You're not on staff here."

He began walking back the way he'd presumably come, down a dark and gloomy corridor, his hand still on her arm. There were paintings crowding the walls, men posed haughtily in doublet and hose, women staring blankly, their fingers beringed, starched ruffs about their necks.

"Then why did you bring me along?" she asked rather tartly, and then, before he could answer, "And I was in the process of seeing to your supper, *Your Grace*. I'd think you'd be more concerned about your comfort."

"I'm always *extremely* concerned as to my comfort and creature needs," Val replied as they came to a wide stone staircase. He turned to her and touched her lightly on one cheek, his azure eyes bright in the low light. "And I brought you along because I *like* you."

She inhaled and all thought fled her mind. He stood so close that they seemed to share the same breaths.

His lips slowly curved and he grasped her hand in his.

"But," he continued as they mounted the stairs, his hand wrapped firmly about hers, "I am not going to wait for my esteemed castle housekeeper to rouse my equally esteemed cook in the middle of the night to find something worthy of my palate. No. Instead I shall simply retire to my rooms and partake of the victuals Mrs. Bram packed for us when we began this journey. There are plenty left, for I instructed her to be generous, foreseeing a situation such as this." He shivered suddenly. "Dear God, the place is even colder than I remembered."

They made the upper floor, where the doors to what were obviously the ducal chambers were thrown open. A small dark-haired maid in nightclothes knelt by the enormous fireplace, coaxing a flame, while another girl turned down the bed—though it looked as if she was merely causing the dust to fly about—and a third was bringing in hot water as they arrived.

Mehmed and Pip were standing by the hearth watching the dark-haired maid work at the fire.

Bridget sniffed discreetly. She could smell mildew and, faintly, something decayed.

Val was less inclined toward discretion. He inhaled deeply. "Ah, the stink of my ancestors' rot. That *does* bring back memories—all of them quite vivid, if not pleasant. Now away, you sprites, and climb into your beds under the eaves. I'll have need of you in the morn, I'm sure."

The maids froze, and the one kneeling at the hearth pushed a lock of hair off her forehead with the back of her wrist and said, "Pardon, Your Grace?"

"Go. Away," Val enunciated quite insultingly.

Bridget glared at him—and then switched to a smile as the maids trudged, yawning, to the door. "Thank you!"

She waited until the door was closed before whirling on him—he seemed to let go of her hand without regret. "You needn't be so rude."

"No," he agreed, rummaging in the provisions basket, "but I'm paying them and I'm a bloody duke besides, so I needn't be polite, either. Apple?"

He held out the piece of fruit with a smile that was both innocent and faintly derisive.

She set her hands on her hips. "You'll find that you'll have better service if you treat your servants as human beings, capable of both thought and feeling."

He threw himself into a chair, one leg over the arm, swinging lazily. "If a servant's service displeases me in any way I have them dismissed. The remaining servants see this and act accordingly. I have the best service money can buy."

He took a large bite of the red apple, chewing as he watched her.

She came to him and knelt by his side. "It isn't *right* to treat other people as things that you can buy and sell."

He smirked. "What is right and wrong?"

"Would you like to be treated that way?" She didn't know why this argument, so late at night after three days of constant, exhausting travel, meant so much to her, but it did.

It did.

He pointed a finger at her, beautiful, confident in his wealth and rank, his gold thumb ring winking in the firelight. "If anyone were to treat me in such a way I'd cut his nose off and make him eat it."

He took another bite of the apple.

"Would you like others to treat *me* in this way?" she whispered. "As a thing to be ordered about, without regard to my feelings or thoughts?"

He froze, looking at her.

Her eyes never leaving his, she took the apple from his hand and bit into it.

Chewing, she rose and left the room.

* * *

VAL WOKE TO a freezing room and the sight of a ginger cat sitting at the foot of his bed. It had a white blaze on its chest and was washing itself quite unconcernedly.

The cat paused and looked up at him and he saw that it had green eyes, like Pretty, his first cat, the one that Father had strangled.

He'd had terrible taste in cat names at the age of five.

Val sneezed.

The cat was off like a shot and gone before he could blink.

And then he wondered: had it been there at all?

He sat up and looked at the spot on the dusty coverlet where the cat had been. It had left no impression.

Madness.

The room, in the light of day, still smelled like death and decay.

He got up, dragging the dusty coverlet from the bed, and wrapped it about himself. It trailed on the floor as he crossed to the diamond-paned window. It overlooked the inner keep, barren save for a gnarled oak tree at the center. Everything was mantled in the night's frost. He remembered men in masks, gamboling by firelight around that tree. Laughter and screeching.

Whimpering and soft crying.

Those masked men had terrified him as a young boy. Had once sent him running from his spying place, high in the widow's tower, back to his room, to hide under his bed. The nursery maid had found him only late the next morning.

Now he saw those masked revelers for what they really were: opportunities pure and simple. Nothing more. And like any opportunity's their benefits and their risks must be assessed.

He'd put that process into motion when he'd written the Duke of Dyemore before they'd left London. Whether the old man had gotten the letter, whether he was interested enough to come to Yorkshire and meet him, wasn't certain, of course. But Val would be very surprised indeed if he hadn't heard from the duke by next week.

A harsh cawing drew his eye upward and Val caught sight of a flock of jackdaws taking wing over the castellated walls.

He'd been created here, the result of as careful breeding as any Arabian stallion's. A dam from bloodlines that came from the Norman invasion and wealth to boot. A sire with a title, land, and beauty.

And he'd been formed here, drop by frozen crystalline drop, until he gleamed, translucent like a diamond, sharp and pure, and without any softness.

That had been frozen clean away.

Those who professed shock, disbelief, nay, even *horror* at the result, had not been paying sufficient attention to the depth of the ice.

Act not surprised when frozen ground yields naught but death.

And now he was returned to the seat of his ancestors. Ah, but it was past time he took his rightful place.

Val turned away from the window and strode to the door, opening it and sticking his head out into the hallway.

To his surprise a footman was actually without, apparently awaiting his appearance.

The man jerked nervously. "Your Grace?"

"Bring hot water and plenty of it," Val said. "A maid to make my fire. Tea, milk, sugar, eggs, ham, kippered herring, sausages, cheese, bread, butter, and jam. Oh, and Mrs. Crumb." He remembered the conversation of the night before. "Please."

"I'm sorry, Your Grace?" the footman said, looking dazed. "Who?"

"Mrs. Crumb," Val repeated. "The woman I came in with last night. About this high"—he placed the side of hand at his chin—"wears dreadfully ugly mobcaps and is probably someplace ordering someone about."

"Oh," said the footman with dawning comprehension. "*Her.*"

BRIDGET HAD WAKED earlier that morning to the stink of mildew and a damp coverlet in a cold, dark room.

She was of two minds about the matter.

One was sympathetic. It was never nice to be the servant in charge of a country house who was expected to be ready with no notice for the whims of a feckless master turning up in the middle of the night. The aristocracy seemed to think that beds made themselves, pantries were magically stocked, and staff could be hired at the snap of one's fingers.

On the *other* hand, mildew, dust, and damp denoted incompetence and *that* was another matter entirely—one that rather scandalized the housekeeper within her.

Right, then.

Bridget rose, shivering in her chemise. This disturbed Pip, who, despite his wiry fur, had been forced to seek warmth beneath the covers. He bumbled about, searching for a way out of the covers, until he found the edge and emerged, looking like some medieval cowled monk.

The dog stretched and then sat, watching as Bridget dressed.

She felt grimy, irritably aware that there was no water to wash in. Nevertheless she tied her mobcap firmly beneath her chin, hung her chatelaine at her waist, and snapped her fingers. She and the terrier ventured forth into the hall outside her room.

She'd been given a little room on one of the upper floors, not a servant's room, but certainly not a guest room, either.

Betwixt and between.

She marched down the unlit hall, noting the finely carved dark woodwork of the walls—and the dust above eye level and on the ceiling. Down the stairs—the carpet needed taking up, beating, and sponging, and the banister a good polishing with beeswax. Paused on the landing—smoke stains from years of candles on the upper walls, definite signs of damp on the lower. Down another flight of stairs—shaky banister. Dangerous, that. Must get in a carpenter at once. The lower hall was flanked by a row of gorgeous high Gothic windows looking out on the inner courtyard, all of which were dusty and smudged.

Bridget tutted under her breath.

Farther back she found the servants' passage and another, much narrower flight of stairs leading to the kitchens.

Great groined ceilings met her gaze, stained a tea brown from decades of smoky fires. Taking up one entire wall was the hearth, big enough to roast a side of beef.

Since this was a castle, no doubt it had been used for that very purpose in its time. A venerable table stood to one side of the hearth, wide and battered. Around it were gathered what must be nearly all the castle staff, with varying shades of belligerence, curiosity, and fear on their faces. To one side, huddled in a little defensive group, the obvious outsiders, were the footmen who had traveled from Hermes House: Bob, Bill, Will, and Sam. Presumably their coachman was either still in the stables or had fled, screaming, from the hostile atmosphere.

Bridget let Pip outside by means of a back door and then turned and folded her hands at her waist. "Good morning. I am Mrs. Crumb. Where is Mrs. Ives?"

Mr. Dwight, the butler, stood, his Adam's apple bobbing nervously in his thin throat. "My aunt went home to her cottage this morning. Said she was too old for midnight comings and goings." He gulped as if swallowing more that his aunt might've said.

Well, that might be easier anyway.

"Whom do you use as washerwomen?" she asked Mr. Dwight.

But a tall, thin woman with brown hair pulled tight against her skull interrupted aggressively, "Who are you?"

Bridget affixed a small, firm smile to her lips. "Mrs. Crumb, as I've said. And you are…?"

"Madge Smithers." The woman folded her arms across her thin chest. "The cook."

"Ah. Then I presume you'll want to start preparations for the duke's breakfast. I know he's particularly fond of eggs in the morning."

The cook didn't move—nor did anyone else.

Bridget sighed regretfully. "You see, the thing is, the duke will need to make decisions about his staff in the coming days: who will remain and who will have to find other places of employment."

"He's a devil, everyone hereabouts knows it," one of the footmen said. His words were over-loud and seemed to echo off the ceiling of the kitchens.

Bridget studied the footman. He didn't look more than five and twenty and she wondered how much personal experience he might have of the duke. "What is your name?"

"Conners."

"Well, Conners, if you think His Grace is a devil then why are you working here?"

"What d'you mean?" Conners scowled. "Only work hereabouts, innit?"

Bridget nodded. "Then I suggest you think on it. If you truly hold the duke in such contempt and fear I suggest you leave. If you wish to remain, then reconcile yourself to the fact that you have made a pact with a man you consider the Devil—and treat the Duke of Montgomery with respect."

She paused, waiting while that thought sank in. She understood working from necessity—didn't they all do that?—but she didn't allow ill talk of their master.

Or mutiny, for that matter.

"Now." She glanced brightly at the cook. "Breakfast, I think?"

Mrs. Smithers didn't exactly skip to her duties but she did start her preparations, with the help of two of the scullery maids.

"We have some women who come from the village," Mr. Dwight said when Bridget again asked him about washerwomen. "But my aunt was in charge of them. I'm not sure..."

"Do you have their names?" Bridget asked.

"Yes?"

"Then please ask them to come today."

"But..." Mr. Dwight looked helplessly around the bustling kitchens. "Today isn't washday. It's not for several days. Are you sure there will be things that need washing?"

"Oh, yes," Bridget said. "In fact, tell the washerwomen that we'll need them for at least a week."

"Very—"

"Now, maids," Bridget said briskly.

"Maids?" Mr. Dwight sounded as if he'd never heard of the creatures.

"Yes, I'll need at least another dozen more," Bridget said. "And I expect you'll want at least a half-dozen footmen." She nodded to herself. "Maids, footmen, washerwomen, carpenters, stoneworkers...really, I think you ought to just send word to the village that we're hiring workers of all types. We'll set up in the hall this afternoon so as not to be in the way of Mrs. Smithers in the kitchens and do the interviewing and hiring together. This morning after breakfast we'll walk through the entire castle, you and I, and make note of what needs to be done. But first, tea. I really can't do *anything* without tea in the morning," she confessed to Mr. Dwight. He seemed like such a nice young man.

But a little scatterbrained.

He gazed wide-eyed at her. "Tea...?"

One of the brutish-looking men from the second carriage entered the kitchens from a door Bridget hadn't even realized was there. "She needs 'er breakfast."

"Who?"

At Bridget's query everyone stilled.

Bridget's eyes narrowed and she addressed the man, who was short, but with a barrel chest and a flattened, scarred face. "*Who* needs their breakfast?"

He sneered. "None of your business."

"It's a lady." The dark-haired little maid from the night before spoke up bravely. "Down in th' dungeons."

But Bridget was already crossing the kitchens and ducking through the door the strange manservant had entered through.

Behind her someone yelled, "Oi!"

There was a narrow passage back here. She hurried along it, ignoring doors that obviously led to storage rooms, until she came to an arched opening with a flight of bare stone steps that led downward in a spiral.

These she took.

The walls were moist and cool and she could see light below her. The circular steps spilled out into an open flagstone floor with a small, cozy fire on one end. Three crude wooden doors were set into the walls, all with small holes cut at roughly the height of a man's head. Four bedrolls were laid out on the floor and a table was next to the fire with four chairs around it.

Bridget was almost relieved. *Dungeons* had sounded quite horrific.

Three men were sitting beside the fire, and all three

looked up at the sight of her, although none seemed particularly alarmed.

Behind her the man from the kitchens ran out of the spiral staircase, panting. "Tried to stop 'er."

Bridget drew herself up. "Where is she?"

One of the men sighed, pushing out his chair. "Now, look 'ere, miss."

"Mrs. Crumb! Mrs. Crumb, is that you?"

The man standing behind her made a grab for her.

Bridget dodged and ran to the middle door, the one from which she'd heard the woman's voice. She stood on tiptoe and peered through the little cutout hole and saw Hippolyta Royle.

Chapter Eleven

But King Heartless still nodded to his guards, indicating that the sentence should be carried out.

That was when the magician cleared his throat. "My liege, I can prove my magic is real."

King Heartless frowned—he frowned a lot—and said, "How?"

"I can help you find your heart."

Well, at that everyone froze, save for Prue, who hissed under her breath, "Father, what are you about?"...

—From *King Heartless*

Val was lying in his dusty bed, clad in a shirt, waistcoat, and banyan, munching an apple and wondering if the footman he'd sent for breakfast and Mrs. Crumb had perhaps fallen down the stairs and broken his neck, when heaven's gates opened and an avenging archangel descended upon him in full fury.

The door to his room was flung open, crashing against the far wall and marring what was no doubt some very fine carved oak paneling. She flew in, all fiery flashing eyes and flushed cheeks, her bosom heaving beneath black wool.

She was magnificent.

"Tell them to let her go!" Séraphine ordered him imperiously. "Tell them to let her go *right now*."

She stood over him, her lips wet, her body shaking with her rage, and he wanted to take her and roll her beneath him and fuck her into the mattress.

But no matter what she thought he wasn't *entirely* insane—he had some small sense of self-preservation.

"Am I to understand that you've discovered Miss Royle?" he asked, keeping his apple prudently out of reach.

She flung out her hand, pointing presumably toward his dungeons. "Those…those *apes* that you hired will not listen to me. They won't let her out. What possible reason can you have to keep Miss Royle locked in your dungeons? Do you hate her so very much?"

"No," he replied, surprised. "Why would I hate Miss Royle? I intend to marry her."

For a moment she stared at him, panting, breathless and wordless, it seemed, with rage.

He'd had no idea she would respond to his capture of her queen so very violently.

It was rather arousing.

"Hippolyta Royle *loathes* you," Séraphine said at last, her voice a little lower. "She'll never marry you willingly."

"No," he agreed, "but she'll not have much choice once she's ruined."

Her eyes widened and her face went white. "You intend to rape her?"

He flinched, remembering a childish face, pale with fear. "I didn't say that. As it happens I find rape and rapists disgusting. No. A week or so in the dungeons should do the job for me quite handily with Miss Royle none the worse for wear. By now all of London society knows that she's gone. Once it's discovered where she's been staying and with *whom*..." He shrugged. "She'll have no choice, as I've said. Even if she won't admit it, her father certainly will. I expect to be affianced within a fortnight. "

"But..." She was looking at him oddly. "If you marry a woman who hates you and you don't intend to rape her, how exactly do you plan to consummate the marriage?"

He arched his eyebrow and spread wide his arms, indicating his own incredible beauty. "She can't hate me forever. Once married I give her a week. A month at the outside."

He shrugged and resumed eating his apple.

"You really are the vainest man in the world," she said wonderingly.

He stopped chewing. "This is the first you've noticed?"

She looked down on him, an angel in judgment. Her eyes *burned* at him. "Val, you *can't* do this, don't you see? It's not right."

Her words splashed against him like acid.

He tossed aside the apple and rolled off the bed. He stalked to her, barefoot, and took her by her upper arms, thrusting his face at hers, feeling her heat, seeing the flames licking the rims of her irises, and said, "What is right? What is wrong? Tell me now, Séraphine. Who makes these rules that others know so well?"

She didn't pull back from his anger—he'd give her that—but she hesitated, her eyes searching his. "The Bible—"

He sneered at her words. “A moldering text written by dead men. They tell me that to spill my seed upon the ground is a sin. Nonsense. What else have you?”

Her tongue wet her lips and his cock jerked, for he’d been erect since her abrupt entrance into his bedroom. He *ached* for her fire, her certainty. “The courts—”

“Old men who live on bribes and their own importance. Is this wisdom? Is this the apex of our justice?”

Her eyes narrowed. “Laws that Parliament—”

“Oh, Séraphine,” he purred, pushing his nose close to her jaw to inhale her righteous scent. “Who do you suppose sits in Parliament? Who makes the laws, runs the government of this great and lofty nation, hmm?” She hadn’t bathed this morning, he could tell, and she smelled of herself: woman, sweat, sex. He licked across her cheek, tasting salt and pure saint, to her mouth. He bit her lips. Once, twice, a third time, wanting, *craving*. He pulled back to see her face only with the greatest force of will. “I, Séraphine. I am the government. Dukes and marquesses, earls and viscounts. Men who have land and money and power and have had it for generations and generations, amen. We decide what is right and what is not. Who shall hang for the theft of a handkerchief and who shall be let go for the rape of a maidservant. We decide how many windows on a house shall be taxed and how many men shall die in a war. We are the ruling class.” He smiled at her as sweetly as he knew how. “Now tell me, do you really think one such as *I* should be making these rules of *right* and *wrong*?”

She stared at him, mute, his burning Séraphine, defeated. She had only to admit the game over now.

He let her go and strolled to the provisions basket, planning to look for another apple or perhaps a piece of cheese with which to tempt her. He could be a benevolent victor.

"That's it?"

"Hmm?" He turned to find her right behind him. What a sneaky thing she was!

Her eyes were narrowed, her nostrils flared, and she didn't seem to have noticed that she'd *lost*. "That's your explanation? You can do anything you bloody well please because you can't tell right from wrong yourself and you don't accept other commonly held standards of morality?"

He cocked his head. "Yes?"

"*No*," she said, quite firmly, quite as if she were no longer a mere housekeeper, a commoner, born to a sheep farmer, a *servant*. As if she felt she were his equal in this.

Perhaps even his superior.

"No," she repeated. "*I* don't accept that. You are hurting others with your stupid philosophy, with your disregard for everyone else. You can hold frivolous balls on a moment's notice if you wish, you can scandalize society on a whim, but you *cannot* marry a woman who doesn't want to marry you. It is wrong."

She was so sure of herself—and him. Reluctantly he was fascinated. His lips began to curve upward. "Who says it is—"

"*I* say it is wrong." She placed her palm flat against his chest, the first time she'd ever voluntarily touched him outside the sickroom, and even through banyan, waistcoat, and shirt, her hand seemed to sear his skin. "Not the Bible, not the courts, not the Parliament, *I* say that it is wrong. Let Hippolyta Royle go, give her a carriage and the footmen from Hermes House, and *send her home.* Do it now, Val, because you can be a better man than this."

He stared into her eyes, flaming so brightly for him, and felt himself on a precipice, wavering, the earth beneath his feet crumbling.

If he fell, would he burn?

He took her hand from his chest and lifted it to his mouth and kissed her palm. "No, my sweet Séraphine," he said very, very gently, "I will not, for I think you have mistaken something grave about me. I may be a philosopher, but it is but one of my faces. Turn me and I'll show another. One I think you'll find less amusing, but nonetheless just as true."

She tried to pull away, but he wouldn't let her.

She scowled up at him. "What face is that?"

He smiled, perhaps a trifle sadly, who knew? "The face of a ruler. Everything I have done, everything I do, is simply to consolidate and gain power. Look around you. This is what my ancestors did. That story I told you as we arrived? About the man who killed the former master of this castle and raped his wife? Did you think it a fairy tale? No, his blood runs in my veins. I was bred to do what I am doing now. Don't fault the viper for striking. It's what snakes do."

Her lips trembled, but her eyes were dry, as if she'd already given up hope of persuading him and he did not mourn at all. *Not at all.* "The blood of that woman who was raped is in your veins, too, isn't it?"

Oh, she knew where to hit. "Naturally. But I think it's

less apparent, don't you? The story says she was dark and small."

She shook her head. "So all that talk of right and wrong—that doesn't matter in the end to you at all?"

He hesitated—just for the smallest fraction of a second—because he had always found the question of right and wrong rather fascinating.

But then he smiled at her. "Only in the abstract. I will keep Miss Royle and I will make her my wife. Because she is the most beautiful and wealthiest heiress in England, because she is a prize, and because I can."

Her eyes seemed to blaze at him. "You don't care what I think."

It wasn't a question so he didn't answer—but he caught his breath. And had she been paying attention that might've been answer enough.

But she was pulling her hand away and turning so she didn't notice.

His empty chest was cold, so very cold.

"Away with you, Mrs. Crumb," he said. "I've made my decision and no pretty words from you will change my mind."

She left.

And took all the warmth from the room.

SOME, BRIDGET THOUGHT late that night, might think it rash to attempt a rescue that same day, what with being a stranger to the district, with few allies, fewer funds, a freezing, desolate landscape, and not much time to plan.

Some were probably not half-blind with rage at a thunderously stupid man, of course.

Wonderfully stimulating, rage was.

She crept down the spiral staircase to the dungeons, trying to make as little noise as possible. In theory the guards should all be asleep due to the concoction she'd placed in their ale.

Theory, of course, was a long way from practice. She just hoped that she hadn't used *too* much of the thick, black liquid she'd purchased at great expense from Mrs. Smithers. She really didn't want to kill one of Val's apes.

Although the thought wasn't worrying her as much as it should, come to think of it.

Val was having a very bad effect on her sense of morality.

As she rounded the last turn, though, she exhaled a sigh of relief. Four burly forms were slumped over the table—and they all appeared to be breathing rather noisily.

Hurriedly Bridget found the key ring—unfortunately under one of the men's stinking arms—and ran to the middle dungeon room. "Hsst! Miss Royle!"

"Is that you, Mrs. Crumb?" Miss Royle's face appeared at the little window.

"Yes, I've come to rescue you," Bridget said stoutly.

She inserted the key and turned it in the lock with a great screech, wincing as she did so. Couldn't the guards have oiled the bloody lock?

"Oh, thank you," Miss Royle said as she came out of her tiny prison.

She was sadly much the worse for wear, her hair coming down in a tangled cloud about her shoulders, smudges on her nose and forehead, and with a blanket wrapped around her. Bridget had noticed this morning that under the blanket she seemed to have on only her chemise, as if she'd been taken in the night. What kind of *swine* had a woman kidnapped in her nightclothes?

"I brought a cloak," Bridget had begun, when Miss Royle's dark-brown eyes widened. She darted around Bridget, picked up a coal shovel, and smashed it over the head of one of the guards who had started to rise.

The coal shovel made a clanging, bell-like sound.

"Oh!" Miss Royle said, and then beamed at Bridget. "You have no idea how satisfying that was after the last five days."

"They didn't *hurt* you, did they?" Bridget asked anxiously.

"No, not in the way you mean." Miss Royle wrinkled her nose and toed the man on the ground. She looked as if she wouldn't mind hitting him again with her shovel. "But they were rough and I don't think they've bathed in the last month or so. And being cooped up with them in a carriage, Mrs. Crumb—*quite* disgusting."

Bridget blinked. "Please. Call me Bridget."

"Really?" Miss Royle said, swinging the coal shovel onto her shoulder as a soldier might a musket. "Then you must call me Hippolyta."

"Very well...erm...Hippolyta," Bridget said. "I've some clothing for you. We should hurry."

"Of course." Hippolyta put on a man's buckled shoes, patched hose, and a too-big cast-off dress formerly belonging to Mrs. Smithers, the cook.

Bridget held out the last item of clothing. "I've a cloak for you, but I'm afraid it isn't... well."

The cloak was huge, dingy gray and variously patched

in dark green, bright blue, and red plaid. It also smelled rather strongly of horse.

"Ah," Hippolyta said. "Thank you." She donned the cloak and smiled brightly. "Warm!"

Bridget nodded briskly and led the way back up the dungeon stairs. This time of night most of the servants were asleep. By dint of discreet inquiry Bridget had learned what she'd already suspected: Val was *not* well liked in the area, even though he'd been gone eleven years. It hadn't been hard to find a few people to either look the other way or help outright with the aid of bribery. Something a master of plots and schemes should've thought about before haring off to his gloomy old castle. Oh, but that was right—he didn't pay attention to his hired *help*.

Swine.

They made their way through the kitchens and out the back door into the inner keep. The night sky was cloudy, but the waning moon was revealed for a moment, the old oak's twisted branches black against her pale face.

"The stables are on the other side," Bridget explained, drawing her borrowed coat closer about her. It was damp and cold tonight, the air heavy with the prospect of rain or snow, and she was beginning to wish she'd brought her shawl as well.

They hurried over the frozen ground to the outer gate and around the side of the castle walls. The stables appeared deserted, but a sturdy pony was waiting for them, tethered outside, as promised.

"I'm sorry," Bridget apologized. "It was the only animal I could get on such short notice."

Hippolyta looked doubtful. "Can he carry us both?"

"I hope so," Bridget said grimly.

Hippolyta nodded and untied the pony and led him to a mounting block. She swung on the pony quite competently, Bridget far less so, and then they headed out into the black night.

"Where are we bound?" Hippolyta asked. She was riding behind, actually guiding the pony.

"To the local village." Dear God, the pony was so slow! She hadn't counted on this, that the animal wouldn't be able to move as fast bearing the both of them.

Bridget glanced behind them. Ainsdale Castle seemed to loom in the night, far too close still. A few lights shone from the windows. She couldn't tell, but she didn't think an alarm had been raised. He was probably still up in his rooms, clad in his flamboyant purple banyan, a glass of wine in one hand, an ancient book in the other.

Unaware that she'd demolished his plans good and proper—or would have once she'd gotten Hippolyta safely away. *Did you really think this was over between us just because you declared it so?*

She faced forward again as the pony headed out onto the desolate moors. Now. If only she and Hippolyta could have a *little* luck…

Half an hour later they crested a little hill and Bridget glanced around, relieved to see that in the far distance lights twinkled. She hugged herself. The wind was whipping her skirts about her ankles and the clouds had completely hidden the moon. "There, you see? That should be the village. All you need to do is keep it in sight and you'll soon be there. You'll want the first cottage with a red door—it's Mrs. Ives's, the former housekeeper of

Ainsdale Castle. She doesn't much like the duke and Mr. Dwight assured me she'd hide you for the night. There's an early-morning mail coach that'll take you to London."

Bridget swung her leg over the pony's neck, sliding to the ground with relief. She hadn't wanted to tell Hippolyta, but Bridget could count on one hand the times she'd ridden a horse.

"Please." It was hard to see in the black night, but she could hear the worried note in Hippolyta's voice. "Don't go back there. He's mad. I'll never forgive myself if he does you harm, Bridget."

For a moment a thrill went through Bridget, perhaps a culmination of the day's tension and plotting and excitement. And then she said, "Don't worry. The duke won't harm me." *Physically, at least*, she amended to herself. "Besides," she added more practically, "I've only money enough for one ticket to London on the mail coach."

"But—"

In the distance a high, almost musical baying could be heard. It was drawing nearer—as it had been for the last ten minutes. The foxhounds of Ainsdale Castle were tracking them.

If Bridget hadn't been expecting them, she might've been frightened clean out of her wits.

As it was, the sound only set spurs to her resolve. "Go!"

Hippolyta finally turned the plump pony's head toward the lights and set off in a bobbing gallop.

Just as icy raindrops began spitting from the sky.

Bridget, meanwhile, picked up her skirts and jogged in the opposite direction. It was crucial to her plan that she draw the tracking dogs away from Hippolyta. She wore a man's coat—all right, one of *Val*'s coats—over her dress and the pockets were well stuffed with diced raw bacon. Every few paces she dropped a few pieces.

She was on a path but it was black, and the rain was making the way slippery. She had to be careful not to turn an ankle or run into the gorse accidentally.

Meanwhile the baying of the dogs was getting louder. It occurred to her that foxhounds weren't trained to merely track an animal and point it out as a gentle spaniel might do. Spaniels left the prey for the hunter to deal with.

Foxhounds usually tore the fox apart at the end of the hunt.

Suddenly her clever plan to throw the hounds off Hippolyta's scent didn't seem quite so clever.

Surely Val would call off the hounds?

Could one call off foxhounds?

Bridget found herself running faster, her skirts caught up in both hands, the bacon entirely forgotten. Her face was wet, her breath was coming in pants, and there was a stitch in her side.

The baying was right behind her, loud and oddly musical and she fumbled at her pockets to throw out all the bacon lest the hounds tear her limb from limb to get at it.

A giant black beast came rushing up to her, the sound of hoofbeats thundering in her ears. She cowered, waiting to be trampled, but instead strong arms reached down and seized her, sweeping her up.

"I have you now, my Séraphine," growled the Duke of Montgomery in her ear. "Did you really think I wouldn't come for you?"

* * *

DOGS HAD BEEN the weapons of his father.

Val watched distastefully as the animals milled in the mud about his mount's hooves, snapping and fighting among themselves over the scraps of meat she'd hidden in the pockets of one of his favorite coats. He'd expected his fair Séraphine to make a rescue attempt, but not so soon—or so recklessly.

He tightened his arm about the warm, wet, breathing woman in front of him and kicked the mare into a gallop. She gave a little shriek and he grinned into her stupid, ugly mobcap. She was a servant and probably unused to riding. Served her right, constantly defying him.

He, however, was a duke and had been made to ride since the age of five. Better to have an heir dead of a fall from a giant horse than one not *quite* up to snuff in his riding, had probably been his father's thought on the matter. Assuming his father had given any thought to his son's instruction at all.

They crested a hill and he gave the mare her head, galloping o'er the stormy moors in the moonlight, his captive maiden in his arms. Oh, it was dangerous to be sure. The mare might put a hoof into a hole and tumble them all into the ground, breaking their necks, but he found he just did not give a damn at the moment.

She'd well and truly provoked him this time. She'd lost him a wife for a second time—first by preventing his blackmailing Miss Royle and now by actually freeing the heiress. It was almost as if Séraphine had something against the matrimonial state. But worse—much, *much* worse—she'd run away herself.

That was unpardonable, unforgivable, *unjustifiable.*

Hit him, shame him, spit at him—anything but turn her back on him. She couldn't simply quit their game. That, *that* was not allowed.

And when he'd realized that she was out there on the stormy night moor, alone save an aristocratic lady and a goddamned bloody *pony*...

He growled beneath his breath.

She stilled against him, like a rabbit under a hound's jaws, her heart beating rapidly, and he was glad. She *ought* to be afraid of him. He was a very bad man and she was completely under his power. He could do anything to her.

Anything at all, really.

Time she learned that.

The lights of the castle were nearing and regretfully he let the mare slow.

For the first time since he'd captured her, she spoke, through chattering teeth. "What are you doing?"

"Bringing my prize home," he said lightly as they drew up before the castle doors, "as my ravaging ancestors did. As I understand it, it was customary to throw the prisoners in the dungeons, feast, and then have a merry time torturing the captives, but I think I'll omit that part."

One of the waiting stablemen ran over in the rain to catch the mare's bridle.

Val dismounted, his boots splashing in a puddle, and reached up and lifted Séraphine down. He picked her up, cradling her in his arms like a babe, and started walking toward the doors.

She stiffened immediately. "Put me down," she hissed in his ear, her hands hovering in the air before her as if she didn't know where to put them.

"No," he said. "You might take a mind to scamper off." He smiled slowly down at her wet face, absolutely delighted by a sudden thought. "You've never been carried in a man's arms before, have you?"

"No," she said, glaring quite fiercely at him through clumped eyelashes. "Why would I?"

"Hmm." He wasn't going to answer *that*—not at the moment anyway. "Well, here's a hint: relax a little. If you don't, I might very well drop you and wouldn't that be embarrassing for us both?"

"Oh, God," she moaned as the doors to the castle opened and the tall gangly butler's mouth dropped open at the sight of them.

"Good evening," Val said to him as they passed. "Dinner for two in my rooms. Please."

She did relax a little as he stepped inside, softening against him rather nicely. Unfortunately, as the light hit them Val got his first real look at the coat she was wearing.

He groaned. "Did it *have* to be the purple velvet?" he asked. "It's almost as if you don't like me."

She folded her arms across her bosom as he mounted the stairs, drawing his eye to that sadly shrouded area. "I don't." Her proud poise was marred by a sudden violent shiver.

"Liar," he said absently, "and not a very good one at that. I suppose I could give you lessons, but then I'd lose what advantage I have."

She sighed as they neared his room. "What about Miss Royle?"

He glanced at her, puzzled. "What about her?"

"Why are you here with me instead of out looking for the woman you say you want to marry?"

He smiled just to irritate her and shouldered open the doors to his room. "Jealous? You needn't be. I've most of my men out searching the moors with the dogs. They'll find her safe and sound before morning."

Her little dog came racing toward them, barking like a demon, and Mehmed turned from where he'd been placing drying cloths near the bath. "Mrs. Crumb! Duke find you. I am so glad! We worry, Pip and I, that you become lost on moors and turn into ghost that haunt Duke all his days forever and ever."

"I'm quite crushed by your lack of faith in me, Mehmed," Val murmured. "Now take that mongrel and go to the kitchens and see if they've made our supper yet, please."

The boy grinned like the imp he was. "Yes, Duke!"

He was out the door with the dog in a trice.

Val set Séraphine before the roaring fire, but kept his hands on her because he'd learned his lesson well…and also because he liked his hands upon her.

She glanced at the steaming bath and suppressed another shiver. "I should leave if you're about to take a bath."

"Why?" he asked as he slipped his sadly ruined purple velvet coat from her shoulders. It had cost more than she'd probably make in a lifetime and now stank of bacon and horses, thanks to her. He threw the sodden thing in the corner.

"You'll want your privacy," she replied nonsensically.

He looked into her dark eyes, amused, as he unhooked her chatelaine and laid it on a table. "When have I ever wanted privacy?"

She glanced away. "Perhaps I wish for you to have your privacy?"

"More likely," he agreed. "But if you'd wanted me to acquiesce to your wishes, you really oughtn't have run from me. Rather burned your bridges there, Séraphine, haven't you?"

He smiled and pulled the ugly white fichu from her neck.

She blinked and looked down at the simple, square neckline of her bodice as if she'd never seen it. Perhaps she hadn't. Perhaps she dressed in the dark like a nun. "What are you doing?"

He sighed. "I confess, I find your naïveté perplexing. *How* have you arrived at the advanced age of six and twenty without having anyone attempt seduction upon yourself? I'm of two minds on the matter: One, utter astonishment at my sex and their deaf disregard for your siren call. Two, glee at the thought that your innocence might signal that you are indeed *innocent*. Why this should excite me so, I don't know—virginity has never before been a particular whim of mine. I think perhaps it's the setting. Who knows how many virgins were deflowered here by my lusty ancestors? Or," he said as he deftly unpinned and tossed aside her apron, "maybe it's simply you."

"I don't…" Her words trailed off and then, interestingly, she blushed a deep rose. Well. *That* question settled, then. His little maiden was really a maiden. "What?"

"I think it's you," he confided, pulling the strings tying her hideous mobcap beneath her chin.

She made a wild grab for it, but he was faster, snatching the bloody thing off—*finally*, and with a great deal of satisfaction. She might've deprived him of a wife that it'd taken him half a year and a rather large sum of money to entangle, but by God, he'd taken off her awful cap.

And underneath . . .

"Oh, *Séraphine*," he breathed, enchanted, for her hair was as black as coal, as black as night, as black as his own soul, save for one white streak just over her left eye. But she'd twisted and braided and tortured the strands, binding them tight to her head, and his fingers itched to let them free.

"Don't!" she said, as if she knew what he wanted, her hands flying up to cover her hair.

He batted them aside, laughing, pulling a pin here, a pin there, dropping them carelessly to the carpet as she squealed like a little girl and backed away from him, trying frantically to ward off his fingers.

He might've taken pity on her had he not just spent an hour on a freezing moor, wondering if he was going to find her dead, neck broken, at the bottom of a hill.

Her hair came down all at once, a tumbling mass, tousled and heavy and nearly down to her waist.

"Wonderful," he murmured, taking it in both hands and lifting it.

She was backed against the wall near the hearth, panting, red-faced, eyeing him wildly. "It's oily. I need to wash it."

He smiled kindly at her. Did she think him so easily dissuaded? "I know. Why did you think I had the bath ready?"

She glanced at the bath, her eyes widening, then back to him.

He nodded. "It's for you. The moor is cold this time of year—even without the help of a storm—and I knew you'd need it. Now let's get the rest off you before the water grows tepid."

He began on the hidden hooks to her bodice as she stood still, her breasts rising and falling tremblingly beneath his fingers. It was like undressing a wild animal. Or an angel who had consented to stand still for a moment. Any false move on his part might startle her into flight.

He smiled into her eyes, aware that his cock pressed hard and hot against the placket of his breeches. Her hair had smelled of earth and her. He was almost loath to replace her essential scent with perfumes.

But she was freezing. He'd felt it in the ice of her fingers, in the chill of her cheeks. He wanted her warm.

He couldn't let his burning angel's fire go out.

The bodice gave and he opened it wide, baring her plain, sensible stays, and stripped it down her arms. He untied her skirts and petticoats with a flick of his fingers and helped her step out of them. He knelt at her feet—he a duke, she a housekeeper—and took off mud-clotted buckle shoes and woolen stockings. Then he stood and reached for the laces to her extremely practical stays and noted that her breath seemed to quicken, for he could actually see the tops of her breasts now, full and mounded above her chemise. Pale ivory in contrast to the ebony of her hair.

He loosened her stays and drew them off over her head and she stood in her worn chemise, a small, neat patch on the left shoulder. He could see her nipples, peaked and dark with cold, through the thin material, and the sight was, perhaps, the most erotic he'd ever seen in his debauched life.

He had his hand on her upper arm, just in case, but she didn't bolt. She raised her chin and met his eyes and he felt his lips curve.

His cock pulse.

He might have to reassess what he meant to do. For bedding a martyr, an inquisitor, a fiery archangel, even if a virgin…well, that might be a bit out of the ordinary, surely?

Might a man find himself somehow changed after such an event?

What an odd thought.

He grinned, wide and hungry, to clear the thought from his mind, and whipped the chemise over her head.

She stood naked: soft white belly exposed, ruby nipples peaked on plump breasts, a black bush at the top of curved, pale thighs. She was without chatelaine, without mobcap helmet, without any armor at all, and she refused to cover herself.

Instead she threw her shoulders back and met his gaze with defiance.

And at that moment something squeezed within him.

"Oh, Séraphine," he crooned to her, picking her up in his arms, feeling all that soft, white skin, "how I shall fuck you tonight."

"My name is Bridget," she said.

Chapter Twelve

King Heartless narrowed his eyes. Many, many wizards and doctors and seers had tried to find his heart, remake his heart, or gift him with a heart. All had failed.

"Very well," said the king in a low voice that made the courtiers step back. "If you find my heart I'll let you and your daughter go. If you don't, I'll have both your heads chopped off and set on the castle gates." . . .

—From *King Heartless*

"*Bridget?*" Val said, aghast, some five minutes later.

It was the third or fourth time he'd said it, each time sounding a little more horrified.

Bridget had decided to ignore him. A bath, in a real copper bathtub that came up to her shoulders when she sat in it, and that was filled with steaming-hot water, was a luxury. She wasn't going to let it go to waste just because Val was having some sort of problem with her first name.

"But *Bridget*," he appealed to her. He'd shrugged off his coat and pulled up a chair to sit by the bathtub, clad in a full-sleeved, lace-trimmed fine linen shirt and a gold-embroidered waistcoat in cerulean blue. She would've been much more self-conscious had he not been so preoccupied with her name. "Are you *absolutely* sure?"

"Yes." She sank a little lower in the tub, letting the warm water lap over her upper arms. This really was Heaven. No wonder he was always calling for a bath at odd hours. She'd have one every day if she could.

"But it's an Irish name," he said. "And you told me you came from the North of England—practically Scotland—if—"

She tilted her head back and sank beneath the water, and his words were muffled as the water blocked her ears.

She emerged to him saying, "—unless you're Irish. *Are* you Irish?"

"No." She reached for the lovely milled soap, and then recollected her shadowy footman father and added, "At least, not to my knowledge."

"It's such a dissonant name. *Brid*-get. Brid-*get*. Brigit-brigitbrigit. It almost sounds like a birdcall. One of those irritating birds that live in bushes and chirp repetitiously and ruin one's picnic. Not that I go on many picnics. Brigitbrigitbrigit."

The soap smelled of roses and was smooth and creamy in her hands. She rubbed it through her hair, almost moaning at the lovely feeling after the dirt and cold and fear of the day. She closed her eyes and let the scent of the soap and his drawling voice roll over her as she massaged her scalp with the tips of her fingers.

It was really rather lovely.

But when she opened her eyes she found that Val had stopped complaining about her name. Instead his gaze was fixed on her, his eyes slowly trailing down her arms to her neck and farther, to where her breasts just touched the water. For a long moment he simply looked at her breasts, and she was aware of the pulse of her heart, of the drip of the water from her arm, and of her nipples, tightening in the cool air.

Then his azure gaze rose to meet hers, shining and intent, and she remembered his words. *How I shall fuck you tonight.*

Her lips parted as her heart began to thunder.

"Let me help you rinse your hair."

His voice had deepened and it made a shock go through her, low in her belly. He rose and crossed to where a pitcher stood on the hearth. She didn't turn, but she could hear him moving behind her, and it struck her that she'd seldom been waited upon before in her life—and never by a gentleman.

"Sit a little forward." He was suddenly close. "Close your eyes and tilt your head back."

The water flowed over her scalp, warm and soothing, but her skin was prickled with goose bumps nonetheless.

"Once more, I think," he said, his voice so near, his hands large and sure, and he poured again. "There."

She sat back, wringing the water from her hair with fingers that trembled. She could hear him setting down the pitcher and she wasn't sure what to do. This was so far outside any experience she'd ever before had or imagined...

Bridget cleared her throat, but her voice was husky when she spoke. "Can you hand me a cloth for my hair?"

"Let me." He expertly wrapped a cloth around her head, keeping her clean hair out of the water. "Now you look like an Ottoman sultana." His fingers lingered on the back of her neck, stroking.

She closed her eyes, feeling her nipples throb. Oh, God, he'd barely touched her yet.

She inhaled and tried a smile, but found she was too tense. "Is...is there another cloth with which to dry myself?"

The fingers left as he reseated himself, his cheek propped on his knuckles. "But you haven't washed yourself, sweet Brid-*get*." He snapped off the *t* of her name with a click of his tongue. "I'm sure you wouldn't want to miss..." His gaze seemed to penetrate the now-clouded water before rising and meeting her own eyes with a devilish gleam. "Well, *everything*."

She felt heat rise from her throat. He meant to *watch* her—was already watching her—as if she were some sensuous, lovely nymph. A lady of leisure and self-indulgence.

Bridget swallowed. She was used to washing with a pitcher and washbasin. How much more voluptuous to do it in this great bath. He'd led her to this—oh, not the nudity, not what they might do afterward in his bed. No, this right here. This reveling in the pleasure quite literally of the flesh. The pleasure of hot water, of soft soap, of subtle scent, of the feel of her own skin, of her hair down and *clean*.

Could she truly be bought for so little?

And yet it wasn't little. Not this. She served others who thought it so. Who regarded a tub full to the brim with hot water as nothing unusual because they'd never had to haul the water, make the fire, fill the pitchers, and carry them up the stairs one after another, bloody, backbreaking work.

She stood in between.

She saw both sides: the life of luxury, summoned at the

snap of one's fingers, and the toil and sweat and *work* that made it possible.

Besides. She wasn't selling herself. She knew that. *He* knew that. Even if others might think money was what lay between them, *she* knew it was far more complicated than that.

So, having come to that conclusion, she stretched her arms above her head, *reveling* in the steam, in the rose scent surrounding her, and met his satyr's gaze frankly.

And *smiled.*

His exotic azure eyes widened and his eyebrows arched as he murmured, "Oh, Séraphine, you are *magnificent.*"

Her smile lingered as she picked up the washcloth and wet it, passing it over the lovely, lovely soap again before rubbing it on her neck.

Heaven.

"Is there more clean water?" she asked.

"I can ring for more," he replied, his voice husky.

"Please."

He got up and went to the door, opening it only far enough to talk to someone outside, presumably one of the footmen. For a moment she wondered what the other servants would think, and then she shrugged.

That she knew already.

He came back with a tray of food.

"It seems I must play footman since I'm too jealous to let any other man in here."

She glanced up, somewhat surprised. He'd never been worried over his own nudity. "Thank you."

He resettled in the chair, lounging back this time, eyes half-closed, legs sprawled apart. "You're welcome."

There was a thickness in his breeches. For a moment she stared witlessly.

Then her gaze rose to meet his.

His face was side-lit by the fire, beautiful and otherworldly, like a fairy prince's, and his lips curved as his eyes seemed to glow. He waved his left hand indolently. "Please. Continue."

She took her washcloth and wet it again, trailing warm water over her collarbone. The scent of roses enveloped her, heady, almost overwhelming.

She could hear his breathing deepen, but she dared not look at him.

The soapy water streamed between her breasts and she followed it down with the washcloth, rubbing gently, sweeping under each breast and then under her arms. She let the washcloth soak in the water and then wrung it out. She lifted her arm to wash it.

Her skin seemed to gleam golden in the firelight.

A knock came at the door and Val swore foully under his breath.

She smiled secretly to herself when he jumped up to get the door. This was an odd sort of excitement that she'd never thought to find within herself. To hold the Duke of Montgomery enthralled while she bathed.

She was washing her other arm when he set the pitcher of hot water down and resumed his seat. She saw him wince and farther widen his legs as if seeking comfort, and that made her duck her chin and smile again. Oh, she was very wicked, but he had only himself to blame for luring her into a world of decadence. For stripping her housekeeperly trappings from her. For revealing the woman beneath.

For revealing what she was to him.

She rinsed the washcloth and then soaped it well before propping her foot on the edge of the bathtub and thoroughly scrubbing her toes.

For some reason *that* was when he moaned.

She glanced at him in mild surprise, which was a mistake.

His head was cocked back, his eyes mere azure slits beneath lowered lashes as he watched her. His bottom lip was caught in strong, white teeth and his cheeks were lightly flushed. One arm was flung behind his head and the other…

The other was pressed frankly on the placket of his breeches, the heel of his hand grinding down.

She swallowed, feeling heat rising in her.

"Oh, Séraphine," he whispered. "Your plump little toes, the arch of your instep, the curve of your luscious calf…" He groaned as if in pain and actually *writhed* in the chair before stilling again. "I think you taunt me apurpose with that washcloth. My oath: I'll give you my title and all I'm worth if you'll but do it once again."

He sounded so very earnest.

Slowly she drew her washcloth over her ankle and up the rounded calf of her leg.

He shuddered.

When had she ever held such power?

She lifted her leg and washed behind her knee, without flourish or seduction, and he gritted his teeth and rotated his wrist on the bulge in his breeches.

Carefully she lowered that leg and lifted out her other foot to the rim of the tub, washing each toe just as diligently. The heat of the water and the rose perfume of the soap had made her almost drowsy. Lax and slow. She felt soft at her middle, warm and liquid, and after she'd finished with her legs, after he was panting in his chair and muttering under his breath, she closed her eyes and dipped the washcloth beneath the water.

Over her belly, through her curls, between her legs. She tilted her hips, swirling the washcloth in her cleft, parting her folds, delicately rubbing down, and then back up, to that little gathering of muscle, nerves, and skin at the top. She circled that spot gently with her washcloth, and felt a smile lift the corners of her mouth. So warm, so clean, so very, very good . . .

He gave a great shout and then she was being lifted out of the bathtub, water streaming off her everywhere. The fire hissed and she dropped the washcloth into the bathwater with a splash.

He wrapped her in a huge drying cloth and bore her to the enormous bed, talking all the while. "Séraphine, Séraphine, *Séraphine*. Will you drive me mad? Scatter my wits to the wind like so much chaff? Leave me a shell of a man, broken, hollowed of brain and soul, left with merely a throbbing prick like a mindless *goat*? Have mercy, I plead, O siren of chatelaines and unlovely bonnets! Let my famished mouth feast upon thy sweet, sweet flesh. I am awash in yearning spunk."

She stared up at him as he laid her on the freshly laundered sheets, still wrapped in the towel, and would've laughed except for the fact that he *did* look half-maddened, his eyes glaring, his brow gleaming, his fine nostrils flared, his beautiful mouth in a stern line. Gone were the flippant smiles, the indolent gestures, and the graceful laziness.

He knelt over her, still in waistcoat and that extravagantly billowing shirt, his muscles taut, his every nerve seemingly on edge.

Dangerous.

Was this what he was like? Underneath it all, the bare man? Was this what he was when he made love? No laughing aristocrat, but a man compelled by his own most primitive urges?

Was he like this with other women?

She watched, fascinated, aroused as he reached out lace-draped fingers and flicked the cloth away from her, unwrapping her like a cocooned butterfly.

"God," he said, "*God.*"

He attacked her throat and she was so startled by the sudden move that she squeaked. He was laving her with his tongue, openmouthed, and she moaned, arching, wondering wildly if this was the same man who wore pink silk coats and black velvet bows. This seemed so *base*, so animal. Not at all like the effete aristocrat she thought she knew.

He bit at her collarbone, licked down across a breast and suckled frankly on a nipple, drawing strongly and suddenly.

She grasped for his head, off-balance as if she were falling, even though she lay on a solid bed. His hair was silky beneath her hands, curling around her fingers.

But then he pulled away, tonguing under her breasts, each one, and down her belly, pausing to mouth her navel, and then thrusting her legs apart, climbing nimbly between, and thumbing wide her labia.

She gasped. "I...wait—"

But he'd already laid his mouth against her flesh, licking her there roughly as if he did indeed intend to devour her.

She'd never...that is...

She screamed, thrusting her hand into her mouth to muffle the sound as she came hard and fast.

But he didn't stop. He was pressing against her clitoris now with his tongue, firmly circling, and his thumbs... his thumbs were stroking her as well, burrowing deeper, gently seeking until one thrust frankly inside her and then out again. He kissed down, licking around his thumb, tonguing the flesh around her entrance, slowly building the pleasure again and it seemed...

She opened her eyes, staring dazedly at nothing, feeling the rolls of delight mounting...

It seemed as if he could do this forever. As if he took pleasure from what he was doing—such a low thing, such a *dirty* thing.

As if he *loved* what he was doing to her.

The thought sent an exquisite jolt through her and she closed her eyes on it, half drawing up her legs. He was... She had both hands tangled in his beautiful hair now, the ribbon had somehow gone and he was suckling on her clitoris and she was crying, moaning, as she came again, this time in a long, near-painful twisting wave.

Oh, God.

He was doing something, moving, but she'd lost her bones and could only half open her eyes.

She looked up in time to see him kneeling upright, his eyes gleaming, as he ripped open his falls. His penis was dark red and angrily erect, standing to his navel. He caught her hips and pulled her until she was on his lap, then he bent and, without ceremony, thrust himself within her.

"Now," he rasped, no grace, no drawl, no civility at all. "Come again for me *now*."

And he pulled her on and off his cock, rotating his hips all the while, his eyes on her, watching, waiting, as if she were the last drop of water in a desert.

As if she were his only hope of life.

His thick cock rubbed against her as she lay, sprawled and nude, a pagan sacrifice to his lust.

His lips parted and he panted, shoving into her faster, harder. "Come."

She shook her head against the sheets, her breasts heaving. She felt herself tingling, quivering, quickening, as if her veins ran with lightning.

His head fell back against his shoulders, his hips still thrusting, his hands hard on her bottom as he kept her wedded to him. "*Please*. Come."

She pushed her hand to the juncture of her thighs, where his penis rubbed in and out of her, and touched herself.

But he batted her hand away, replacing her fingers with his thumb, pressing down hard.

And she arched, screaming, the lightning blazing from her center, sparking through her limbs, flying out her fingertips.

She was incandescent.

He fell atop her, heavy and male, pulling her legs up around his narrow hips, and ground down into her, once, twice.

His cock jerked within her and she could feel every muscle in his body tense. He groaned into her ear like a man dying and then fell senseless and limp.

And as she followed him into exhausted slumber she heard his single word:

Mine.

THIS MORNING COPERNICUS Shrugg was attired in a brown coat over a high-necked, long, dark-red waistcoat, both of expensive material but of such a cut and with so few embellishments that they were nearly Puritan in style. In contrast his white wig sported a row of delicate little curls framing his sad hound's face.

Hugh found his gaze kept straying to those fairylike curls.

"I thought the matter finished, Your Grace," Shrugg was saying, his brows drawn together lugubriously as he poured tea. They were in his office at St James's Palace, though this time, since he hadn't been sent for in secret, Hugh had availed himself of the front entrance. "It didn't work out the way we would've liked, but you did your best and Himself is satisfied that it is over."

They both glanced reflexively overhead.

Hugh's gaze dropped back to the other man. "But is it?"

"What do you mean?" Shrugg asked, handing him a cup of tea.

Hugh nodded his thanks, though he'd never much liked tea. He sat back, holding the fragile teacup carefully in his big hand. "I've done some discreet questioning."

"And?"

Hugh ran his tongue over his teeth. "Did you look at the letter? The one Montgomery delivered in exchange for the King's nod?"

Shrugg looked nervous. "That was destroyed. There can be no point in—"

"Shrugg," Hugh said.

The other man stopped speaking.

"Humor me. What was in the letter?"

Shrugg licked his lips and motioned Hugh forward.

Hugh sighed and leaned in.

The older man whispered hoarsely. "It was a letter written in Prince William's own hand, discussing the Lords of Chaos and their next meeting. It talked of two very dissolute aristocrats and of the desecration of a church by satanic rites. There was"—Shrugg grimaced—"a rather graphic reference to the deflowering of a girl."

"And?"

Shrugg stared. "And? What do you mean, Your Grace? Is that not enough?"

"Was there any mention of Prince William's initiation?"

"No, not that I can remember. Why do you ask?"

"Because," Hugh said grimly, "according to my sources the Lords of Chaos always have an initiation for new members. And whatever happens at the initiation binds the man to the Lords forever."

Shrugg shook his head. "I don't—"

"Damn it, man, *think*," Hugh said impatiently. "Whatever they do, the initiate is afraid to leave the Lords of Chaos lest they inform others about both his involvement in the heinous cabal and the terrible act that was done at the initiation—*and Montgomery has this information on*

Prince William. He can still blackmail the King should he wish to do so."

"I don't..." Shrugg blinked rapidly. "I don't follow. He gave us the letter. *That* was the blackmail material."

"But was it the *only* blackmail material Montgomery had?" Hugh thrust his dainty teacup onto the desktop and set his elbows on his knees as he thought aloud. "He always keeps something back, Montgomery does—most blackmailers do—and you must admit the letter he *did* surrender, as you tell it, sounds damnably weak."

"But the deflowering..." Shrugg muttered.

Hugh shot him an exasperated look. "If deflowering maidens were blackmail material, the entire aristocracy would have its pockets to let. No"—he shook his head, leaning back in his chair and ignoring the protesting creak it gave—"this entire matter has been a mess from the start. Mostly my fault, I realize—I shouldn't have tried to burgle Montgomery's house, though there wasn't much choice at the time—but whoever gave the order to have him poisoned was a rank fool."

Shrugg started. "*What?*"

"Ah. Didn't know that, did you?"

"No, of course not."

Hugh arched an eyebrow. "Montgomery was vomiting and shaking for three days. Almost didn't make it, as I understand it."

For a moment the older man had a vague, calculating look in his eye, as if he were doing sums in his head.

"It must've been..." But whatever name Shrugg had been about to say was cut off when he pressed his lips firmly together. He shook his head. "You know how these things work. Upstarts with their own circles of information, jockeying for favor. Someone thought he could simply cut out all the intrigue and diplomacy and kill the root of the problem. Literally, unfortunately."

"Yes, well, imagine had he succeeded," Hugh replied. "*That* would've done nothing but rouse interest in Montgomery—and, through him, possibly Prince William. Who knows where he's put his blackmail letters? What if they're with a man of business and set to be published on his death? The whole thing could've blown up in our faces."

Shrugg actually shuddered at the thought.

"As it is," Hugh murmured, "we only have to wonder what happened to the footman."

"I... what?"

Hugh looked at him. "The footman, my informant—and someone's paid poisoner. He's missing and I'll lay money on what's happened to him."

"Surely not." Shrugg looked truly distressed, which rather amused Hugh, considering how much scandal and intrigue the man must've seen in his lifetime in his position. "Montgomery's a *duke*. He can't be a murderer."

Hugh lifted his shoulders. "He's also a blackmailer. Many would prefer the former to the latter, given the choice."

Shrugg had gone white to the lips. "Dear Lord."

"Probably the bottom of the Thames," Hugh mused. "If he was weighted well enough."

There was a short silence.

Shrugg broke it finally, looking just a little green around the edges. "Wh... what do you suggest we do, Your Grace?"

Hugh raised his eyebrows. He would've thought it was obvious, but maybe not to a deskman such as Shrugg. "I'll have to keep after him, won't I?" He stood, looking down on Shrugg's little curls. "We can't rest until the Duke of Montgomery is stopped." He thought a moment more, and added, "And the Lords of Chaos as well."

VAL WOKE TO a cold, empty bed and the realization that he'd done something incredibly stupid.

It was an odd sensation—he rarely if ever regretted a decision or action once made. Why bother? What was done was past changing. But this one... well, he had the feeling this one might very well haunt him.

And where the hell was she?

He stared at the indented pillow beside his head. He had the memory of a warm body in his arms all night, round buttocks snuggled tight to his loins, hot and soft, and now?

Now there was only cold.

He had the vague recollection that it was the chill that had waked him, and that was her fault as well.

He sat up and met the green eyes of the demon cat, standing upon the tray of cold food from the night before. It had a chicken wing between its fangs and at his yell it jumped down and dashed away out the cracked doors.

The inner door that led to a dressing room opened and Mehmed and the dog came running in. The dog immediately rushed to the tray and tried to gulp down the rest of the food.

"Duke!" Mehmed exclaimed as he attempted fruitlessly to pull the terrier away from the tray. "Are you hurt?"

"No." Val ran his hand over his head, feeling the tangles in his hair. She'd threaded her fingers in his curls last night as he'd tongued her. She'd tasted of salt and woman and want.

He pushed the memory aside as he climbed from the bed. He still wore his clothes from the night before, rumpled and—he sniffed beneath his arm—sadly smelling. He buttoned his falls.

"Call the footmen. Tell them to empty the bathtub and send up fresh hot water, tea, eggs—" He waved his hand impatiently. "And all the usual. Damn it, where is Mrs. Crumb?"

Mehmed shrugged. "I don't know, Duke. You take her to bed, huh? Maybe make her your sultana now?"

"What?" For a moment Val stared absently after the boy as he went to the doors and spoke to the footman outside.

When he returned Val was frowning. "It's *duchess*. And no, Mrs. Crumb won't be my duchess. She's a bloody housekeeper." Despite that telling white streak in her hair. *Oh, Séraphine, what secrets you have kept from me*...

Mehmed began picking up the debris from the night before. "Many great sultanas come from lowest ranks of the harem. They are slaves when first they enter the harem."

"Yes, well, that is in the lands where the Ottomans rule. This is England, which is entirely different," Val said, feeling increasingly irritable. "And besides they are allowed three wives while we poor Christians are accorded but one."

"Is sad for Christians," agreed Mehmed. "Maybe you become Muslim, yes? And then you can take Mrs. Crumb as wife and also two others."

Val winced. "Thank you, Mehmed, but I rather like my foreskin where it is. That price is rather too rich for my tastes. Not to mention I'd probably have to forfeit my dukedom."

"You not notice," the boy said earnestly, throwing his arms wide. The dog took the opportunity of his distraction to steal the last bit of cheese off the supper tray. "I not notice when they cut it off me."

"You were a *baby*," Val shouted, and then, in normal tones, "Oh, thank the gods," as the footmen *finally* brought in fresh hot water.

With them, though, came the butler, whose name Val had already forgotten. The man's face was dolorous. "Your Grace."

"What?" He really wasn't in the mood for more bad news. He watched avidly as a parade of footmen drained the tub—taking away the cold water—and began filling it with fresh hot water.

The butler cleared his throat. Perhaps he had a cold. "The…erm…master of the hounds bid me tell you…erm…"

Slowly Val swiveled his head, pinning the butler with his gaze. "Ye-es?"

The butler went into a paroxysm of throat-clearing and coughing. Perhaps he had the ague. Perhaps Val would need a new butler soon.

"I…" The man finally got out, "I…I…I…he couldn't find her. The lady on the moors. She disappeared and the master of the foxhounds couldn't find her and is too much of a coward to tell you so himself. Erm. Your Grace."

For a moment Val only breathed quietly, his eyes turning to slits as he stared at the bringer of very bad news indeed.

Then he flung his arms wide and bellowed. "Away! Away, you pestilence, you flies, you midges of ruination! Get thee back to thy kitchens of destruction and God damn thy lips and thy words and thine eyes! Away, I say, and never come again! A plague and a flood of amphibians upon the lot of you!"

There was a general rush to the door and then silence.

Mehmed, who hadn't moved, looked sorrowfully at the bathtub and the surrounding steaming pitchers. "The bath, it is only half-full, Duke."

"Well, then fill it," Val snapped, and went to sulk in the bed over the perfidy of women and one woman in particular.

Chapter Thirteen

Well, Prue gave her father a worried look, but the magician merely said, "In order to find your heart, you must complete three trials, the first of which is to spin a wagonload of wool into yarn by the light of the moon."
King Heartless stared at the magician. "Spinning is women's work."
"Yes." The magician beamed. "My daughter, Prue, can help you." . . .
—From *King Heartless*

Washing tons of linens was a backbreaking chore, but an oddly satisfying one, Bridget thought. She'd found the washhouse—an ancient low room beside the kitchens. Three great kettles were boiling merrily away and three of the dozen or so washerwomen she'd hired yesterday were stirring the pots slowly with long wooden paddles. At one end of a long table, several women were laboriously wringing the wet linens, while at the other end, two women were ironing the laundry that had already dried to just damp.

They'd been working since six this morning.

Bridget raised the edge of her apron to blot the sweat on her brow and upper lip.

"Naturally I find you surrounded by warm clouds and billowing white cloths," Val drawled in her ear, making her jump.

She whirled to find him standing right behind her. He wore slate blue today, the color nearly severe on him, his curling golden hair clubbed neatly back, his azure eyes watching her alertly for any weakness.

Oh, God, he'd had his *mouth* on her most intimate parts last night. What had possessed her to let him do that? It was as if she'd been in some sort of sensual dream. The hot bath, his words, his hands, his *lips*...

He smiled and she knew, she absolutely *knew* that *he* knew what she was thinking about.

She turned and nearly ran from the washhouse.

The courtyard of the castle was bright this morning, but sadly neglected, she noticed absently as she hurried along the path to the kitchens.

"I rather thought to have a stroll as well," he said from beside her. He wasn't even out of breath, the knave.

He reached over and plucked off her mobcap.

She stopped and glared at him, her hands flying to her hair. The white streak was there for anyone to see. He must've noticed it last night, but he hadn't mentioned it. Perhaps he didn't realize the significance.

Her mother's hair was completely white, after all.

For some reason he grinned, flashing perfect teeth. He tossed the mobcap over his shoulder and she started for it, but he grabbed her arm. "No. You've cost me a wife. They told me this morning that Miss Royle was not to be found. The least you could do is forfeit that bloody cap."

She swallowed, staring at him. She was glad, of course,

that Miss Royle had escaped, but she wondered what he really wanted of her.

It was morning now. The fairy dust of the night had blown away. She was a housekeeper and he a duke. He couldn't possibly...

"Stop thinking," he said, and started walking, compelling her to do so as well. "It's dreadfully tedious. Do you know that this morning Mehmed suggested I amputate my foreskin?"

"I...*what*?" She would've stopped and stared at him again, but they'd reached a door to the inside and he was pulling her along.

"*Amputate* my *foreskin*," he repeated loudly just as they passed a carpenter working on the stairs. Val, naturally, didn't seem to notice the man, but Bridget felt herself flush and the carpenter dropped his hammer. "You *do* know what a foreskin is?" he asked kindly as they mounted the stairs. "It's the—"

"I *know* what a foreskin is," she hissed. "*Why* are you so loud?"

"I'm a duke?" He shrugged. "Why should I lower my voice? It's a lovely voice, resonant and mellow. I should think everyone would like to hear it."

"Oh, for—"

"But since we're making general complaints," he continued over her mutter, "*why* weren't you a virgin?"

"I never said I was a virgin," she retorted primly as they gained the upper floor. She was rather surprised when instead of turning toward his bedroom they went left along a corridor.

"There was a clear implication."

"Only by you." She sighed, feeling a bit grubby next to his usual elegance, but oddly exhilarated that he'd sought her out. That he cared enough to come and... bicker with her? "Why does it matter anyway?"

"Well, it really doesn't," he admitted, "at least not to me. Although when one goes into the act with expectations of one thing and instead finds quite another... well, it doesn't seem exactly correct, does it?"

"You could have stopped if it upset you so much," she said sweetly.

"*Could* I have, though?" he replied, sounding not a little troubled. "The problem is, I really don't think so. And that, dear, dear Brid-*get*, is not only unprecedented but also alarming."

He was silent a moment as they turned down another passage, which gave her time to think about his words and wonder if they were a compliment. As with practically everything that fell from his lips, it was nearly impossible to tell.

"*And*," he said suddenly as if there'd been no momentary lapse. "How did you lose your virginity anyway?"

She glanced at him sideways under her eyelashes. "I thought you said it didn't matter to you."

"It doesn't," he said vehemently. "I put to you, what is a maidenhead, after all, but a tiny bit of flesh so insubstantial that a hard ride—no pun intended—can destroy it? Now a *foreskin*, that's a sturdy bit of flesh, much more significant, and, really, quite important to my own life, I feel. No, your virginity, or lack thereof, doesn't affect me. But *how* you lost it might be of grave interest, for there are many ways to lose a hymen, some *quite* unpleasant." He looked at her and smiled that sweet little boy's smile. "Do I need to kill anyone?"

And she knew he would.

That realization really ought to appall her—that this insane man would, on her word alone, somehow find a stranger and kill him.

Just for her.

She took a deep breath, remembering the spotty-faced young butcher's apprentice from so very long ago now. "No, you don't have to kill anyone."

"Oh, good," he said. "Who?"

"What?"

"Who was it?" he asked as they reached a door at the juncture of two corridors. He opened it and gestured her in.

"I don't think that's any of your business," she said absently. The door led to a winding staircase that went up. They must be at one of the castle towers. She glanced over her shoulder to find him right behind her, his head cocked and his eyes on . . . her ankles?

His gaze met hers. "Of course it's none of my business, but that's not the point. I want to know."

She faced forward again and began the ascent. "How would you like it if I asked about all of your lovers, Your Grace?"

"Oho, we're 'Your Grace'-ing now, are we? As it happens, I wouldn't mind at all reciting my paramours. No, the problem comes when we get to the sheer *size* of the list. I started at twelve, you see."

She stopped and turned on the wedge-shaped stair.

He was looking up at her, both hands casually braced

on the tower walls. The circular stairwell had deep slit windows set into the stone and a beam of sunlight was striking his head, haloing his golden hair.

He looked absolutely angelic.

"*Twelve?*" she demanded, appalled.

He winked. "An upper housemaid, all of nineteen, if I recollect correctly, and an enterprising sort. I believe she was after a Montgomery bastard. She gave the most magnificent tongue-lashing to my infant loins. Which reminds me, how do you stand on the matter of—?"

But she'd already turned and was hurrying up the stairwell. *Twelve.* How could parents let a child be ravished so? Even if he'd apparently enjoyed it. That was far too young an age to lose one's innocence.

Bridget felt tears prick at her eyes as she emerged into the tower room itself.

Had Val *ever* been allowed to be innocent?

She went to a window to stare out, sightlessly.

He came up behind her. "I used to watch them from this tower."

She swiped at her eyes with her sleeve, trying to steady her breath. "Who?"

"My father." She felt more than saw his shrug. "And others. They called themselves the Lords of Chaos. A secret society. They still exist, d'you believe it? I didn't know until recently. Anyway, my father was their leader. Their Dionysus. They'd hold their revels here once a year."

She looked over her shoulder and saw that the smile was gone from his face. "What did they do?"

Another shrug. "Drink. Dance. Rape." He sighed like a forlorn little boy. "The usual."

She swallowed, keeping very, very still lest she disturb his words.

He inhaled. "I was supposed to be the next Dionysus—it's hereditary, the title shared between the Montgomerys and another family in turn. So you could say it was part of my inheritance: the title, the lands, and the mastery of a mad band of idiots, dancing and fucking in the moonlight. I was readied on the appropriate night, tattooed with Dionysus's dolphin, all prepared to go through with it. But then, you see, Father brought down Eve..." He looked at her finally and his azure eyes held no light in them. "She grew up here, Father's bastard by my nursemaid, and five years my junior. I'd hide her from the revels because... well. It was best to do so. But that night I was supposed to be initiated and I'd left it to her mother, and..." He shook his head, glancing away, his nostrils flared. "*Stupid.* So stupid."

She laid her hand on his sleeve and he stared at it, talking. "I looked up from the banquet table and there she was in a lady's dress, far too fine for her, and I knew, I knew, I *knew* what was to happen, but I was seated next to Father and when he released the foxhounds I *couldn't*—"

He was gasping as if he were drowning, his hands clenched into fists, and Bridget did the only thing she could.

She took him into her arms, holding him steady, holding him tight.

He was shaking against her as if he'd been poisoned again and she let herself slide to the floor, taking him with her so they ended in a pile on the cold stones.

He didn't seem to mind, though. Or even notice.

Dear God, setting foxhounds on a *child*, his *own* child…

"She was…," he choked into her hair. "When I finally got there. A grown man. With his fingers *in* her. Hurting her. There was blood. And her face. Her little face…"

He shuddered once more and suddenly stilled.

Bridget had to remind herself that she *knew* Eve Dinwoody. That the woman was whole and well and about to be married. That she was happy, whatever had happened to her in the past.

They sat for at least five minutes on that hard, cold floor and she began to think that he'd gone to sleep.

And then Val sat up.

He smiled at her and there was no trace of tears on his face or in his clear, bright eyes. "Well. I beat that man to a bloody pulp you can be sure. And got Eve out of England and away from Father, of course. First time I'd traveled to the Continent—and I found my schoolroom French quite inadequate." He glanced around the room. "I've always wondered if this might once have been a lady's solarium."

She stared at him. Had…had the emotional storm been entirely fabricated? But the shaking, the anguish in his voice…

He'd risen and was holding out his hand to her now.

"Val," she said as he helped her up. "How old were you?"

"Hm?" He was poking at a crumbling bit of masonry. "What?"

"When you were initiated into…into the Lords of Chaos," she asked. "How old were you?"

"Oh, I was never initiated," he said. "Ran away with Eve instead, which ruined the whole thing. By the time I returned Father was in a snit and not talking to me. Just as well, really. The initiation is meant to bind one to the Lords, so they usually make it particularly nasty. I think Father meant for me to rape Eve and then kill her."

Her mouth opened, but no sound came out. How could it? She'd never conceived of such evil.

"Oh, and I was seventeen." He smiled at her, all azure eyes, dimples, and golden hair. "Hardly learned to shave, really."

She couldn't stop them this time. The tears overflowed her eyes and coursed down her cheeks. *Seventeen.* And what had happened in the years between? What had those wolves, his *parents*, done to him?

His eyes widened almost comically. "What is it? Why are you crying? Was it something I said? I lied: I started shaving at fifteen, but there really wasn't much point. Took me *forever* to grow in a decent beard. Séraphine. *Bridget.* Please don't cry."

But she couldn't stop. She simply couldn't.

They'd broken him, those wolves. They'd taken a beautiful, bright boy, and broken him with their depraved cruelty until he didn't even know how to respond to his own sorrow.

Worse, they'd tried to turn him into one of them.

He wrapped his arms around her and he held her as she'd held him and as he did so, she looked through watery eyes at the tower. He was right: it did look like a lady's solarium. Dainty Gothic arches marched all the way around the walls, with narrow windows inset between. Most held diamond-paned glass, but two panels were stained glass. The first depicted a knight, helm under his arm, golden head bowed. Opposite him was a black-haired lady, weeping. Perhaps the lady wept for the same reason Bridget did.

Because he couldn't.

VAL WAS NOT used to waiting on a lover.

On anyone, really, but on a lover in particular. Oh, there had been the odd lady playing catch me if you can, but once caught, once bedded, most had been quite biddable.

It'd been he who had wandered away. He who had kept others waiting.

To be at leisure all day, impatient and longing, turning at every feminine heel click, at the close of a door…it was very odd.

And all for such a reason!

Madness.

He said as much to her when at last she deigned to join him that night.

"I don't see why you're in such a bother," Bridget replied, eyes closed, head resting on the high back of his bathtub. "I am your housekeeper. What else would I be doing but keeping your house?"

He regarded her with disfavor. Well, not her *body*—that he regarded with fine favor indeed—but her, well, the *rest*. Something wasn't right when the housekeeper lectured the duke on her proper position.

"Yes, but can't you find someone else to do all"—he waved his hand vaguely—"*that*?"

"No," she said, sounding distressingly *un*-distressed about his distress. "We have nearly all the washing done and most of the lower floors aired. The carpenter finished on the banister and I've had the stoneworkers in to look at the masonry around some of the windows. All in all it's been a lovely day. So much done."

"But not with me." He crossed his legs and his arms in his now-customary chair.

The remains of their supper lay beside the bathtub. He'd had visions of feeding her from his own hand before she'd said very practically that he'd make a mess of beef pie dripping with gravy and it'd be much better if she just ate it herself.

"I don't see why you're so intent on cleaning the castle in any case," he said a bit sulkily. "It's not as if I'll be spending long here."

"It's my work," she said, her voice even, "and I *like* my work. It's quite satisfying."

Well, *that* was patently sheer nonsense. He threw up his hands even though her eyes remained shut and thus were deprived of his gesture. Perhaps she was attempting to drive him mad with delayed lust.

If so, her plot was working.

"How long has it been since someone has lived here anyway?" she murmured drowsily.

He narrowed his eyes. If she fell asleep from all her ridiculous work, he might have to commit an act of somnophilia. "My mother died two years ago."

"And you never bothered coming back?"

He was silent.

She opened her eyes, looking at him. Lately he'd noticed that her glances had a sort of…searching quality to them, but what she was looking for, he hadn't quite determined.

"Why?" she asked softly.

He shook his head.

"When were you last here?"

He glanced up at the ceiling and was surprised. Some enterprising maid had dusted and polished it during the day, no doubt under Bridget's direction. The wood had taken on a mellow, almost honey gleam in the firelight. It looked... warm. He cocked his head, staring. Odd. He'd never thought Father's chambers warm.

"Val?" she murmured.

"Hm?" His gaze drifted down to her breasts, floating, plump and savory, on the water. Her nipples were soft and rosy. He wanted to lick them.

"Val?"

He blinked and met her eyes, fiery dark. Ainsdale Castle. That's what they were discussing. Right. "Oh. Well, I left England shortly after Father died. That was in '30, so nearly twelve years ago."

"You haven't been home since you were..."

"Nineteen." He nodded.

"I see." Her eyes burned intently.

What did she see? Madness, murder, mayhem, and misery? Or merely a chest hollowed out, desolate of humanity and kindness?

Did it matter to him?

"And your mother?" she asked, the quiet pop of the fire the only sound in the room. "Did you come back for her funeral?"

"No," he said. "Neither final illness nor funeral. She would have wished it so. My mother hated me."

"I..." She blinked. At his words? At the steam from the bath? Because she was sleepy? He couldn't tell and didn't know. It was like trying to understand the song of the birds—completely incomprehensible and completely frustrating. "I'm sorry?"

"Are you?" He cocked his head. Was this how people communicated? Mostly with his lovers he fucked. But he wanted...he *wanted* to somehow...talk...to his... housekeeper. "I'm not. I didn't particularly like her, either. She tended to tell me that I was just like my father, whom she *also* hated." He shrugged. "We looked very alike."

"Oh."

She stared at him a moment, burning eyes wide, and for a moment he wondered if she would weep again. That had been very distressing to him and he very much wished that she wouldn't.

"Did you know," he said rapidly, "that in Istanbul they smoke their tobacco pipes through water?"

She leaned a little forward. "What?"

"Yes." He nodded earnestly, pleased he'd caught her attention. "The men in their turbans and draperies, quite colorful, really, lounge about on great cushions and smoke through enormous pipes." He drew with his hands in the air. "Tall contraptions made of bronze and very elegantly chased. There's an upper bowl where the tobacco is placed and lit, and then a long, hollow tube, which leads to the base, also hollow, where a basin of water lies. A thin pipe extends from the base and the smoker must suck very strongly in order to draw his smoke."

She was watching him with a little half smile, his Séraphine, and were he not an empty man he might feel joy.

"I would like to see such a thing," she said. "Did you try this water pipe?"

"Of course," he replied. "I took to wearing the Ottoman's loose, flowing breeches and shirts as well. And a long overcoat. It was white striped in purple and quite lovely." He glanced at her amused eyes. "I brought it back with me, along with one of the water pipes. I'll show it to you one day."

"Will you?" she whispered, and turned her head so he could see only her profile.

"Yes," he murmured, watching as her eyelashes lowered, veiling her expression. "Perhaps I'll take you there, to far-off Istanbul. You can see the bearded men smoking their water pipes, and the domed buildings, and the tall minarets from which their priests sing their prayers, and the spice markets, and the quiet tiled inner courtyards where fountains play." He got up and moved behind her. "They keep harems, those sultans, you know. Their women live behind beautiful screens so that no other man may see them."

She shuddered. "That sounds terrible."

He shrugged. "It's their way, so I suppose they don't see it as terrible. Sometimes I would glimpse a woman's eye, peeking from behind a screen in my host's courtyard. She'd have kohl smeared around her eyes, and silk draped over her face and head."

He knelt behind the bathtub and leaned over her shoulder, bringing his hands around to cup her breasts. He watched as he circled her nipples, slowly awakening them from their slumber.

"It's tempting. I can see why those Ottomans hide their women. If I could, I might dress you in silk—deep-red silk—and put you away where no other man might see you."

She turned her head to glare at him, those dark eyes sparking. "I shouldn't like that."

He smiled at her fondly, almost sadly. This woman—why did he want *this* woman so very much?

"I know." He sipped at her lips lightly—so lightly. "And yet, as I say, tempting."

He caught her lips with his, widening her mouth, tasting red wine and gravy, apples, and her, all her. Bridget, Séraphine, *her.*

Her.

Her.

Her.

He groaned into her mouth, thrusting in his tongue, taking advantage, *wanting*, lusting, his cock rampant. He took her, lifting her out of the bathwater, a repeat of the previous evening, he'd lost all the finesse he'd ever learned apparently, and, wrapping her in a drying cloth, he backed into the chair, sitting down with her in his lap.

Still kissing her.

He'd kiss her until the day he died, if he had his druthers.

The drying cloth around her body fell to her hips. He tugged off the cloth wrapped around her head and let her damp hair fall about her shoulders, spreading it with his fingers.

She drew back, panting. "Oh, you shouldn't."

"Oh, I should," he retorted. "I desire your hair. If I could, I'd wrap it about my cock and pull till I spilled."

She looked at him a little oddly. "It's so coarse. Like a horse's mane."

He laughed. "Then I desire a horse's mane."

He spread the heavy strands between his fingers and then drew a lock over his lips.

She smelled of roses.

"Are you going to take off your clothes this time?" she asked.

"No," he replied, quite certain. "It seems I've regressed to fifteen with the attendant urgency and if I pause to divest myself of raiment, I run the risk of quitting the table too early."

"That hardly seems very fair, considering how many times you paraded around nude in front of me."

"You noticed!" he said, delighted. "Was I not magnificent? I shall make you a bargain. You may see my body *afterward*."

And then he lifted her a little and fastened his mouth on her nipple, for he hadn't been lying about his urgency.

She moaned, all warm, damp woman in his hands, breasts in his face, thighs over his legs, astride him like a female dragoon, and he wanted to *inhale* her. To drink her in and keep her.

Possibly forever.

He wanted to lick her cunt again, make her cream for him, make her scream and writhe, but the angle was wrong and he made a vow: no more baths before bed—they were just too much for his frayed nerves. Instead he drew hard upon her sweet little nipple and plunged his hand between her thighs.

She was wet. Oh, sweet, wonderful woman! She was wet already, slippery and soft and ready for him.

He turned his hand in the confined space between their bodies and she groaned.

He looked up and saw her, his archangel, head tossed back, black hair a cloud, burning, burning bright.

He caught the back of her neck and kissed her, deeply, ruthlessly, because there was nothing else to do.

Keep her. Hold her.

He worked the falls of his breeches with his other hand and freed his grotesquely engorged cock, weeping, pleading for surcease.

Raised her arse a little, placed himself at that hot, wet paradise, and thrust.

She opened her eyes as he pulled his face away, watching her.

He thrust again. The way was tight. Narrow. She was wet, but she hadn't yet come tonight.

Her mouth opened, a strand of hair caught on her shining lips.

God.

He thrust again. *Hard.* And was home.

Burning fire surrounded him. He'd never be cold again.

He could stay like this, cock beautifully lodged in her, all night. Watching her. Perhaps he'd enjoy a glass of wine.

He smiled a little at the thought.

She swallowed, the line of her throat moving.

And then *she* moved.

Kneeling up a bit.

Oh.

Well...

She brought herself down again. Gently. Firmly. Sliding him into her passage. She even swiveled a bit once she'd settled herself fully.

He gasped.

That. That wasn't fair at all.

He reached up to still her, but...

She was doing it *again*. But faster. And harder.

And she was *magnificent*, riding him, beautiful and stern, and...he tried to think of words. To tell her. But they flew away.

So instead he brought her face to his and kissed her helplessly as she ravished him, body and soul. Kissed his nemesis, his salvation, maybe his death.

He watched as she went up in flames.

Burning like an archangel, glorious, frightening, awesome.

And when he caught fire as well, when he emptied his loins into her furnace, in groaning, exquisite jerks, all he could think was this:

His Séraphine thought that deep inside him was a golden core—a good man who could be redeemed.

She was wrong.

And when she plumbed his depths and discovered instead a frozen hollow, she would do what she must.

She would leave him.

Chapter Fourteen

So that night King Heartless and Prue went to the castle gardens. Prue nervously took a spindle and some wool and showed the king how to spin.

"You aren't very good at this," the king said as his yarn broke.

"Well, neither are you!" Prue retorted before thinking. After that the king hardly spoke save to swear horribly and in the morning Prue was very happy to still be alive....

—From King Heartless

The Duke of Montgomery slept as he did everything else: easily, elegantly, and gracefully.

More beautifully than any other person living.

Bridget gazed down thoughtfully on the sleeping man the next morning. He lay sprawled upon the freshly laundered sheets, one arm arced over his head, his golden curls tumbled upon the pillows, his straight nose profiled against the sheets. His lips were a little parted, but he did not snore—no, not he. His stubble was gilt and merely highlighted the perfect angles of his jaw. The bedcovers were pushed to his thighs, his other hand resting on a taut belly. His chest was smoothly muscled and unblemished, the few golden hairs between his pectorals highlighting his masculinity. One leg was bent and his cock, thick and long this morning, lay along the crease of his thigh. The foreskin—his precious foreskin, she remembered with some amusement—was stretched a bit taut, revealing the very tip of his head, gleaming and pink.

He was perfect. Her lover.

Bridget pursed her lips, giving that lovely penis one last lingering glance before turning to the door and leaving the room quietly.

It seemed very strange that this man should be her lover, for however short a time it might be. Even if he were not a duke, even if, in some other world, he were a footman or a butler—a man of her own rank and station in life—it would be a strange fit. He was a beautiful, otherworldly creature, and she?

She was just ordinary. From her horse's-mane hair to her sturdy, practical feet, she'd never turned men's heads. Oh, she wasn't ill-favored—her features were regular enough—but she knew, too, that she wasn't the sort of woman whom men flirted with. Whom men stared at. She'd had a few admirers in the past, but they hadn't been a multitude.

She was unremarkable.

The Duke of Montgomery was anything but.

Perhaps, then, that was what drew him to her—her very normality. Val was just quixotic enough to become fascinated—for a short time—by the prosaic.

That was quite a depressing thought, but Bridget faced it practically. She knew that whatever else happened they were not meant to be together for any length of time. It was too ludicrous a concept—like a racehorse yoked to a plow horse.

And what drew her to him? Oh, she could try to fool herself. Pretend that she sought out the duke only in order to try to help him recognize right from wrong, try to mend his wicked, wicked ways.

But that was a child's game—because while she did want to help him find the better part of himself, that wasn't the real reason *she* stayed.

The truth was much simpler. For the first time in her life she was doing something strictly for herself: she was letting go of propriety, reason, logic, even morality, she supposed.

She was making love to Val. Selfishly. Because she *wanted* to. Because he was everything she'd been denied in life—everything she'd denied herself: laughter and wit and books and adventure. Lust and sensuality. Silks and hot baths. Warm dogs and warmer bed linen.

He was sin itself and if she was a sinner for a little while, she'd pay the price and gladly.

And if that price was a child?

Oh, that wouldn't be so very bad, either.

She was a bastard herself. If she had a child by him, she'd *keep* her babe and no matter how hard it might be to make her way in the future at least she'd never be alone again.

Bridget made the kitchen door and checked as always that her apparel was in order—minus her mobcap. By this time no doubt the entire staff must suspect that she was sleeping with the duke, but she wasn't going to flaunt the fact, and she certainly wasn't going to let any rumors affect her authority in any way.

She opened the doors and sailed into the kitchens. "Good morning."

"Morning," grunted Mrs. Smithers as she kneaded dough of some kind.

While she hadn't the same rapport with the Ainsdale cook that she had with Mrs. Bram, nevertheless Mrs. Smithers was far more accommodating, in her own taciturn way, than she had been when Bridget first arrived.

Which she proved immediately by jerking her chin at one of the scullery maids. "Quit yer dozin', Ann, and get a cup of tea for Mrs. Crumb."

Bridget accepted her teacup gratefully, smiling her thanks to the little maid as she took a seat at the kitchen table across from Mr. Dwight.

"Good morning, Mrs. Crumb," the butler said cheerfully. Bridget had noticed he was rather alarmingly awake in the mornings. "Will you be seeing to the upper floors today?"

"I think so, yes, Mr. Dwight," she replied, tucking into the porridge set before her. She had to admit that Mrs. Smithers made a fine, hearty porridge. "I understand many of the rooms haven't been opened in years?"

He shook his head, pursing his lips. "My aunt said they were shut up before Her Grace took ill."

Bridget nodded. It was a money-saving measure she approved of—why heat and maintain rooms not in use?—but there were bound to be vermin and other unpleasant surprises in such places if they weren't at least checked once in a while.

The kitchen door opened and Mehmed bounded in with

Pip at his heels. The little dog made a beeline to Bridget, setting his paws upon her knees for a good-morning pat.

She took the last bite of her porridge. "I'll be just a moment," she told Mr. Dwight, and then went into the inner courtyard with the boy and the dog.

Pip immediately trotted over to water the ancient oak.

"It is very cold here," Mehmed said mournfully, both arms wrapped around his shoulders. "I think I shall freeze in the winter. The duke says the sky will turn to ice and bits of it will fall in tiny pieces of white."

"The duke likes to be dramatic," Bridget murmured as she watched Pip race about the inner courtyard.

She glanced up at the widow's tower standing sentinel over the castle, and remembered Val telling her what he'd watched from that tower. This place had witnessed debauchery, vice, and cruelty beyond her imagining and yet they had left no mark upon the old gray stones. The castle stood immune and impartial.

Were she the housekeeper of this place, she'd plant a vegetable garden here, right by the kitchen door. Herbs and lettuces, peas, carrots, and radishes, all bounded neatly by tiny box hedges. And farther on she would hire gardeners to lay down straight, level paths of gravel, train pears and apples and plums against the inner walls, and plant roses and irises for the lady of the house to admire as she walked her paths.

That's what she would do if she were the housekeeper of Ainsdale Castle.

"Mrs. Crumb!"

Bridget started from her reverie at Mehmed's happy shout and turned to the boy.

He was standing with Pip. "Mrs. Crumb, I forgot to tell you. Yesterday I teach Pip to sit."

Bridget raised her eyebrows, because the little terrier wasn't in fact sitting. "Yes?"

"Watch!"

The boy turned toward the dog and thrust his hands straight in the air above his head. "Pip!"

The dog barked and went into a play bow.

"Pip! SIT!" Mehmed shouted, bringing his hands down commandingly before him.

Immediately the terrier leaped up, barking madly, ran around the boy three times...

And sat in front of him.

"Oh." Bridget pressed her hand to her mouth because she did *not* want to laugh at the boy. "How very extraordinary."

Mehmed beamed. "I think this is much better sit than you try, yes?"

"Oh, yes indeed," Bridget agreed.

"Pip very good at sit now," Mehmed said, looking at the dog, who had almost immediately risen from his sit to wander about again.

"Yes, well, I'm afraid I shall have to start my work now," Bridget said. "Will you attend the duke?"

Mehmed looked a little glum. "He not wake up for long time still. He say only pli-bee-un wake up before noon." He looked at her and shook his head. "I not know what pli-bee-un is."

"Us," Bridget growled. "And he *would* say that."

"Dukes can sleep all day. We can't." He darted her a rather sly glance. "But he very sad when you not there yesterday."

She did not reply to that, but her heart skipped a beat, silly thing.

"Would you like to help me air and clean closed-up rooms?" she enquired as she walked toward the kitchen door.

"Ye-es?" Mehmed replied doubtfully.

"Or," she added, "you and Pip could see if there's any work to do in the stables."

"Yes, very well!" he said, immediately brightening and starting for a different door to the castle, one that was much closer to the back and the stables. "Come, Pip, come!"

The dog raced after him.

"Don't let him be trampled by horses!" Bridget called after the boy.

He waved cheerfully and disappeared into the door with the dog.

Bridget sighed and turned to the kitchen door. She had her troops to gather.

The morning was spent in opening and cleaning three rooms in the upper west wing, at the opposite end of the castle from Val's bedroom. It was quite filthy work and Bridget mourned her mobcap, which had been missing since Val had torn it from her head yesterday.

She suspected that he'd burned it.

At the moment she was supervising the clearing of the third room, which evidently had been used as a catchall, as it was full of tables and other unused furniture. Two footmen carefully moved a heavy mahogany sideboard from the wall, revealing something cloth-draped leaning against the paneling.

Bridget gingerly pulled off the cloth, mindful of the layer of dust on it.

Then she froze, staring.

It was a life-size portrait of a boy. A beautiful, golden boy, not more than seven or eight years old, but already wearing a sky-blue suit, white lace falling at his throat and wrists, diamond buckles on his shoes. He was formally posed, a foot outthrust, the opposite hand on his waist, a pink velvet cape with ermine trim draped over one shoulder and arm. The other hand held a small, jeweled dagger, offered to the viewer.

The boy stood in a stateroom of some sort. Draperies and formal furniture on either side of him. Bridget had seen portraits of aristocratic children in other homes. Unlike those children, this boy had no pets, no toys, and no trappings of childhood about him.

He stood alone in a world of adults.

And his azure eyes were unbearably sad.

"She hated me even then."

Bridget turned to find Val eyeing the sad little boy dispassionately. "I would've thought she'd have that burned years ago. I remember sitting for the painter. I couldn't stand still, but my father wanted the portrait. She told me if I didn't stand still she'd chop off my ears." He smiled at Bridget as if sharing a joke. "I was too young to realize she'd never do it. Father would've killed her had she marred his heir in any way. So I stood still. I think it took him three weeks to paint it."

Bridget wanted to weep. Could he not even say the word *mother*?

She glanced behind him and was relieved to see that

the other servants had left the room. "*Why* did she hate you so much?"

"I'm my father's son." He shrugged. "I look exactly like him and she rather hated him as well. I suppose that was enough."

She stared. "But you aren't your father."

"Aren't I?" he murmured, his eyes weary. "He did make me in his image, after all."

She caught his hand impulsively. "Just because you look the same doesn't mean you're the same man as your father. You're not. You're *not*."

He cocked his head at her, his eyebrows drawn together as if he were considering her words doubtfully.

If the old duchess had been alive, Bridget would've given her a piece of her mind.

She cleared her throat. "Shall I have it hung again, perhaps in the dining room?"

"What?" He glanced at the painting. "Oh, if you want. It certainly cost Father enough and the painter is supposed to be good." He looked around the room. "I wonder why she put it here, though. She was such a vindictive old thing. Hated my father. Hated this castle. Hated me." He kicked a small stack of packing crates. They fell over and something smashed. "You should've heard her yelling after me when I left. I was the very Devil, the spitting image of Father. Just like him in every—"

He was interrupted by a thin but very clear cat's meow.

Val froze, his eyes rolling to her.

Bridget frowned, looking around. Where—?

The meow came again.

"Can you hear that?" Val hissed.

She waved at him to be quiet. The room held two tables—heavy medieval things and quite worm-eaten—the fallen crates, what looked like more paintings under cloths—

Another meow.

She moved toward the only remaining large piece of furniture, a sort of cupboard, as tall as a man and intricately spindled and carved. Two doors stood at the front and she tried them, but they were locked.

"Here." Val shouldered her aside and brought out his curved dagger.

"Don't—!" she started.

But he'd already shoved the blade between the doors and levered them open by breaking the lock from the wood.

"Oh," she said with deep disapproval, "you needn't have done that."

"No, but I thought you wanted to look inside," he said. "And I've seldom seen such an ugly cupboard. I think it's one my mother had in her rooms. Do you want to look in it or not?"

"I do," she said, but when she opened the doors all she found was an empty mouse nest and a lot of dust.

The meow came again, quite close.

She leaned her head inside the cupboard. She would've sworn the cat—or kitten, for it sounded quite small—was right in front of her, but there was nothing there.

She straightened and glanced at Val.

His azure eyes were alight with amusement. "Phantom cats and ghostly kittens."

She frowned at him. "I don't believe in ghosts."

"Boring." He kissed her on the nose and, while she was still blinking in surprise, leaned down and did something to the back of the cupboard.

Suddenly one of the boards came away in his hands.

She leaned down again to look.

Staring back at them was a ginger cat, her green eyes wide, and at her teats were a row of wriggling kittens in a rainbow of colors. She was curled in the small space of what was evidently a false back to the cupboard.

"But how did she get in?" Bridget breathed, enchanted. The kittens were at that wee fluffy stage and absolutely adorable.

"Magic," Val said promptly, and then, more prosaically, "or the back of the cupboard's rotted away."

Bridget laughed. "What shall we name them?"

But that made him stiffen and pull away. "Nothing. They're not ours, are they?"

"No," she said slowly, watching him. She remembered what his father had done to him, the long litany of pet cats—cats he'd named—and her heart nearly broke. "But..."

"Then leave them be," he said, crossing the room and toeing the fallen packing crates again. "No cause to be imposing names on cats, is there? Seems rather rude if you ask me. No one asks the *cats* if they like being named."

She glanced at the mother cat, who was purring, her eyes half-closed, and then back at him. She should leave it be, she knew, but..."You liked cats as a boy, didn't you?"

He whirled on her, looking outraged. "Who told you that?"

"You did," she said gently. "When you were delirious from the poison, remember?"

"No." He shook his head decisively. "I've found that it's much easier if one forgets certain things, so I've made a habit of it. Sometimes when I'm introduced to a man I forget his name immediately, just to stay in practice. It's wonderfully useful, forgetfulness."

She didn't know whether to laugh or cry at that. How much had he forgotten over his lifetime? How much had he been made to endure?

"Well." She inhaled. "You did tell me. You said you had four cats, Pretty, Marmalade, Opal, and—"

"Tiger," he said, stalking toward her, "Tiger whom I strung up and murdered so Father wouldn't. Are you absolutely certain you want to go down this path, Séraphine, mine?"

"My name is Bridget," she said, holding her ground bravely.

"Oh, no," he replied, catching her upper arms, holding her tight, almost hurting her. "Right now you are burning Séraphine, sitting in judgment, and I am the unholy Duke of Montgomery and if you want to know, if you really, *truly* want to know with all your pure saint's soul, there were many more than Pretty, Marmalade, Opal, and Tiger. Dozens of cats. He made sure there were cats. Who do you think kept me supplied in cats as a boy? Father did. He'd bring me a pretty fluffy kitten and place it on my pillow at night so that I'd wake with it curled against my face, trusting and purring and soft, so soft, just for me. Innocent and lovely. I'd name it—I named *all* of them. And he'd wait until I loved that cat, until it was my best friend, my *only* friend, and then he'd wring its neck in front of my eyes." He leaned his forehead against hers, his eyes closed and still—still!—incredibly dry. "Until I was old enough and strong enough and smart enough and I knew I knew I knew that you *have* to kill the thing you love, Séraphine, or they'll use it against you. They'll wring its neck before your eyes and you'll *hurt*. Your insides will bleed screams and despair and you'll want death, you'll *love* death."

He stopped, panting, openmouthed and still, and said very quietly and precisely, "So you see. It's better. *Much* better. Not to love at all."

Slowly, carefully, she inched her hand up his heaving chest, up his neck and to his dry, dry face. "I do see, yes. I see."

She stood on tiptoe and kissed him, softly, on the lips. A gentle brush, a sweet reminder that she stood here and his father did not.

She cupped his face in her hands and leaned back to look up at him.

His azure eyes were drowsy and a little calmer.

He inhaled.

And then his gaze went past her to the open cupboard and he started laughing. Deep, racking guffaws that made her stare in horror.

He held his belly and pointed.

She turned and looked, expecting something awful.

All she saw was that the cat had left her kittens. They either slept or stood on trembling legs, exploring their small box at the back of the cupboard.

"What?"

"Look," he rasped. "Oh, look. That *bitch*." He went off again, laughing and staggering about the room as if possessed.

She bent to look again.

There was something white under the kittens.

She reached and took out an oblong ivory box, intricately carved all over. It looked very old and very dear and she tutted under her breath at the thought that it had been used as a cat's bed.

"Is this what you mean?" she asked the maddened man.

She tried to open it, but the lid appeared stuck.

"No, no," said Val, suddenly beside her. "You know nothing of Montgomerys and their intrigues."

He took the box from her hands, turned it upside down, and pressed his thumbnail to a carving on the bottom. A sliver popped out of the side of the box and he slid it sideways, and then opened the lid.

Bridget peered over his shoulder.

Inside was a sealed letter.

"She never smiled," he said, staring at the letter, "not even on the day I left. She sat in her bed, Cal by her side, and I watched her place this letter in this box. She swore she would keep it and would have it published if I ever returned to England before she died. But I never truly believed her. What a fool I, it seems. Her venom was true. One can't fault her for that. Eleven years later and it poisons me still, though she rots in the ground. Brava, madam, brava!"

He contemplated the letter for a second longer.

Then he looked up at her and handed her the open casket. "Here, take it. This is my heart, blackened, my soul, unshriven. Do this in remembrance of me."

She stared at the ivory box. "I can't take that!"

He cocked his head. "Why not?"

"Because..." Because she didn't want to have the means to betray him. She looked at him. "What is in the letter?"

He shrugged. "I don't know."

"You just said that your mother cursed you from the grave with it," she retorted, exasperated.

"And she most likely did," he said. "But I don't *know*. The letter is sealed. I haven't read it."

She narrowed her eyes. "But if she wrote what you *think* she wrote...?"

He smiled. "Then the contents will hang me."

She stopped breathing. He'd said, "will." Not "might." So certain. So *sure*. Very few crimes resulted in the death penalty for a duke.

And he wanted *her* to take the evidence of his crime.

She wanted to tell him to destroy it instead. It was on the very tip of her tongue.

But Bridget was a morally upright person at heart. If he'd done something so truly terrible...

"Ah, there's the inquisitor," he whispered.

And placed the awful casket in her hands.

Chapter Fifteen

Prue and King Heartless brought their baskets of yarn to show the magician.

He glanced at their lumpy yarn and smiled. "What fine work, Your Majesty!"

The king and Prue looked at each other, then the king arched a disbelieving eyebrow.

The magician hastily cleared his throat. "Now you'll need to weave a fine cloth by moonlight."

The king swore again while Prue merely sighed. . . .

—From *King Heartless*

It was a whim. Perhaps a fatal whim, but whims often were—at least *his* certainly were.

Val watched his burning angel take the vile little box, his mother's bitter bile neatly and elegantly condensed and contained. She'd been a stickler for what she considered the societal refinements, his dam. Séraphine's countenance was troubled. She didn't like taking the burden of his sins—of one rather damning sin in particular, though she did not know it—but she bravely clasped the disgusting thing to her bosom nonetheless.

He'd expected nothing less from a grand inquisitor.

It satisfied him somehow, knowing she held his destruction, his peril, in her plump, practical little housekeeper's hands. That if he riled her too much, if she woke one day and found him completely objectionable, then she could, with the flick of her wool-clad wrist, have him obliterated. It seemed to balance the world somehow. After all, she had a conscience, while he did not.

Besides. Even Achilles had his heel.

"Come," he said gently, for he knew she'd been through travail. "I sought you out amongst your labors to bend my knee and plead that you leave the dust and spiders and mouse droppings to come and lounge awhile and perhaps partake of luncheon."

Interestingly, she blushed. "I can't do that," she hissed under her breath.

"Why not?" he asked, deeply diverted by her reaction.

"The other servants."

He blinked. "I assure you, I do let all my servants partake of luncheon."

"But if I am with you . . ." Her blush deepened.

He cocked his head, studying her, entirely baffled. "I didn't mean luncheon as a euphemism; however, I'm entirely happy to adjourn to my rooms right at this moment if that is—"

"*No*," she said with what some might take as unflattering emphasis. She rolled her eyes as if *he* were the one being difficult, which, to be fair, he often *was*. "Let's go have luncheon."

He smiled. "Splendid!"

She looked at him a little shyly. Absolutely enchanting.

"I'm dusty. I'll go wash first and meet you in the dining room, shall I?"

He bowed with a flourish. "I await your presence."

She looked flustered at that and he was *very* tempted to perhaps lean her up against one of the tables and—

"No," she said, very firmly, backing away, and, much lower, "It's *the middle of the day*!"

So very Puritan! Who knew the lower classes were so staid in their lovemaking?

Val contemplated this as he made his way to his dining room. He'd always vaguely imagined the servants having at it at all hours behind the kitchen doors. Well, when he thought about it. Which wasn't often because they were *servants*. But it was one of those old canards the pamphleteers were always going on about—that the lower classes were too sexed and too fertile—and yet here was his housekeeper refusing him her favors, bizarrely because it was the middle of the day.

What, exactly, he wondered, was wrong with the middle of the day? The light? Surely being able to see the person one was about to tumble was a *good* thing? Was it the lack of bed? But no—last night she'd ridden him in a chair. And very enjoyable it'd been.

Or at least he'd thought so.

Val paused on the stairs, a sudden and *very* unwelcome notion having come into his mind—one that had never, ever occurred to him before. What if Bridget *hadn't* found it enjoyable?

He contemplated the notion for two seconds.

No. She'd come all over his cock—he'd both felt it and witnessed it. And besides.

He was Valentine Napier, the Duke of Montgomery. There simply wasn't a better lover in the world.

Satisfied, he continued his descent.

The butler—whose name he still couldn't remember—met him at the bottom of the stair. "The Duke of Dyemore to see you, Your Grace. He's waiting in the library."

Ah, fate had come to call. The old man had traveled to his country seat—in the next county to Ainsdale—faster than he'd expected. Well. He must be eager, then.

To business, to business.

But for a moment Val hesitated. He *could*...he could simply send Dyemore away. Spend the afternoon luxuriating with Séraphine.

Séraphine...he blinked. Oh, but there was Séraphine, now. Someone to protect from the masked men of the world. No. Nonononono. Better to go through with it.

The one with the power did not have to grieve the next day.

Val nodded to the butler. "Ask him if he cares to take luncheon with me."

He entered the dining room and found a room polished and clean and not as dour as he remembered. Of course his memories were mainly of bacchanals that ended in rape and ravage.

It'd once been the castle's hall and the ceiling was high and bore ancient painted coats of arms along the eaves. The table was long and nearly black, the walls hung with paintings of various no doubt demonic ancestors. Father had pride of place over a gray stone fireplace, attired in gray periwig and silk hose, his sapphire-blue robes draped about his elegant form.

Val took his seat and contemplated his father's blank azure eyes. He supposed he could have the bloody portrait burned, now that he was master of the castle.

"Montgomery," Dyemore croaked in his old man's voice as he tottered across the dining room. "You're looking in good health. I heard rumors that you were taken ill after your ball."

"Ah, rumors," Val said, standing to greet his guest. "They're best left to old women and those that are soft in the head, don't you agree? Unless, of course, they can be verified."

"Of course," Dyemore said, shaking his hand with a lingering touch. "But then I did have the tale from one of your maids."

"*Did* you?" Val smiled as he took his seat again. "Tell me her name so I might have the wench tossed in the street."

Dyemore chuckled. "Ah, you remind me of your father."

"So my mother was wont to tell me," Val said lightly as he poured the old man a glass of wine.

The door to the dining room opened. Bridget stepped inside and Val immediately realized his mistake.

She was dressed in her usual ugly black wool, white pinned apron, and white fichu, all quite modest, but Dyemore had already made allusion to gossip and informing servants. Did the old man know who, exactly, had nursed him through that illness?

Val smiled very slightly over his wineglass and damned himself for a bloody fool.

"Is this the lovely Mrs. Crumb?" Dyemore asked, examining Séraphine as if she were a salted herring presented for his consumption.

Briefly Val contemplated stabbing him with his dinner knife. It would be so very easy. But then the disposal of the body, et cetera, et cetera. So tedious and he really did rather want the power of the Lords.

Oh, very well.

"Mrs. Crumb is indeed my housekeeper and will be joining us for luncheon," Val said, holding out his hand for her.

She, to her credit and quite unsurprisingly, kept her composure and strode, head held high, to his side. She eschewed his hand, but did take her seat. It occurred to Val in passing that he'd seen princesses with less aplomb.

Val let his hand fall to the table and smiled at her. "This is Leonard de Chartres, the Duke of Dyemore and a great friend of my late father."

Her eyes widened a fraction but in no other way did she demonstrate her comprehension of that statement. "Your Grace. A pleasure to meet you."

"The pleasure is all mine," Dyemore replied, sounding as amused as if he sat chatting with a talking cat. He turned to Val. "A novelty for you, eh, Montgomery? I remember your father liked his outré diversions as well. Why, one entire winter—was it 1712 or 1713?—there was this little—"

Fortunately for the state of Val's appetite, Dyemore was interrupted by the advent of luncheon. The butler preceded three footmen, bearing trays of salmon, beef, and a variety of stewed fruits and breads.

"Never much liked fish," Dyemore said a short time

later, bloody beef juice seeping from the corner of his mouth as he masticated. "Now beef's a man's meal."

"Oh, quite," Val agreed, stabbing a fork into his salmon.

"Now," the old man continued. "We'll have to get you properly initiated."

Bridget banged her knife onto her plate and glared at him. Val wondered if she'd make it through the meal without going off like a Chinese firecracker.

"Really? An initiation?" Val asked, turning to Dyemore. "Tedious, that. I thought, as one of the founding families…?"

"Sacred rules," Dyemore intoned—rather comically, considering what they were discussing. "But the sooner the better. 'M not getting any younger. Ha!"

"I would've thought your son…?" Val asked, purely for his own curiosity's sake. He had no intention of letting anyone else shoulder him out the seat of power.

"Raphael?" Dyemore made a very unpleasant face. "He's…not appropriate for the role."

Indeed? Well, that was certainly interesting. Val vaguely remembered a boy of about his own age, and wondered if Raphael were crippled or mentally deficient. Surely he would have heard rumors if so?

"No, you'll do much better," Dyemore continued as he fished a bit of gristle from between his teeth. "Young. Strong of limb. Comely."

His eyes had gone half-lidded.

Val might've felt himself violated had he been inclined.

He smiled. "When?"

The other man shrugged. "Spring is our usual time, you know that."

Val shook his head. "Too far off. I'll want to take my place sooner."

Dyemore grinned. "Perhaps something can be arranged. We've been a bit more…liberal since your father's time with our revels."

"And where have you been holding them?"

But Dyemore shook his finger at him roguishly. "Now, now. I can't tell you that, as you well know. Not until you're initiated." He sat back in his chair, eyeing Val almost lasciviously. "You're eager to join us, I know, but you must be patient, my boy."

Val smiled and drank his wine, content for now to let the old man think that the Lords' rather pedestrian sexual debauchery was the reason he wanted to join them.

The meal was finished in a congenial, if not pleasant, atmosphere, Dyemore making none-too-subtle references to Father's perversions, his mother's hatred of Val, et cetera, et cetera. Really, it would do the world good if the old man just choked on one of his gobbled bites, but such was not to be. Val was soon escorting his guest to his doors.

Which was when it happened.

He could blame the wine, his own preoccupation with Séraphine, and the cloud of disapproval that had been growing around her all through the meal, but when it came right down to it, it was nothing more than stupidity.

Bloody stupidity.

Dyemore was at the door, his hat and cane in hand, saying his final, doddering, malicious farewells, when Bridget turned away from Val.

He caught her hand.

Merely that. Completely without thought. He didn't

want her to go stalking off to who knew where to clean any more of his goddamned castle when he just wanted to have a quiet discussion with her and perhaps, after that, a nice round of midafternoon lovemaking.

Such a little thing, and yet so telling. Because he could explain away a housekeeper at his luncheon table as some strange sexual perversion. A sudden desire to roll about in the muck of the lower classes. But holding a woman's hand meant something completely different, even to a jaded, pox-ridden, soulless old roué such as Dyemore.

It meant affection.

And *that* meant weakness.

He saw Dyemore's bloodshot gaze dart to the hand that held Bridget's plump little fingers. The old man's liver-colored lips twitched in a satisfied smile, and Val felt something odd in his frozen hollow chest. Something that took his breath away.

It felt almost like...

Well. *Fear.*

And Val thought, *You have to kill the thing you love or they'll use it against you.*

Wasn't it good, then, that he didn't love Bridget?

"WHY?" BRIDGET WHIRLED on Val the moment he closed the door to his room. She was *shaking*, she was so upset. "What would possess you to dine with the Duke of Dyemore and *ask* to be initiated into the Lords of Chaos? Are you that perverse? Do you like sex with all sorts of women that much?"

"Actually," he drawled, "it's often boys—very young ones—and little girls."

For a moment she simply stared at him, unable to believe her ears.

Then she said, very precisely and flatly, "You want to rape little boys and—"

"*No.*" He actually had the *gall* to look hurt. "I already told you how I feel about rape and rapists. Of course I wouldn't do such a thing to a child."

She looked at him. Took a deep breath. And then another. Pushed aside the images, and the words, the terrible old man, and having to remain quiet through that *ghastly* luncheon—all the things that had made her so very angry. Put them all to the side for now, and just looked at Valentine the man.

He stood several paces from her, his golden hair clubbed back, wearing a marine-blue suit with red embroidery and a terra-cotta waistcoat. Rather subdued for him, really. He was watching her as if she were a woman from a strange, foreign country. One he'd never encountered before.

He often looked at her that way, she thought a little sadly.

"Why do you want to join the Lords of Chaos?" she asked.

"Because they all have a common vice," he said promptly. "And they're all men of rank and privilege."

She nodded. "You want to blackmail them."

"Yes." He smiled as if she were a bright pupil and he a schoolmaster. "Think of the opportunities! Not just among the Lords, but their families as well." He spread his hands wide as if imagining a network of spider webs, interconnecting, entangling entire communities.

"And then, they have a tradition, you know, of helping one another secretly, in business, marriage, Parliament, the church, the army, the navy, well, anywhere, really. They're everywhere, the Lords."

He smiled cherubically while she tried not to show the horror on her face.

"How can they know who the other Lords are if they wear masks?"

"The tattoos. If one Lord shows another the dolphin the second is supposed to do anything the first asks of him."

She frowned. "But your tattoo is on your..."

He shrugged. "I never meant to use it. I wasn't going to be indebted to one of *them*."

And there, finally, was the clear loathing of the Lords she'd heard the other day.

"But you'll *join* them," she said carefully. "You'll sit next to men who...hurt young boys and girls."

He looked at her, all trace of humor gone from his face. "I sat next to a man like that just now at luncheon."

She swallowed down the acid rising in her throat. "Yes. Yes, you did."

"You can't escape them, Séraphine, those sorts of men. They're all around everywhere."

"But you don't have to join them," she said, her voice hard. "Val. *Valentine*. *You* don't have to be one of them."

"I'm not," he said, clearly confused. "I just told you—"

"Joining them is as good as *being* one of them," she said. "In the end, it *is* the same."

He stared at her, his straight, beautiful brows knit. "It is?"

"Yes." She crossed to him and placed her hands on

his face, holding his azure gaze, trying to impart . . . well, *humanity*. It'd been blown out of him as a child, but she could try, couldn't she? "Don't join the Lords of Chaos. Please."

"But the opportunities for blackmail . . . the power."

"You have enough power as it is," she assured him gently. "You're the Duke of Montgomery."

"No, Séraphine," he said, sadly, *wearily*, and without smiling. "There's never enough power, not even for the Duke of Montgomery."

"Why?" she whispered. "*Why* would you need more power?"

He squeezed his beautiful azure eyes shut and raised a shaking fist to his temple. "You don't understand!"

"Then make me!"

He opened his eyes wide and seized her arms, spinning her in a circle, his gaze boring into hers. "Don't you comprehend? Can't you *see* them? They're all around us—wolves and birds of prey and jackals, baying at the moon, jaws agape. So close, Bridget, so close you can smell the fetid stink of their breath, and if you don't have power they'll drag you or Eve or me from beneath the bed and tear the meat from your bones, and leave you a weeping skeleton." He inhaled, stopping their dizzying whirl so suddenly that she gasped and staggered against him and he wrapped his arms around her, clutching her tight. He whispered in her ear, "I'm not mad. I know they don't wear the masks anymore, but that doesn't mean, my burning Séraphine, that they aren't still out there, in banal old-man form. So you see, I *must* have more power. It's the only way to survive them."

He was shaking and she didn't completely understand him, but she cared for him, even though she knew she shouldn't.

So she kissed him, this flamboyant man who refused to name cats and entrusted her with a beautiful, stinking box that contained a sin so great it could hang him. And as she did so she told herself that no matter what else happened she mustn't fall in love with him.

Even if it might be far, far too late.

She pulled the tie from his hair, threading her fingers through the curling golden strands, luxuriating in their silkiness.

He groaned, the sound vibrating against her lips, and bent her over the crook of his arm, as he reached up with his left hand and pulled the pins from her hair.

She felt them come out, one by one, and the mass of her hair fell over his arm. His hand moved to her face, holding her as he angled his mouth over hers, biting her lower lip and then thrusting his tongue into her.

He tasted of red wine when she suckled him.

He picked her up and the room whirled for a moment before she found herself on the bed.

She looked up at him and said, "I want you naked this time."

He nodded very seriously, and said, "Of course."

But a smile twitched at his lips when he pulled the lace neckcloth free from his throat.

She sat up, watching as he shrugged off his marine-blue coat and flung it onto a chair, then toed off his shoes. He flicked open the buttons of his waistcoat deliberately, staring at her from beneath golden eyelashes. The waistcoat soon joined the coat.

Then he bent and stripped the stockings from his legs. He straightened and unbuttoned the tiny shell buttons at his wrists, and then the ones down the front of his shirt. He paused, looked at her, reached both hands behind his back, and with one fluid movement stripped his shirt over his head.

The muscles of his shoulders gleamed in the sunlight streaming in the window. He might've been a god come to frolic with her for the afternoon.

He watched her, eyes gone heavy-lidded, as he flicked open the falls of his breeches, letting them simply drop to the floor when they were loose enough.

He stood now in his smallclothes—*silk* smallclothes, she noted with no small amusement—and waited while she looked her fill.

Finally he dropped those as well.

She'd seen him thus before, of course. He made a veritable habit of nudity, it seemed, the vain, vain man, but he'd not been her lover then.

She'd not . . . cared for him then.

He was beautiful. Naturally. Perfect of limb, smooth of complexion, his cock pointed, full and heavy and ready for her.

How often had he been admired thus by lovers? How often had he posed in his perfect beauty?

The thing was, she would've been enticed even had he not been beautiful. At least she thought so. For instance, that little white line on his right knee. Was it a scar? Who knew? But the fact that it was just a bit off, that it was imperfect, and thus made him human?

That was erotic to her.

That was the real intimacy, wasn't it? Of seeing another person nude. At heart it was the intimacy of the imperfect and human. And all those other lovers? Well, she wondered if they'd ever seen her Val as anything other than a perfect, beautiful *thing*. Had they ever seen the man beneath the beauty?

Would they like him as well when that taut belly began to sag? When the guinea-gold hair faded, when lines drew themselves around the azure eyes?

Because, on the whole, she thought she might like him *more*.

Not that she'd ever have the chance to see him age.

She bit her lip, blinking away tears at the thought. Oh, how she'd like to age with this man.

"Séraphine?" he asked. "Where have you gone?"

"Nowhere," she said. "Help me undress, please."

And he did, pulling her to her feet and efficiently divesting her of all her clothing in much less time than it would have taken her.

She didn't think about how much practice he must've had.

When she stood nude before him, she took his hands and led him to the bed, lying down on her left side so that he might lie facing her but with his left hand uppermost.

He tucked his arm beneath his head and watched her. "You're in a strange mood."

"Am I?" she asked. "Do you know all my moods?"

His lips curved then. "Only those you deign to show me."

She didn't answer, but reached out a finger to trace those lips, fine and shaped in a classic cupid's bow. "If you had all the power in the world, Valentine, what would you do?"

"I told you," he replied, each word a kiss to her finger, "one can never have enough power."

"Humor me," she commanded, she who had grown up the foster daughter of a sheep farmer. "What would you do?"

His dark eyelashes dipped slowly. "I would travel the world, I suppose, and learn to speak all the languages, the better to work intrigues at royal courts."

She laughed under her breath at his answer because it was so essentially him.

"What would you do?" he asked. "Were you not a housekeeper? If you could do anything, be anyone, in the wide, wonderful world?"

She raised her eyebrows. "I don't know. I've never thought about it. I like being a housekeeper."

"Humor me," he said, echoing her words.

She smiled at him, a little whimsically. "Perhaps I'd be a sailor and sail to China and India and uncharted Africa."

"Would you?" he asked, sounding delighted.

"Hmm," she whispered, bringing her mouth to his. "Perhaps I'd sail to Istanbul and see these Ottoman gentlemen in their flowing robes smoke their water pipes myself."

She kissed him softly, the press of her lips unhurried in the afternoon sunlight, the tips of her breasts brushing his chest. She wanted to remember this moment, this idle time so unlike any other in her life.

This golden man in the golden light.

He drew her hair over her breast, brushing the strands against the tip of her nipple, using it to paint a point of pleasure as their kiss deepened.

She groaned a little, moving closer, letting her arm drape over his, feeling the smooth expanse of his back, the glide of his muscles beneath his skin as he tugged her uppermost thigh over his legs.

She felt the blunt head of his cock nudge against her folds and she tilted her hips.

It was a strange position, and yet a blissfully relaxed one.

He pulled her more firmly against him, his hand spread frankly over her bottom, and entered her on a gentle thrust.

She opened her eyes and found him watching her as they kissed.

He drew back, his mouth open and wet, his eyes half-closed, still watching her.

His hand flexed on her bottom and he tilted his hips into her. "Hard. Soft. Male..."

"Female," she whispered, scratching her fingernails down his long flawless back.

His lips twitched a smile. "Dark. Light. Evil..."

"Good." She bit the side of his neck delicately.

He gasped and his penis jerked within her. "*Ahh.* Cold. Hot. Despair..."

"Hope." She rolled, using the full force of her weight as leverage, and pushed him flat, climbing atop him, finally sinking fully on his cock.

She looked down on him from her position of triumph and placed both palms on his chest, scraping her thumbs across his pink nipples.

"Ahh!" He bared his teeth, tossing his head back, his arms flung above his head, a Prometheus tortured by the eagle.

She slid her palms down his gorgeous torso until she felt the bones of his hips. She braced herself there and she began to move. A subtle rocking, a delicious little wave. She hardly shifted his hardness within her, but ground her folds against him.

It was...oh, it was sweet, watching him in the sunlight as her breasts swayed, as she felt the heat build between her legs, as his cock ground inside her.

His hands were clenched in fists, the tendons in his neck stretched taut, his head tilted back as he watched her from slitted eyes. He was motionless and she wondered when he'd break.

When he'd be unable to stand any more.

She leaned a little forward so that she could grind her clitoris against him as she rolled, rocking back and forth. And the spark that gave her made her groan.

He answered in echo.

She opened her eyes, smiling at him. "Ugly."

He gasped, blinking. "Beautiful."

She laughed, on edge, close, so close. "Bitter."

"Sweet." He heaved himself up, wrapped his arms around her, and rolled them both, so that he was thrusting into her, hard and fast, almost before they'd settled. He braced himself over her, his golden curls falling into darkened glittering azure eyes, lines imprinted on his pale beautiful face, and gazed down at her with awful, terrible foreboding. "Death."

She was falling apart under his assault, sparks flying behind her eyes, warm honey in her limbs, but she forced herself to meet his gaze, to keep her eyes open even as her mouth went slack with pleasure. "*Life*."

His hips faltered, and his head rolled on his shoulders as if he'd been hit, as if he were in great pain, his lips drawn back from his teeth. He groaned, continuing to thrust, but more slowly, less gracefully, a man in his death throes.

And as she watched, he opened his eyes and gasped, "*Séraphine*."

She answered as naturally as breathing, "Valentine," and felt his hot seed fill her.

Chapter Sixteen

That night Prue and King Heartless went again to the gardens, where a loom was being built. The king yelled at the workmen for being lazy, but Prue shushed him. "They won't work any faster for being scolded." So the king instead thanked the workmen when they were done. Then they wove and wove, and though neither was particularly good at it, every once in a while Prue would lean over and tighten the king's weft and he would grunt in acknowledgment. . . .

—From *King Heartless*

The next morning they set off for London. Not because Val was in any hurry to return to that teeming metropolis, but because of that single glance Dyemore had given Val's hand linked with Bridget's. It made him ever so slightly nervous and he felt it best to put as many miles as possible between Séraphine and those awful liver-colored lips. And since the main reason for journeying to Ainsdale in the first place—namely, Miss Royle—had slipped his net, there was really no cause to stay.

Of course there were the other, more minor incentives

for returning: to discover how his affairs were progressing and what news and scandals were muttering and murmuring in the alleys and salons of London, and to satisfy his own prodigious curiosity.

Which was why, on an afternoon four days later, he was shown into Lady Amelia Caire's sitting room.

"My lady," he said, sweeping his gold-lace-trimmed tricorne wide in a deep bow, "I beg your pardon for such a disgraceful leave of manners. I know I have not the pleasure of an introduction, but I hope your gentle feminine mercy will take pity upon such a poor wretch as I and grant me an audience."

Lady Caire's lips curved coolly. "Your Grace. What an unexpected surprise."

"People keep telling me that," Val said, taking a seat, for he rather thought that if he waited to be offered one, he might stand for the entire encounter, "but I ask myself: *can* a surprise be expected?"

"Mm." Even her frosty smile had disappeared. "Amusing as this conversation is, Your Grace, I wonder why you've chosen to come to my house."

"Do you?" He sat back on her very elegant and very uncomfortable settee. He approved: style should always come before function, although personally he enjoyed *both*. "I think we have a mutual acquaintance."

She was a beautiful woman. Her nose was narrow and small, with delicate little nostrils. Below, her lips were a perfect cupid's bow. Her eyes had been almond-shaped and large. The lids had creped a little with age, fine lines radiating from the corners, but in some ways it merely gave her face more command.

Her hair was snow white.

She looked nothing like her daughter. Even when Séraphine's hair became pure white in several years, she would not look like her mother. She'd merely look like herself: a burning angel, even more fierce and strange.

He could hardly wait.

He watched now, though, as the woman who had conceived and borne his Séraphine looked back at him, bored.

She raised a perfectly arched eyebrow. "I'm sorry, but we no doubt have many acquaintances in common."

"Yes," he said, smiling, "but this one is special. Very special."

He took her letters from his pocket and very gently placed them on the low table between them.

She glanced at the letters.

The spring before he'd used them to blackmail her into introducing his sister to a group of aristocratic ladies, so she knew full well what they were. He had to admire her composure. She neither made a move toward the letters nor changed her expression.

She simply looked at him.

What a fascinating woman! Val had the impression that she was quite prepared to wait him out—interesting, since she *must* know he held all the cards. She might not look anything like her daughter, but perhaps they were alike in their bravery.

In their defiance.

Into their silent battle of wills came the sound of boot heels and then the scrape of the sitting room door opening.

A man stood there, tall and broad, his hair quite as

white as his mother's, left long and clubbed back with a black velvet bow.

His hawk's gaze darted from Val to Lady Caire. "Mother?"

She went white to the lips, still facing Val, her back to her son. Her eyes widened in a clear plea.

Val smiled and rose. "Lord Caire, I presume."

Caire didn't move an inch. "You are?"

He made another sweeping bow because, among other reasons, he was very, very good at them. "Valentine Napier, the Duke of Montgomery, at your service, sir."

Caire inclined his head. "Your Grace." His eyes were narrowed as if he'd heard Val's name and was trying to place it.

Oh, good.

Caire's mouth opened.

The door burst open again and a small female child came pirouetting into the room, crying shrilly, "Gwandmama! Gwandmama! We've been to the fair and saw a dog in a dwess that danced on its paws. Can *I* have a dog?"

The tiny devil came to an abrupt stop at her father's knees and stuck a finger in her mouth at the sight of Val, muttering rather indistinctly around it, "Oo're oo?"

"I," Val said, staring down his nose at it, "am the Duke of Montgomery. Oo're *oo*?"

The finger came out of the mouth with an audible *pop*. "'M Annawise Hun'ington."

"Charmed, I'm sure," Val said, distracted by the dark-haired woman who had entered behind the child. She wasn't a particular beauty, but she had a Madonna-like poise.

Lady Caire stood. Somehow the letters on the low

table had disappeared, possibly into one of her sleeves or a pocket. "As you can see, Your Grace, my son's family has arrived and while this has been an interesting visit—"

But the day's entrances apparently weren't done. Rapid, determined, and quite familiar feminine heel-taps approached.

Val's breath caught in anticipation.

She came in, grim and alert, and probably ready for anything.

Anything, of course, but what she found.

For his bright burning Séraphine had taken off her hat between the front door and the sitting room.

And whatever else Caire was, he wasn't a fool.

He took one long look at her and without taking his eyes from her said, "Mother, who is this woman?"

BRIDGET HAD FOUND where Val was headed only because of an offhand comment by Mehmed made half an hour before: "I do not understand this. How can a lady be a *care*?"

It had taken her perhaps a minute to work through the implications—and less than that to realize that Val was going to interfere where he should not.

She'd nearly run here.

All the while worrying that he was going to blackmail her mother again—after they'd become lovers. She was by turns hurt and angry. How dared he betray her?

Which was why she didn't actually have a plan when she entered Lady Caire's sitting room. She'd been so anxious to get here and prevent Valentine's mischief that she hadn't thought about *how* she was going to do so.

Five people turned at her entrance. Valentine, wearing

a beautiful, wicked, anticipatory smile; Lady Caire, cool and watchful; a dark-haired lady with a curious expression; a darling little girl with her finger in her mouth and her hand on the knee of a tall man.

A man who had hair so white it looked silver.

She knew at once who it must be, of course. He had the white hair of their mother, the aristocratic bearing, and...

Well, he *was* an aristocrat, wasn't he? A baron.

He stared at her with clear blue eyes—the same color, technically, as Val's, but so very different—and said, "Mother, who is this woman?"

Oh. Lady Caire.

Bridget couldn't even look at her. She felt heat crawl up her cheeks, for she knew that the lady hadn't ever wanted this, to be confronted by both her...well...in the same room together.

She very much wanted to burst into tears.

But she couldn't, so she bobbed a hasty curtsy to Lord Caire. "I'm Bridget Crumb, sir."

For some reason that made Val's smile twist down.

"Bridget Crumb," Lord Caire said slowly. He was staring at the streak in her hair and she damned herself for a fool for removing her hat when she'd come in.

For rushing here at all.

Val caught her eye and arched an amused eyebrow.

She scowled at him.

And then hastily ordered her face.

"Well," she said brightly. "I must be going."

"Oh, but you've only just got here," Val, the wretch, said smoothly. "And in such a hurry. I can't have my housekeeper rushing all about London so very agitated."

"*Your* housekeeper," Lord Caire said, his head snapping alarmingly to Val.

"Oh, yes, and rather more," Val drawled, taking her hand and kissing her knuckles in the most horrifying manner.

Bridget could only stare. What on *earth* was he doing?

"Shall we go together?" he asked solicitously, looping his arm around her waist and drawing her against his side in a far too intimate manner.

She stiffened, trying to wriggle away without causing a scene, but the problem was he was quite strong and she couldn't move an inch.

The little girl chose that moment to take her finger out of her mouth and point it damply at Val. "I don't *wike* you."

He looked down his nose at her. "No, nor does anyone else, yet they all seem to be happy enough to let me take sweet Séraphine off to be debauched at my leisure. D'you suppose they would stand around twiddling their thumbs were I to take *you* as well?"

"Val!" Bridget said, horrified.

While at the same time the child opened her mouth and wailed for her "Mama."

The dark-haired woman hurried over to pick her up, casting a very intense glare at Val.

"Let's leave, *please*," Bridget muttered to him, tugging at his arm. This was a farce, a ridiculous comedy, but at any moment it would turn to tragedy, irreversible and permanent, and she was suddenly frightened. "*Please*."

He was an obdurate rock, though, staring at Lord Caire, a mocking smile curling the corner of his mouth.

"Mother?" Lord Caire whispered.

Bridget couldn't help it. She glanced at the older woman.

Lady Caire was staring at her, the oddest expression in her blue eyes. It was almost one of... longing? That couldn't be, surely?

Then the lady closed her eyes, hiding their expression, whatever it had been, and said, "She's my daughter."

Suddenly everyone was quiet. Even the little girl stopped crying.

Lady Caire opened her sapphire eyes and looked into her son's eyes. "She is your sister, Lazarus."

He nodded, almost calmly.

Then he pivoted and struck Val full in the jaw.

VAL FELT HIS jaw cautiously ten minutes later in his carriage. All in all it'd been a quite exciting afternoon and thoroughly enjoyable, despite the slight pain.

"It's a very good thing I know how to take a blow, otherwise Caire might've broken my jaw."

The woman across from him—she'd absolutely refused to sit with him—remained sullenly mute.

He eyed her a moment. Darling Séraphine's color was still rather high and her breasts were rising and falling rapidly.

No doubt it was best to proceed with caution.

Too bad he never did.

"I agree it *would* be a tragedy to mar this visage," he mused. "A sin to the sight of women everywhere—and many men as well, let me assure you. And did you notice how quickly he moved, that brother of yours? Not many men of his size and years can get around a settee that fast. I'll have to watch myself tomorrow morning or I might lose an ear or an eye or my nose or my—"

"Stop it," she said in what sounded very like a growl. "Just stop it. You're not going to duel Lord Caire!"

"I assure you I am," he said earnestly. "We aristocrats take these things very seriously, you know—or rather you *don't* because your mother went and copulated with, what? A stable lad? A traveling tinker? A tall and brawny footman? Ah," he breathed, for she'd flinched on the last. "A footman. How very boring of her—*every* titled lady wants to tup a young footman. I'd thought she might be a little more original than that."

"Why are you being so awful about this?" she asked.

"Why aren't *you*?" he shot back, some of the clean, clear anger bubbling up that had been simmering beneath his skin for the last several days, ever since he'd seen that glorious white streak and known—known *instantly*—what it must mean. "What did she do? Hide herself away in some isolated cottage when she began to show, drop you in secret like a *kitten*, and hand you to the first farmer she came upon? 'Oh, I say, mind bringing up my *daughter* while I return to my life and pretend she never *happened*?' "

A rose flush climbed her cheeks and her dark eyes began to burn. "That's...that's not how it was."

He crossed his legs and assumed an exaggeratedly interested expression. "Oh? *Do* tell."

She lifted her chin, stubborn and proud, and, though she was unaware of it, looking more like her mother than at any other time. "My Mam was a good woman and my foster father was...not unkind."

He was having a very hard time keeping his anger from boiling over. "A rousing endorsement if ever I've heard one. Did he hit you?"

"*No.*" She scowled. "I told you, he wasn't unkind."

He waited.

"He used to tell me I was a cuckoo in his nest." She hurried on, "But Mam loved me, I know she did. Lady Caire made sure a good family raised me. And she visited me."

"Really?" He drawled. This was much too easy. "How often?"

Her nostrils flared. "Four times that I can remember. She couldn't do it any more than that. It would've roused suspicion."

He clapped his hands mockingly. "How generous. And yet you went into service at the age of twelve."

"I wanted to work."

"Did you?" He leaned forward, and this time he couldn't manage even the mocking smile. "Don't *lie* to me, Séraphine, not to *me*. Would you really have preferred work at the age of twelve to *books*? She could've sent you to a family of her own rank, or one just a little below. Such things have been done before. You could have been raised as a lady. Schooled as one. Seen the world as one. You could've worn silk and brocade instead of wool. You could've danced your nights away instead of scrubbing the floors of indolent, stupid aristocrats. She *stole* your rightful life from you."

For a moment she stared at him, breathing hard, as if she were the one who had whispered the litany of poison and hatred.

Then she closed her eyes as if weary. "And if I had—if I'd been that lady in silks, dancing at balls, unused to work or labor—I'd never have met you." She opened her eyes. "You do know that, don't you?"

"Oh, yes," he breathed. "And that, *that* may be her worst crime of all."

She shook her head and sat forward. "It doesn't matter. *If*s and *but for*s and *what might have been*s. This is who I am and this is the life I have lived. It may be hard for you to understand, but I've rather enjoyed it. I *like* being a housekeeper. I don't blame Lady Caire for my life and neither should you, Val."

"And yet I do," he said quite honestly.

"*Please.*" She closed her eyes. "You cannot duel Lord Caire."

He smiled without any humor at all. "I can and I will, I assure you."

She inhaled, her face going white. "I'll take your mother's ivory box to the Duke of Kyle."

A thrill went through him at the thought, but he shook his head gently. "Oh, Séraphine."

"I will," she said, staring straight at him, her mouth firm, her chin lifted and resolved. "I don't want to, but I will if you go through with this. Call it off and I won't have to."

He sighed. She was such a wonderful woman. He could've spent his entire life searching the world and never found her. Who would've thought such a marvel was right under his nose in his own house? "I am not going to call off the duel because you will not betray me."

Tears glittered in her eyes and the sight made his frozen chest ache almost as if something awoke inside him.

"Don't make me do it, Val, *please.* I don't want you dueling Lady Caire's son."

"Your brother," he said.

"Lord Caire."

"Your. Brother."

She looked at him. "Does it really matter?"

"Oh, yes," he said grimly. "And tomorrow I'll prove it—if I have to kill him to do it."

Chapter Seventeen

In the morning the magician viewed the resulting misshapen cloth and said, "And now, Your Majesty, you must embroider this cloth by—"

"The light of the moon," King Heartless snapped. "Yes, I know. But despite two nights' lost sleep I feel exactly the same. Where is my heart?"

"Closer than you think," the magician replied, looking wise.

Prue rolled her eyes. . . .

—From *King Heartless*

She tried reasoning. She tried shouting. She tried begging.

Nothing worked.

Oh, he was charming. He was witty and beautiful and he was mad, but he was stubborn and bent on his own wicked and strange path.

And he meant to kill Lord Caire, who, after all, was indeed her brother.

Even if Bridget couldn't bring herself to call the tall aristocratic stranger that.

So after hours and hours of arguing and shouting and

weeping until she was hoarse, she did the only thing left to her.

It was long after dark and she was hurrying along a brightly lit London street, the wind trying to catch at her hat and bringing tears to her eyes.

That was what she told herself, anyway.

It was just that she knew Val was doing all this for *her*, that in his own way this was a bizarre show of…of… *loyalty*, perhaps even affection. To Val, killing her brother was a bit like handing her a bunch of posies.

She laughed bitterly under her breath and swiped at her cheeks. She was almost to St James's Square.

She stepped into the square, looking nervously around. Even at night London's streets teemed with people. The square was flickering with shop lanterns and small bonfires, lit to warm waiting carriage drivers, chairmen, and loiterers, but she couldn't see him. What if he hadn't received her message? What if he wasn't here? She'd have to somehow—

"Mrs. Crumb."

She started a little, for she was that nervous, and turned.

She'd forgotten how big a man the Duke of Kyle was. He loomed from the shadows and she wondered how he'd come so close to her without her knowledge.

He bent his head as if trying to peer into her face and she very much hoped that he couldn't see her countenance clearly. "Mrs. Crumb?"

"Your Grace," she replied. "Thank you for meeting me."

"My pleasure," he replied, a polite man lying. He didn't say anything more, merely waiting for her to speak.

She inhaled. "Val... that is... the Duke of Montgomery was challenged to a duel today by... by Lord Caire."

"Indeed?" His voice held calm curiosity and she was grateful. Dueling was, strictly speaking, quite illegal and punishable by banishment from England for life.

"I did try to get him to apologize to His Lordship or... or to somehow decline the duel, but His Grace was quite stubbornly adamant that he will duel Lord Caire tomorrow morning."

Kyle cleared his throat. "Yes, well, such things are normally rather binding, you understand."

She peered at him in the darkness. Were *all* men idiots?

He seemed to sense her silent criticism. "Was that why you called me here, Mrs. Crumb?"

"No," she said, fumbling with the soft bag she carried. Now that it came to the point, she found she was shaking. "I have something for you. If you show it to the Duke of Montgomery he will be forced to quit the duel."

She drew out the ivory casket from the bag.

Kyle went very still.

She tried to see his expression, but it was impossible in the flickering light. "You must promise me, Your Grace, that you won't use the contents of this box against the Duke of Montgomery. I'm entrusting you with his life, you see, and he's..." She closed her eyes and swallowed. "He's very dear to me indeed."

"Mrs. Crumb," he said sternly. "What makes you think I would undertake this task for you?"

"Because," she said, "once you've got him to quit the duel, you can exchange this box for the rest of the King's blackmail letters. The contents of this box are very important to the Duke of Montgomery. And..." She bit her lip, *ordering* herself not to cry. "*And* I think you'll help me because you're a good man, Your Grace. You'll do what's right and you'll keep your word to me."

There was a slight pause.

Then Kyle took the ivory casket from her hands. "Quite correct, Mrs. Crumb. Quite correct."

She clasped her hands before her. "I only know that the duel is on the morrow—not when or where exactly."

"I will find the place and time, never fear." He turned to go and then abruptly turned back again and bowed. "Take care of yourself, ma'am. I would not wish anything ill to befall you."

And he disappeared into the shadows.

Bridget wrapped her arms about herself and hurried back to Hermes House, even colder now. She felt empty inside, as if she were missing something.

She wondered a little despairingly if this was how Val felt all the time.

A carriage rumbled by, splashing freezing muck on her skirts. Her eyes were dry—dry and aching—and she kept thinking that she could still run back and catch him. Explain that it was all a mistake and beg Kyle to give her back the casket.

But she didn't. She stumped on toward Hermes House instead.

Once, when she took a narrow, dark lane, nearly deserted now that it was close to midnight, she thought she heard footsteps behind her. She almost picked up her skirts and ran then. The night and dark and grief overtook her, but she firmly fought down her own hysteria and made the outlet of the lane, which came to a brightly lit street.

And then she was at Hermes House, the front entrance this time, which as a servant she rarely entered.

She looked up and saw the grand pediment, lit eerily from the lanterns at the front door below. Within the pediment was a bas-relief of the god Hermes, holding his snake staff and with a cloak over his arm.

He looked just like Val.

Because, of course, he had been the one to build the house. He'd ordered his likeness carved into stone above his own doorstep for all of London to see—in the nude.

She bit her lip, staring at the sculpture, half smiling, half trying not to cry. Such a vain man. Such a beautiful, mercurial, vain man.

And she was going to be the one to bring him down.

She climbed the front steps and knocked softly.

Bob the footman answered almost instantly—he was on duty in the hall tonight and she'd alerted him that she'd be out on an errand.

"Thank you," she said to the footman. "Be sure to lock up, please."

"Yes, Mrs. Crumb."

She took off her hat and shawl, walking back to her little room next to the kitchens.

The Hermes House kitchens were dim this time of night, the bootblack boy asleep on his pallet by the hearth. He had a pallet-mate now—the ginger cat from Ainsdale Castle, curled with her eight multicolored kittens in an old basket lined with cloths. Mehmed had smuggled the cat and her offspring into the carriage on the ride home to

London—something they'd discovered only after several hours' travel from the castle, when the kittens had waked and begun mewling. Pip, who had been sniffing suspiciously at the covered hamper beside the boy, had jumped back comically at the small sound and begun barking frantically.

It seemed the terrier had run across cats in his wanderings about London and regarded them with a combination of wariness and awe.

Bridget pushed open the door to her room and was greeted by Pip, standing on her bed and wagging his tail. Despite his friendship with Mehmed at Ainsdale Castle, he'd reverted to sleeping in her bedroom once they'd returned to Hermes House.

Even if she didn't retire here.

Bridget hung up her hat and her shawl and went to the small looking glass beside the door. Her reflection regarded her soberly. Her brows straight and a little too heavy, too dark. Her nose narrow and unremarkable, her mouth as well. Her chin just a bit too aggressive. She wasn't at all like her elegant mother. She wasn't plain, but she wasn't a beauty, either.

She looked working-class.

And yet this was the face the gorgeous Duke of Montgomery had chosen to bed. Would fight a duel for tomorrow. Silly, wonderful, beautiful man.

Bridget sighed wearily.

Her eyes were a little reddened, her cheeks and nose pink from the cold outside.

She turned and splashed cool water on her face, then blotted it with a cloth.

She returned to the looking glass, carefully smoothing a few errant strands of her coarse hair back into place with her fingers. She tried a smile. There. That almost looked natural.

She gave the sleeping Pip a last pat and closed her bedroom door quietly behind her. The house, *her* house, really, for she was the one who cleaned and polished and maintained it—*cared* for it—was sleeping. She walked the hallway, noting where the paint was becoming grimy from repeated brushing by passing bodies. Out into the main entry—the pink marble floor should be polished soon. Up the grand staircase, her gaze meeting the eyes of Val's formal portrait at the landing. He'd been painted draped in yards of ermine, his lips with a faint, mischievous curve. Sometimes, in the months when he'd been supposedly abroad, she'd stood staring at that handsome face, wondering where he'd hidden Lady Caire's letters.

It occurred to her now that she could have asked him where he had hidden them, for he'd told her during one of their arguments earlier that afternoon that he'd given the letters to Lady Caire.

She made the upper hall and walked to his bedroom door. Opened it. One swift glance proved that he wasn't inside—and neither was Mehmed nor Attwell. Both valets must've gone to bed already.

She walked down the hall toward the library, remembering the first time she'd seen it, the thousands upon thousands of books, the rows of black marble columns, crowned by golden Corinthian capitals, marching down the sides of the room. It had been simply spectacular.

Like the man himself.

She'd worked for ancient families before, but never a duke and never such a flamboyant one. The library had taken her breath away, though she'd not shown it, of course.

Servants didn't have emotions.

She opened the door and glanced inside.

He was by the huge, ornate fireplace, lounging on a pile of jewel-colored velvet cushions. He wore his favorite purple silk banyan. The one with the gold-and-green dragon on the back. At his side on the floor was a glass of red wine. As she neared, she saw that he held a small book in his hand, the gold covers encrusted with jewels.

She came to a halt by his elbow and at last he looked up. "Bridget."

She shook her head slowly. Tonight she would be everything she might've been to him. "Séraphine."

He drew in his breath sharply and she could see his pupils dilate. "Really?"

"Yes." She unhooked her chatelaine and paused, looking at it. "Lady Caire gave this to me. When I came to London."

"Ah," he said, and he almost sounded… gentle.

She smoothed a thumb over the red-and-blue-enameled central disk, remembering how proud she'd been when she'd opened the gift from Her Ladyship. "She gave me a book, too, when I was small. *Gulliver's Travels.* I don't know how many times I've read it."

She glanced up at him, expecting mockery for her confession, but he merely watched her a little sadly.

She set the chatelaine down carefully and unpinned her apron and let it drop to the floor, kicking it aside. "What are you reading?"

"Hm?" he murmured distractedly as she began unlacing her bodice. "Oh, the Koran. It's the holy book of Mehmed's people and mostly very boring, but maybe that's because my Arabic needs work."

"Then why are you reading it?" she asked, pulling her bodice off.

He smiled. "Because my Arabic needs work. And because nearly everyone in that part of the world quotes from this book. It's rather like being illiterate not to know it."

She nodded. That made sense. She stepped out of her skirts. "Will you be traveling there again? To Istanbul and Arabia and the places where they follow the Koran?"

"I hope so," he said, laying aside the golden book very carefully. "The air is so hot there, warm and fragrant, the sky so blue, and the food tastes like nothing here. They have olives and dates and soft cheeses. I think you would like it, my Séraphine. You could dress in pink and gold and mahogany and lounge on silken pillows, listening to strange music. I'd buy you a little monkey with a vest and a hat to make you laugh and I'd sit and watch you and feed you juicy grapes."

She smiled sadly and drew off her stays. "And how would we get there, Val?"

"I'd hire a ship," he said taking a sip of his red wine. "No, I'd *buy* a ship—one of our very own. It'll have blue sails and a flag with a rooster on it. We'll take your mongrel and Mehmed and all his cats and set sail with fifty strong men. During the day we'll sit on deck and watch for mermaids and monsters in the waves, and at night we'll stare at the stars and then I'll make love to you until dawn."

"And after far Arabia?" she whispered as she drew off her chemise and stood nude save for her stockings and shoes. "What then?"

His smile faded and he looked very grave as she took off her shoes and stockings. "Why, Séraphine, then we would journey on to Egypt or India or China or indeed wherever else you please. Or even come round about here, back to foggy, bustling London, where, if nothing else, the pies and sausages are quite good, if that was what you wished. Just as long as I were with you and you with me, my sweet Séraphine."

She closed her eyes and wondered how serious he was, for this was her dream, really. To be with him always.

She opened her eyes and knelt before him. "That sounds wonderful."

She reached up and, one by one, took out the pins from her hair, placing each one beside his book. Then she shook out her hair, combing her fingers through the strands and pulling them forward over her shoulders.

He was propped on one elbow, watching her, his face nearly expressionless, and she wondered for the first time if he knew what she'd done. But if he did, would he have let her in? Would he have talked of Istanbul and olives and ships with blue sails?

Maybe he would. He was Valentine, after all.

Perhaps it didn't matter. She'd done it and could never undo it.

She leaned forward and crawled to him, nude, her hair brushing the floor. When she reached him, she curled beside him and carefully, delicately, unbuttoned his purple silk banyan from the bottom. Then she spread the edges wide so that he lay on the smooth, glossy fabric nude save for his arms.

He arched one eyebrow at her.

She began at his pink nipples, licking softly, only that, one at a time.

Then she drew back and blew on them, eyeing her work as they tightened under her breath.

He swallowed, but didn't say anything.

She bent and grazed her teeth over the jut of his hip. He smelled of cloves and some exotic perfume, and she imagined him in those faraway lands, smoking from his water pipe, lounging on his colorful silken pillows, speaking in a foreign language.

Without her.

She tasted salt at the corner of her mouth as she licked to his navel, his belly contracting under her tongue.

She inhaled and moved downward without raising her face, without letting him see her eyes, and cupped him between her hands. Such a beautiful cock. Straight and pale, though it was growing ruddy at the head. Veins wrapped the column around as he stood between her palms, hard and proud, his foreskin pulled back, the broad tip a little wet.

She kissed him there, mingling their salt, mingling their tears, though he didn't know it. Her hair fell forward, shielding her. Giving her a little privacy as she pressed her lips against his heat. Slowly she opened her lips over him, letting him in, until he lay on the flat of her tongue.

Then she suckled, her eyes closed, concentrating on his taste, the feel of him in her mouth, more intimate in a way than his penis between her legs. This was an act that *she* chose, one she didn't have to do, one that gave her no innate pleasure.

And yet it did.

She could feel herself grow wet as she sucked and sucked again, moaning a little, her mouth filling with water and his taste, her thighs clenching, her fists squeezing along his shaft.

He muttered something and she felt him brush her hair aside.

She opened her eyes and saw him watching her, his face flushed.

Slowly, as if she were a deer that might startle, he reached out and took her head between his hands. Gently but firmly.

"Careful," he whispered, his voice cracking. "Your teeth..." He pushed his hips up, shoving himself a little farther inside her mouth. "Can you..." He swallowed. "Can you move your hands? Up and down."

Watching him, still holding him in her mouth, she did as he asked, moving the soft skin along the hard shaft.

"*Yesss*," he said on a hiss. "Like that. Just like that, Séraphine. Oh, but suck me, my darling one, suck me as well. Dear, sweet *God*."

She watched him as he threw his head back, giving himself over to his pleasure. How many women had seen him like this before?

How many would see him like this in the future?

Oh, but now, at this moment, only *she* did. *She* was the one who commanded him. *She* was the one whose hair he tangled his fingers in.

She was the one who licked and licked and licked his cock until he moaned in lost abandon.

Until he broke.

He sat up and, in a tangle of purple silk, grasped her and pulled her into his lap, her thighs wrapping around his back. Still sitting, facing her, he thrust into her, rocking hard, his azure eyes gleaming in triumph and lust.

She wound her arms about his neck and rocked with him, watching him, trying to clutch, to hold this moment: the smells, the sounds, the sight of him gazing up at her.

He leaned over and picked up his half-full wineglass and splashed the cold liquid on her breasts.

She let her head roll on her shoulders, gasping as he licked the red wine from her nipples and thrust his cock into her.

He took one nipple into his mouth and suckled and she caught her breath, falling, despairing, the tears suddenly washing over her eyes.

"Valentine. Valentine. Valentine," she whispered as the shocks quaked through her. "I love you."

And he shouted his own release.

DAWN WAS A very good time to hold a duel, in Val's opinion. First, one was wide awake, having never gone to sleep the night before. Second, everyone *else* was sleepy, having awoken at an unaccustomed hour. Third, most people were actually asleep at dawn—well, most people of any consequence—which made for less of a chance of witnesses. And fourth, dawn was generally a very pretty time of day—mists, the rose-tinted light just peeking o'er yon horizon, et cetera, et cetera.

Fourth, he found, did not actually pertain to dawn in late October.

Val shivered on his black mare as he made his way through the park. The dawn was looking more gray than rose-tinted and there was the definite threat of rain in the air. He very much hoped that he might quickly stab Caire in the arm—or another appropriately painful, but not actually fatal spot—and then hurry home to a hot pot of tea.

Up ahead, through the gloomy mists, a few individuals were standing about. Either he'd found his dueling partners or he'd happened upon someone *else*'s duel. If so he'd offer to trade just so he could get the thing over with before it rained. Séraphine had been warm and, now that he thought about it, rose-tinted, when he'd left her curled in his bed.

If he was lucky she'd still be there when he returned.

"Montgomery," Caire called as he neared. "Where is your second?"

"Don't have one," Val said as he swung his leg over the mare's neck and dropped to the ground. "If you kill me, your second will just have to be satisfied with kicking my body."

That surprised a laugh from one of the other two men, a bespectacled gentleman wearing a gray wig.

Caire grunted. "Well, I brought one. Godric St. John, this is Valentine Napier, the Duke of Montgomery."

St. John seemed to suppress a sigh as he made a bow, his gray eyes grave.

Val made his usual elegant sweep as he was introduced to the third man, the doctor.

"May I examine the blades?" St. John asked.

"If you must," Val said, unsheathing his and holding it out over his forearm, hilt first. He met Caire's eyes. "I hope we can finish this soon. I left your sister in my bed."

St. John swore under his breath and stepped between them, facing Val. "Are you insane?"

"Many think so." Val was watching Caire, his lips twitching.

Caire hadn't moved. Only his eyes, hard and staring and trained upon Val, showed that he'd heard Val's words. Those eyes burned a bit like Séraphine's, Val mused, and he wondered if the other man truly meant to kill him this morning.

Well, he could certainly *try*.

He grinned. "Shall we begin?"

St. John handed them back their swords.

In the distance galloping hoofbeats could be heard, drawing closer.

Val assumed his fencer's stance, muscles readied, arms gracefully extended, death at the point of his sword.

He smiled into Caire's eyes.

The other man had a longer reach.

But Val would lay money he was the quicker of the two.

And he was the younger by at least eight years, maybe more.

He shifted his weight to his back leg, ready, waiting…

"En garde!"

Caire sprang, ferocious and fast, and Val laughed out loud as he parried, retreating, looking for the opening…

"Stop! Stop at once!"

The roar came from the mounted man, on a horse so

huge it looked like something used to pull a brewer's cart. The horse half reared, protesting the abrupt halt, and Val came within inches of having his brains dashed out by an enormous hoof.

Both duelists backed quickly away, their swords lowering.

"What's the meaning of this?" Caire demanded.

While his second asked more calmly, "Who are you, sir?"

"I'm Hugh Fitzroy, the Duke of Kyle," said the rider, who certainly was. He looked at Val. "And I need to speak to you."

Val waved his sword. "Busy."

"Now."

Val arched an eyebrow, but walked over, out of curiosity if nothing else. He'd had no idea Kyle had such a flair for the dramatic.

Kyle took something from his cloak and it was a moment before Val recognized it.

Perhaps a killing blow was always a surprise.

"You know what this is," Kyle said.

"I do," Val said, tasting blood in his mouth, though that might've been his imagination. "The question is, do you?"

Kyle glanced at the casket in his hands. "I know that whatever is in this box is enough for you to forfeit this duel." He looked up. "And that I can trade it for the prince's letters. *All* of the letters."

"Ah," said Val, drawing back his head. "No, you don't know what is in the box, then. If you did, you'd use it for far more than paltry letters."

He turned and looked at Caire, unsmiling. "I forfeit the duel. I do apologize most abjectly. I am a cad, a bounder, a rogue, a liar, a thief, a blackmailer, a murderer, and, yes, the seducer of your sister. I regret causing offense to your house and to your honor."

Caire looked at him and nodded curtly.

Val bowed and turned to Kyle.

The duke was watching him speculatively. "What's in the box?"

"Oh," Val said as he mounted the black mare. "That. It's my heart—or what's left of it. She gave you my heart."

Chapter Eighteen

That night King Heartless and Prue trudged wearily to the garden. "I think your father plays me for a fool," the king growled. "If he does I shall cut off his head."
Prue threw down the needle she was trying to thread. "This is why people say you're heartless."
"I am heartless," said King Heartless. "What more should you expect?" . . .
—From *King Heartless*

She didn't know what to do next.

Funny. Bridget had spent most of her life placing one foot in front of the other, one task after another, going from one situation to the next, methodical, precise. Her day was ordered from when she rose to when she blew out her candle, a series of chores and lists and arranged events.

And now?

Now she was walking down a London street, very early in the morning, a soft bag with all her worldly possessions held in one hand, and Pip trotting on her other side.

She didn't even know where to *go*.

Around her London was waking, maids coming out to sweep the front steps, delivery carts rolling by, and she… she didn't know what to do.

She'd received the note from the Duke of Kyle with its curt message: "Done. All safe." And then she'd fled. She'd not even had the courage to wait for Val to return. To bear his recriminations and anger for betraying him.

What a coward she was.

A carriage pulled up beside her.

Bridget halted and for a moment her heart squeezed so tight she thought it might stop altogether.

But then the door opened and Lady Caire peered out.

Bridget blinked.

A footman got down from the back and set the step.

"Well, get in, dear," said Lady Caire, and Bridget did.

Pip hopped in as well, the door shut, and the carriage started forward.

"I didn't know you had a dog," Lady Caire said, staring at Pip.

Bridget looked at him.

Unfortunately he was trying to bite his hind leg.

She glanced up again. "I do."

"I see," said Lady Caire.

Pip jumped on the seat beside Bridget and the carriage rumbled on for a bit.

Lady Caire cleared her throat. "Montgomery forfeited the duel."

Bridget nodded.

"I understand," Lady Caire said, "that we have you to thank for that, Bridget."

Bridget looked at her. "Did you name me?"

Lady Caire looked startled. "I'm sorry?"

"Did you name me or did you just drop me with Mam and my foster father and leave them to pick a name? Did you know them at all?" Bridget's hands were twisting in her lap and she half laughed as she remembered Val's words. "Or perhaps you put me in a basket like a kitten and sent me off with a servant to find someone to raise me. Did you even *care* if they were good or bad people?"

Lady Caire's face had gone white. "I stayed with a girlhood friend up there. She knew your…Mam and foster father. I went to interview them in their cottage when… when I was close. Your Mam was there when I had you. She was the second to hold you. After me. I held you first. I cradled you in my arms and saw that you had black hair—*my* family's black hair—and a red scrunched face. You were very quiet. My son screamed at birth but you just lay and looked around with wide eyes. We swaddled you. And then I gave you to your Mam." Lady Caire looked down at her hands. "I named you Bridget because… because I knew that I couldn't give you one of my family's names. Bridget was my old nanny's name. She was from Ireland and I loved her dearly."

She looked up and tears were silently streaming down her proud aristocratic cheeks.

"There are many, many things that I regret doing in my life, but nothing that I regret more than what I did to you, Bridget."

At that Bridget burst into tears.

SHE WAS GONE.

Gone.

Gone.

Gone.

His housekeeper, his archangel, his inquisitor, his Bridget.

His Séraphine.

Burning light. Warmth in the darkness. Stealer of both heart and soul.

Though he had that back. He'd bartered it for a handful of royal letters.

Val stared at the ivory box as he drank from the bottle of wine. *Straight* from the bottle of wine, for he seemed to have misplaced his wineglass and none of the servants would come near him no matter how loudly he bellowed.

Such were the things that happened when one's housekeeper left.

She'd said she loved him. Loved *him*. What a strange and wondrous thing. And how it hurt, this love! What pain it caused, like tiny knives in the veins. He didn't think he liked it much, but he'd endure it, yes he would, if only she'd return and stab him again.

He held out his arms and looked at the ceiling of his library, his grand library, his very favorite room in his magnificent house, the house he'd had built to his very, very specific plans. The ceiling was painted and gilded and grand, very grand.

And cold.

Everything was cold.

The fire wasn't hot enough, that was the problem. So he took some of his books—his beautiful, beautiful books—and burned them, gilt edges curling, illuminated pages turning brown, fine leather smoking and stinking, and thought that must be a shame. Séraphine would scold him were she here. She would snatch them from the fire and never burn her plump fingers for she was a creature of fire herself, burning, burning.

But she wasn't here.

Gone.

Gone.

Gone.

And when he looked up from the embers of his precious books, he saw that he'd somehow smashed the bottle of wine. He'd trod on the glass in his bare feet and his blood had mingled with the wine on the floor.

Or perhaps it was the opposite. Perhaps the wine had mingled with the blood in his veins and now he was part grape.

Fair Séraphine had tried to explain to him the difference, right from wrong. It made sense to her because she burned and was an angel. But to him, a creature of hollow ice and pain, it was sound and confusion without her to filter it for him.

And she wasn't here to care anyway, either for him or for his victims.

So he wrote to Dyemore.

"I'M SO GLAD you agreed to stay with us," Temperance Huntington, Lady Caire said the next morning at the breakfast table to Bridget.

Bridget bit her lip, looking up from the eggs she hadn't touched. Yesterday, after an incredibly awkward carriage ride, the elder Lady Caire had deposited Bridget at her son's town house and then almost immediately left.

Bridget had been a very poor guest so far, having spent the previous day mostly in her room, exhausted and sleeping, too depressed to venture forth and confront strangers who must think the very worst of her.

This morning, though, she'd determined not to be such a coward. "Thank you for letting me stay, my lady. I do appreciate it very much and I promise it won't be for long. Just until I can find a new position and—"

"Oh." The lady's brows knit over her gold-brown eyes. "First of all, you're more than welcome to stay as long as you wish—indefinitely, really. You're Lazarus's sister. And please. Call me Temperance." She smiled, her entire face lighting. "We're sisters, after all, aren't we?"

"I . . ." Bridget had to look away from the kind face. The tears threatened again, damn it. She'd never been one for weeping and now she was a veritable watering pot. She inhaled shakily. "You're very kind."

The sudden scrape of a chair made her look up.

Temperance was standing. She held out her hand. "Will you come with me? I want to show you something."

The elder woman led Bridget up a staircase, splendid but not as flamboyant as dear Val's—push that thought aside. Down a passage that obviously held the private apartments of the family, and to a set of large double doors. She opened them and Bridget blinked.

This was the master bedroom, and most obviously used by both the lord and the lady of the house.

Bridget looked at Temperance, but the other lady was calmly walking to a tall chest of drawers. On top were arranged a few items and she picked up one and turned, holding it out.

"This is Annalise," Temperance said. "The *first* Annalise. Lazarus's younger sister—and your elder, I suppose."

Bridget took the miniature—for that was what it was—and looked. A small girl peered up at her, dark-haired, brown-eyed, wearing a severe, square-necked bodice and a ribbon around her throat.

She looked all of four.

Bridget glanced up and met Temperance's sad golden eyes.

"Their father was... well, as far as I can gather he was quite awful," Temperance said matter-of-factly. "Very strict. Possibly mad. And he ruled the household with an iron fist. When Annalise was five she caught some sort of fever. He refused to call a doctor. Amelia, Lady Caire, pleaded with him, but he..." Temperance shook her head, pressing her lips together. "Annalise died. Lazarus was ten years old."

Bridget swallowed and looked Temperance in her golden eyes. "I'm not Annalise."

"No," Temperance said at once. "Oh, no. I didn't mean that. You can't replace her, of course. It's just..." She sighed. "He never had anyone else, you see. He rather blamed Lady Caire for Annalise's death, even though... well. Children can be so stubborn in their prejudices, can't they?" she said somewhat obscurely. "Anyway, it's only been recently that they've been able to talk at all. For years he was so alone. So lonely. I know he can seem quite intimidating, so sharp and, well, *looming*." She rolled her eyes. "And he didn't exactly make a very good first impression, calling out your... well... the Duke of Montgomery, which," she muttered under her breath, "*really* is a bit hypocritical, considering how he courted *me*, but I hope you'll give him a chance. You're actually rather a miracle, you see."

Bridget looked down at the miniature of a long-dead half sister and wondered if she'd found her family at last.

Chapter Nineteen

Prue had rather come to like the king in the last two nights, despite his foul temper, so she said, "I expect wisdom, fairness, and kindness from a king. Just because you haven't a heart in your chest doesn't mean you can't act *as if you had one."*

The king scowled quite ferociously, but Prue tilted her chin and stood her ground. "Fine!" he finally shouted.

They set to work and little more was said that night, but the king looked thoughtful as he labored. . . .

—From *King Heartless*

Everything was so gray without Val, Bridget thought morosely a few days later. She'd decided to take a short walk with Pip, who was trotting along jauntily beside her. Apparently now that she was the sister of a baron, she merited a footman to follow her. Something that she might find amusing were it not for the fact that everything was so *gray*, despite the fact that the sun was shining.

If only . . .

If only she could have one more chance to talk to him, to try to explain while he painted swirls of colors with words, to kiss him tenderly while he told her she burned.

To tell him again and again that she loved him even if he couldn't quite return the words yet, his head cocked, his azure eyes glittering and alive.

But she'd betrayed him, given his worst secret, his most terrible vulnerability, to one of his enemies, and even with all his wonderful, beautiful, mercurial madness, Valentine would never be able to forgive that.

Never.

She felt the tears threaten her already-sore eyes again. She bent her head to hide them, which was probably why she didn't see the carriage until it was already beside her, the door flung open.

Pip was barking madly, the footman shouting behind her, but she was grabbed by rough hands and thrown inside, a hood pulled over her head.

And then she felt the carriage pull away as she fought to breathe, to free her arms from the strong hands, as Pip's barks faded into the distance.

THE PROBLEM WITH dreary old secret societies was that they must have their ridiculous revels in arcane places, the better to invoke the supposed mysteries, et cetera, et cetera.

Val stared out his carriage window four nights later near midnight and thought that really, now that he was almost to the Dyemore estate in Yorkshire, he'd rather be at Hermes House, reading a book he hadn't yet set alight. Or staring at the wall.

He'd been staring at the walls quite a lot recently.

It was all rather... well, dreary, really. He wasn't sure he'd be able to make it through whatever revolting ceremony Dyemore had concocted without yawning and nodding off.

He kept wanting to turn and ask Bridget her thoughts on matters and she wasn't there, was she?

She was never there.

Even fulfilling his vow to go through with it, to become the center of the Lords of Chaos and gather all that raw power and illicit knowledge for himself, now seemed... a tedious chore. Without Séraphine there to rant at him with burning eyes, to tell him why he shouldn't do this or that, and to explain so seriously that it was *wrong* of him and that he really, truly ought to try to do the right thing, the whole procedure was really rather tiresome.

He'd turn the carriage round and head back to London if he weren't fearful that he'd set fire to the entire library and leave himself without any source of relief in this life at all.

Oh, Bridget.

He closed his eyes and thought that had he not cut out his blackened heart and left it in that foul ivory casket long ago, it might—it just might—be a broken thing in his chest right now.

The carriage shuddered to a stop.

He opened his eyes as the door was thrown wide on the nightmarish sight of torches and naked men in animal masks.

Might as well get on with it, then.

BRIDGET HAD SPENT a hellish three days and two nights being jostled and bruised on the carriage floor as it had journeyed to where she didn't know. She'd had time to be terrified, imagining rape and murder, to become so tired she'd dozed on the quaking floor, almost uncaring, only to be awakened, terrified once more, every time they'd stopped.

She'd been allowed to relieve herself at intervals, humiliatingly, at the side of the road, in front of whatever men had kidnapped her.

They'd given her water and bread.

They'd not offered anything else.

Which, on the whole, rather alarmed her. If they meant to keep her for ransom from her brother, surely they'd want to feed her better? She didn't want to think about what they might want her for if not ransom, but it had been a *very* long journey.

They didn't talk much, but she could discern four voices: two within the carriage and two riding outside. All, to her surprise, sounded refined.

That didn't make sense.

They'd bound her wrists behind her back when they'd first caught her. The rope was rough and tied quite tight. She was lying on her side on the carriage floor and she'd tried several times to surreptitiously rub the bindings off. All she'd succeeded in doing was tightening the rope around her wrists, with the result that her fingers now felt thick and nearly useless, which frightened her more. On the second day her kidnappers had noticed her movement and she'd been kicked in the side for her trouble. Her side still ached.

By the time the carriage stopped for the final time she'd moved past terror, past exhaustion, past terror again, and on to determination.

Bridget decided that really, this wasn't how she was going to die.

So when the carriage door opened, when they took the hood off her head, and she saw the torches burning and the nude men in masks, she fought. She kicked and she bit and she lowered her head and brought it up violently into the chin of the man standing over her.

He swore and staggered back, blood dripping from beneath the rabbit mask he wore.

Three others seized her bound arms, though.

One in a fox mask stood in front of her. He held a knife and he had a dolphin tattoo on the inside of his elbow.

He was also horribly erect.

She twisted, throwing her weight against the men behind her, and caught them off guard. All three of them went down to the ground. She rolled, elbowing one in the stomach, but the other held firm. The fox brought the knife down.

Cutting, slicing her clothes from her body.

A thrill of horror went through Bridget. She raised her legs, kicking, twisted her neck, biting. But more hands joined the first ones, holding her down, keeping her immobile as the fox cut every piece of clothing from her body. She lay on the hard, cold ground, naked, with scalding tears streaming into her hair.

One came to stand over her, his body wrinkled and old, his mask, in cruel contrast, portraying a beautiful young man with grapes in his hair. "Bring her."

She clenched her thighs together. Bared her gritted teeth. She wouldn't make it easy for them, these savage aristocrats, these bloody Lords of Chaos, for it had to be them.

But they lifted her, held her high above their heads among the burning torches, and carried her somewhere. She could feel their hard hands on her bare body. On her shoulders and legs and buttocks, holding her aloft like a slaughtered doe at some medieval feast. What were they doing?

They bore her into a circle of torches and lowered her onto a great stone, freezing against her skin. The fox was there again, cutting the ropes at her wrists finally. But before she could move, her hands were seized and her wrists were tied to posts at the upper corners of the stone. Her ankles were spread and tied to posts at the lower corners.

She was a sacrifice, spread-eagled and bound, ready for the priest.

She stared up, horrified, stunned, terrified, and a man came to stand over her. He wore a wolf's mask, his body was beautiful and without flaw, his nipples pink, with just a scattering of golden hair between his pectorals. She couldn't see his dolphin tattoo, but she knew that was because he wore it on his left buttock.

Oh, God, *no.*

The old man handed the wolf-masked man a long knife. "This is your initiation sacrifice. Enjoy her in whatever manner strikes your fancy. You can share her, if you wish. And then kill her."

And all Bridget could think of were Val's words, whispered as he leaned his forehead against hers: *you have to kill the thing you love.*

Val raised the knife above her...

Chapter Twenty

In the morning Prue and King Heartless showed their embroidered cloth to the magician.
"Well," said he, turning the cloth this way and that. "This is quite a fine... er..."
"Lion," said the king, yawning.
"Or possibly a pig," muttered Prue.
"I've finished the three trials," the king said. And he summoned the royal physician to listen to his chest. But though the physician tried and tried, he heard no heartbeat....

—From *King Heartless*

Val raised the knife above Bridget, *his* Bridget, and gazed into her burning eyes, and thought, *You have to kill the thing you love.*

She might never forgive him this. Never, ever, in all eternity.

But he must do it anyway, for though he'd lost her love, he couldn't lose all of her. Not now. Not ever.

He whirled and plunged the knife into Dyemore's gut. Looked into the old goat's wide eyes, growled, "*Mine*," and twisted the knife, drawing the blade up and out, disemboweling him.

Val stepped nimbly back to avoid the entrails, kicked over two of the torches, and bent down to slice through Bridget's bindings and pull her into his arms. The wooden stage around Dyemore's graceless altar caught flame as Foxy came at him with his knife. Val swung at his balls—sadly missing, but carving a nice slice into the meat of his thigh.

Foxy went down in a gush of arterial blood.

That stopped the rest of them short. They milled in confusion, leaderless, unable to decide quite what to do. The thing was, even in masks they were a cowardly lot. Why else hide their vile desires in a secret society?

Val ran with Bridget, nude as Adam and Eve, into the night. They passed more revelers in masks, either rushing toward the commotion or unaware that anything had happened. Two more nudists on this night and at this place weren't anything out of the ordinary.

Dyemore had used the ruined abbey on his own estate as the location for the revels. Val hadn't far to go before he found the old road where the carriages had been left to wait.

Aristocrats, even nude reveling ones, don't like walking far.

His carriage was, thankfully, already pointed in the right direction. Val tore off the wolf mask.

"Ainsdale Castle!" he shouted at his startled coachman before bundling sweet Séraphine into the carriage.

He immediately turned to her as the carriage rocked into motion, wrapping her in his cloak and examining her. She had bruises on her shoulders and on her arms. Her wrists were bloodied—he growled under his breath as he examined them, picking away the remains of the ropes. Her plump little toes were muddied and cut and cold. He warmed them with his hands, crooning to them. She had quite a nasty bruise on her left side and he tenderly pressed his fingers around that, soft sounds leaving his lips helplessly. Oh, that he had been there when this had been done! He would have put their eyes out. He would have cut off their noses and made them eat them. He would have—

"Valentine."

He blinked and realized that she had the palms of her hands on his face and was looking at him. "Valentine. I'm all right."

His eyes narrowed as he looked at her face, for he was no fool. They must've had her for several days to bring her here. "Are you, though?"

She looked at him very firmly. "Yes."

"They didn't rape you?"

"No."

"Or touch you in any way?"

She sighed. "They grabbed me when they took me. They tied me up."

He thought about that. He didn't like it. "Did they make you do anything you didn't want to?"

She hesitated.

He went icy cold. "Tell me."

"They..." She went a deep red and looked away. "They...when I needed to...to urinate they didn't turn away."

"Ah." Well. That settled that.

He wrapped his arms around her. "I am truly sorry you had to endure such horrific events, my Séraphine. Had I the ability, I would travel through time and strangle these men as infants."

"That's..." She gulped and laid her head against his bare chest and began to shake.

Perhaps she was having some sort of fit brought on by the nightmare of this evening? He looked at her with alarm.

She raised her head and she was laughing. "Oh, Valentine, whatever shall I do with you?"

He looked at her calculatingly. She seemed soft, amenable, perhaps even open to suggestion after her shock.

He smiled as charmingly as he knew how. "You could marry me."

She smiled back, a little sadly. "Could I?"

"Yes," he said earnestly. "You could."

But she merely shook her head and laid it again on his breast.

He thought and thought—many considered him quite a genius, including himself—and at last he thought of something he could say. "I'm sorry."

She lifted her head. "What?"

Yes, this was obviously the correct thing to say. "I'm sorry for killing Dyemore." He remembered the pool of blood around Foxy. "And possibly the man wearing the fox mask."

He thought about the men who had kidnapped her. But he hadn't done anything to them...*yet*. He glanced out of the corner of his eye at her. Surely she didn't have some nonsensical rule about *future* murders?

Just in case he crossed his fingers.

And smiled at her.

But she was looking at him rather oddly now. "You don't have to apologize for killing the Duke of Dyemore—or the man in the fox mask."

He blinked. "Come again?"

"You were acting to save me—and yourself." She knit her brows. "Although I do hope you won't be charged with his murder."

"Who is going to do so? All the witnesses were at a naked pagan orgy. Try explaining *that* in court." He came back to the more important point. "But I don't understand. You're saying that at times it's perfectly all right for me to kill a man."

"Well..." She bit her lip and he could tell she was trying not to say it, but in the end she had to. "Yes."

He smiled very slowly at her. "Séraphine, are you making these rules up?"

"Noooo," she said. "No, I am not."

And her burning saint's eyes were so earnest that he had to draw her back into his arms and kiss her, moving his mouth over hers possessively because he'd lost her once already. Lost her and he might not have regained her.

She drew back finally and looked up at him, all dark eyes in her pale face, and said, "What is in your mother's letter, Val?"

OVER AN HOUR later Bridget sat before the fire in Ainsdale Castle wrapped in Val's purple velvet coat—the same one she'd worn to escape him on the moors. It had been rescued by Mr. Dwight, who had seen to its cleaning. It smelled only faintly of bacon now and was deliciously comfortable.

She'd had a warm bath and eaten a meal hastily prepared by Mrs. Smithers, and now she was sitting with her hands in her lap, contemplating the terrible ivory casket. Apparently Val had kept it with him ever since Kyle had traded it back to him.

Val had given the casket to her, after the bath, after the meal, and then left the room. She had the suspicion that he couldn't bear to stay and watch her read the letter. That made her very sad.

She sighed and reached for the thing, turning it over and finding the carving on the underside as she'd seen him do only weeks before. She pressed into it with her thumbnail. The sliver of ivory popped out and she slid it over, and then opened the box.

The letter within was still there.

Opened.

She blinked and then narrowed her eyes. Well. At least the Duke of Kyle had returned it.

She picked it up and unfolded it.

His mother had had a beautiful hand. Flowery and precise, like beautiful embroidery upon the page. She'd used it to describe her son as demon-possessed since birth and a patricide, giving a date and details that sounded quite truthful.

Bridget let the letter fall to her lap as she stared into the flames thoughtfully.

Then she nodded and put the letter into the fire.

She watched it burn and then went in search of Valentine, her true love.

THE WIDOW'S TOWER was cold and dark, the stars in the sky a thousand miles away, and Val thought that this was how he would always be if she left him. So very cold and dark and alone, forever gazing at the stars, burning bright and too bloody far away to reach.

Then her arms wrapped around him, warming him, and he turned, clasping her to his chest, relieved, so relieved that he wouldn't have to gaze at the stars all alone forever.

He buried his face in her black hair, still damp from her bath, and said in a rough whisper, just this once because she deserved to know, "He found her. Eve. I'd taken her to Geneva. Far away—or so I thought. But Father found her somehow two years later, and he was going to bring her back to his Lords and... so I had to... I *had* to... I took a dagger and I killed him in his sleep. Thrust it through his throat. But mother knew. She told me I must leave England while she lived or she'd give the letter to the magistrates." He drew in a breath, thinking wildly. It wasn't enough. She would consider killing a parent too awful a crime. "It was him or Eve, Séraphine. You must understand. If I hadn't killed him I would have had to kill Eve... and I couldn't do that. I *couldn't.* Not Eve."

"Hush," she whispered, pulling back from him, though he tried to keep her close. "Hush. I understand. Do you hear me, Valentine? I understand."

And then he saw her burning eyes. They gazed at him calmly and he saw in them benediction.

He fell to his knees before her, pressing his face to her purple-velvet-clad belly. "Séraphine, Séraphine, Séraphine. O most beloved of women, most fiery of saints, never leave me, please. I'll erect columns of white marble to you, build gardens of delights for you, cause ships to sail and warriors to rise for you, if you'll only remain by my side."

She smiled down at him and cupped his cheeks. "Valentine, do you love me?"

Ah, God, it was like a shot to the gut.

He squeezed tight his eyes. To come so close and lose her because of *this*. "If I were able I would love you as no man has ever loved a woman since the beginning of time."

She knelt then to face him and whispered, "But you *are* able."

He clutched her. He *wouldn't* let her go, no, not even when she realized…"Séraphine, my darling, burning one, do you not remember? I told you, so long ago now, that I lacked that part. I *cannot*—"

"But you can, Valentine." She touched a finger to his cheek and then showed it to him.

He blinked.

Her finger was wet. His *eyes* were wet.

She smiled at him, his burning Séraphine, and it was as if the night sky were ablaze. "You love me."

"I love you," he said in wonder, and felt his chest fill with warmth. "*I love you.*"

"And I love you," she whispered, her hands cupping his face.

So he kissed her until she was limp and pliable and so very hot against him, and then he purred into her ear,

"Does that mean you'll become my duchess, darling Bridget Crumb?"

And when she sighed back, "Oh, yes, Val," he picked her up and carried her off to have his wicked, wicked way with her.

Because he might have a heart now but some things weren't *ever* going to change.

Epilogue

Well, all the courtiers and counselors cowered, for they expected the magician and his daughter to be dragged away at once and executed. This was always how the king acted—swiftly and ruthlessly—and since the magician had not found him a new heart, they expected nothing else.

But the king looked weary and sad. "You promised me a heart," he said to the magician. "Yet I do not have one."

The magician cocked his head, his eyes twinkling. "Are you sure, Your Majesty?"

The king gestured to the physician. "There is no heart in my chest."

"But a heart needn't always be in one's chest," the magician said.

The king narrowed his eyes at that. "You talk nonsense."

"Indeed I do not," the magician said. "I promised you a heart and I gave you one." He nodded to his daughter. "Didn't Prue help you and guide you in the last three nights?"

"Yes," the king said slowly.

"And didn't she advise you to gentle your manner?"

"Yes."

"And are you not a better man for knowing her?"

At this the king merely nodded, for he was staring at Prue, who blushed and glanced away.

"Prue is your heart, my liege," the magician said, "And I have found her for you."

Well, the king might once have been heartless, but he'd never been foolish. He bent his knee to Prue and took her hand. "Will you marry me, Prue, and be my queen and heart and helpmeet all of our days?"

Prue opened her mouth and closed it. "But I'm not a princess. I'm just Prue."

At that the king smiled for perhaps the first time in his life. "Aye, but you're my heart, sweet Prue, and a man cannot live without his heart."

Prue could only agree to that and so she married the king in the most splendid wedding anyone had ever seen. The king was no longer Heartless, but became King Heart instead.

And as for the magician? Well, 'twas said that he never did any true magic, but I think the gossips wrong, for what better magic is there than to bring two hearts together?

Don't you agree?

—From *King Heartless*

TWO MONTHS LATER, AT ST JAMES'S PALACE...

"Ambassador to the Ottoman Empire?" Hugh stared at Shrugg. "The *Duke of Montgomery*? Surely that's like sending a lit powder keg over there?"

"He might be a lit powder keg, but he's *our* lit powder

keg." The older man took a sip of his tea. "Besides, Montgomery's usually a bit more subtle than that, especially now that he's got that wife by his side. Have you met her? Used to be his housekeeper, apparently, but you know Montgomery. Went and married her, scandalizing everyone, never mind that it's the most sane thing he's ever done. Which reminds me. He gave me this to give to you."

Shrugg rummaged in his desk until he found a rather grubby bit of paper, which he shoved across the desk to Hugh.

Hugh peered down at it. The paper held the names of four gentlemen, all aristocrats. He could see no particular connection between them.

He looked up inquiringly at Shrugg. "What am I supposed to do with this?"

"I'm not sure exactly," Shrugg said slowly. "But Montgomery wanted you to know that they're all members of the Lords of Chaos."

MEANWHILE . . .

There were a great many children in his garden, Val thought with disapproval. He'd come out only because there were a great many adults in his house, a large number of whom had, at one time or another, actively tried to kill him. They were celebrating Eve's wedding breakfast at Hermes House and Bridget had forbidden him from poisoning anyone, not even Wakefield.

Val thought he really ought to have special dispensation for Wakefield.

"I don't *wike* you," said a familiar infant voice.

Annalise Huntington gazed up at him, the pink bow in her hair only giving a certain élan to her scowl.

Val looked down thoughtfully upon the spawn of Lazarus Huntington, Lord Caire, one of the many who had once tried to kill him. Despite Val's making an honest duchess of his sister, Caire still seemed to hold him in much dislike, and Val had often caught the older man watching him with a disquieting look of contemplation on his face. Rather like a hawk deciding how best to dismember a cat.

Val smiled evilly at the child and reached into his pocket.

"Do you," he asked, "like kittens?"

And he held out a black, fluffy kitten with a white chest.

Annalise blinked at the kitten's green eyes.

The kitten blinked back.

"Oh, *yes*!" said Annalise.

Val deposited the kitten into the plump little arms and strolled to the kitchens, where Hecate and her kittens were in residence, swinging his gold walking stick.

There were seven more kittens remaining and a garden full of his enemies' children…

ONE MONTH LATER IN ISTANBUL…

The bright Mediterranean sun shone outside, but the interior of their vast bedroom was pleasantly cool, thanks to the deep arches shielding the floor-to-ceiling windows. The arches were intricately tiled in blue, yellow, and white, with a motif that continued on the floor, over the ceiling, and atop some of the thin columns that marched across the floor. Somewhere an imam was calling the faithful to prayer from high atop one of the minarets that dotted the city, his voice rising and falling hauntingly.

Bridget adored this time of day. It was hot and lazy and most often Val spent it with her.

Today she lay across a bed draped in ochre silk sheets, nibbling on honey cakes, and perusing a letter written by her sister-in-law, Lady Temperance Caire. Pip lay curled on a tasseled cushion on the floor at the foot of the bed.

"Annalise has named the kitten you gave her Lord Sneaky."

Val, who was engrossed in a letter of his own, grunted. "Her cat-naming abilities are as awful as my own were at that age."

Bridget wrinkled her nose. "I think it's sweet."

"*Oh*," said her husband, sounding deeply pleased at something he'd read in his letter.

"What?" Bridget sat up, inadvertently spilling several drops of honey on her breast.

Sadly, she'd succumbed to her husband's fondness for nudity soon after their marriage.

Valentine glanced up, but his gaze was immediately drawn to the honey slowly dripping down her breast.

"Val . . ." Bridget moved to scoop the honey up with her finger.

His hand darted out, catching hers.

"Oh, don't," he breathed, leaning over her, forcing her flat on her back.

He bent, closing his azure eyes, and licked her breast almost reverently.

She shuddered.

"It's the middle of the day," she whispered.

His eyes opened, wicked and amused. "I know. Your favorite."

She smiled up at him, threading her fingers through his golden hair. "I love you."

"And I love you," he murmured against her lips, before taking her mouth hard and possessively.

Their letters fell to the floor, abandoned, but Bridget didn't care at all.

She was with her true love and the world outside could wait.

THE SIZZLING MAIDEN LANE SERIES CONTINUES…

PLEASE SEE THE NEXT PAGE FOR A PREVIEW OF

Duke of Pleasure.

JANUARY 1742
LONDON, ENGLAND

Hugh Fitzroy, the Duke of Kyle, did not want to die tonight, for three very good reasons.

It was half past midnight as he eyed the toughs slinking out of the shadows up ahead in the cold alley near Covent Garden. He switched the bottle of fine Viennese wine from his right arm to his left and drew his sword. He'd dined with the Austrian ambassador earlier and the wine was a gift.

One, Kit, his elder son—and, formally, the Earl of Staffin—was only seven. Far too young to inherit the dukedom.

Next to him was a linkboy with a lantern. The boy was frozen, his lantern a small pool of light in the alley. The youth's eyes were wide and frightened. He couldn't be more than fifteen. Hugh glanced behind them. Several men were at the entrance to the alley. He and the linkboy were trapped.

Two, Peter, his younger son, was still suffering nightmares from the death of his mother only six months before. What would his father's death so soon after do to the boy?

They might be footpads. Unlikely, though. Footpads usually worked in smaller numbers, were not this organized, and were after money, not death.

Assassins, then.

And *three*, Hugh had recently been assigned an important job by His Majesty's government: bring down the Lords of Chaos. On the whole, Hugh liked to finish his jobs. Brought a nice sense of completion at the end of the day, if nothing else.

Right, then.

"If you can, run," Hugh said to the linkboy. "They're after me, not you."

He pivoted and attacked the men behind them. There were two men in front, another to their rear. The first raised a club.

Hugh slashed him across the throat. That one went down in a spray of scarlet. But the second was already bringing his club down in a bone-jarring blow against Hugh's left shoulder.

He juggled the bottle of wine, just catching it again before kicking the man in the balls. The second man stumbled back against the man at his back.

There were running footsteps from behind Hugh.

He spun.

Caught the descending knife with his blade and slid his sword into the hand holding the knife.

A howling scream, and the knife clattered to the wet icy cobblestones in a splatter of blood.

The knifeman lowered his head and charged like an enraged bull.

Hugh flattened all six foot four inches of himself against the filthy alley wall, stuck out his foot, and tripped Charging Bull into the three men he'd already dealt with.

The linkboy, who had been cowering at the opposite wall, took the opportunity to squirm through the remaining three standing men and run away.

Which left them all in darkness, save for the light of the moon.

Hugh grinned.

He didn't have to worry about hitting his compatriots in the dark.

He spun and rushed the man next in line after the Bull. They'd picked a nice alley, his attackers. No way out—save either end—but it did have one small advantage for Hugh: no matter how many men were against him, only two could fit abreast in the alley at a time. Any left over were simply bottled up behind the others, twiddling their thumbs.

Hugh slashed the next man and shouldered past him. Got a blow upside the head for his trouble and saw stars. Hugh shook his head and elbowed the next—*hard*—in the face, and kicked the third in the belly. Suddenly he could see the light at the end of the alley.

Hugh knew men who felt that gentlemen should never run from a fight. Of course many of these same gentlemen had never *been* in a real fight.

Besides, he had those three *very* good reasons.

Actually, now that he thought of it, there was a *fourth* reason he did not want to die tonight.

Hugh ran to the end of the alley, his bottle of fine Viennese wine cradled in the crook of his left arm, his sword in the other fist. The cobblestones were iced over and his momentum was such he slid into the lit street.

Where he found another half-dozen men bearing down on him from his left.

Bloody *hell.*

Four, he hadn't had a woman in his bed in over nine months and to die in such a drought seemed a particularly unkind blow from fate, god*damn* it.

Hugh nearly dropped the bloody wine as he scrambled to turn to the right. He could hear the men he'd left in the alley rallying even as he sprinted straight into the worst part of London: the stews of St Giles. They were right on his heels, a veritable army of assassins. The streets here were narrow, ill lit, and cobbled badly, if at all. If he fell because of ice or a missing cobblestone, he'd never get up again.

He turned down a smaller alley and then immediately down another.

Behind him he heard a shout. Christ, if they split up, they would corner him again.

He hadn't enough of a lead, even if a man of his size could easily hide in a place like St Giles. Hugh glanced up as he entered a small courtyard. Overhead the moon was veiled in clouds, and it almost looked as if a boy were silhouetted, jumping from one rooftop to another…

Which…

Was insane.

Think. If he could circle and come back the way he'd entered St Giles, he could slip their noose.

A narrow passage.

Another courtyard.

Ah, *Christ.*

They were already here, blocking the two other exits of the courtyard.

Hugh spun, but the passage he'd just run out from was crowded with more men, perhaps a dozen in all.

Well.

He put his back to the only wall left to him and straightened.

He rather wished he'd tasted the wine. He was fond of Viennese wine.

A tall man in a ragged brown coat and a filthy red neckcloth stepped forward. Hugh half expected him to make some sort of speech. Instead he drew a knife the size of a man's forearm, grinned, and licked the blade.

Hugh didn't wait for whatever other disgusting preliminaries Knife Licker might feel were appropriate for the occasion. He stepped forward and smashed the bottle of very fine Viennese wine over the man's head.

Then they were on him.

He slashed and felt the jolt to his arm as he hit flesh.

Swung and raked the sword across another's face.

Staggered as he was slammed into by two men.

Another hit him hard in the jaw.

And then someone clubbed him behind the knees.

He fell to his knees on the icy ground, growling like a bleeding, baited bear.

Raised an arm to defend his head…

And…

Someone dropped from the sky right in front of him.

Facing his attackers.

Darting, wheeling, spinning.

Defending him so gracefully.

With a sword.

Hugh staggered upright again, blinking blood out of his eyes—when had he been cut?

And saw a boy? No, a slight *man* in a half mask, and floppy hat, and boots, fighting with two swords. Hugh just had time to think: *insane*, before the man was thrown back against him.

Hugh caught the man and had another thought, which was: *tits*?

And then he set the woman—most definitely a *woman* although in a man's clothing—on her feet and put his back to hers and fought as if their lives depended on it.

Which they did.

There were still eight or so of the attackers left and although they weren't trained, they were determined. Hugh slashed and punched and kicked, while his feminine savior danced an elegant dance of death with her sword. When he smashed the butt of his sword into the skull of one of the last men, the remaining two looked at each other, picked up a third, and took to their heels.

Panting, Hugh glanced around the courtyard. It was strewn with groaning men, most still very much alive, though not dangerous at the moment.

He peered at the masked woman. She was tiny, barely reaching his shoulder. How was it she'd saved him from certain, ignoble death? But she had. She surely had.

"Thank you," he said, his voice gruff. "I—"

She grinned, a quicksilver flash, and put her left hand

on the back of his neck to pull his head down to her face to kiss him.

She might be a deadly sword fighter, but her lips were soft and spicy. He groaned and pushed closer.

But she laughed—a low, husky sound that went straight to his cock—and skipped away. She disappeared down one of the tiny alleys leading off the courtyard.

And as Hugh stared after her, he had but one thought: when had the Ghost of St Giles become a woman?